PRAISE FOR *Terrible Virtue*

Winner of the ELLE's Lettres Readers' Prize
An Amazon Best Literature & Fiction Book of the Month

"*Terrible Virtue* is captivating, powerful, headlong, and inventive—just like its subject. A beautifully wrought, compulsively readable novel. Ellen Feldman can do anything."
— Stacy Schiff, author of *The Witches: Salem, 1692*

"A highly topical novelization of the life of Margaret Sanger. . . . We need her story now more than ever." — *Elle*

"Margaret Sanger was passionate about birth control, freedom, a surprising number of men, and her daughter. Ellen Feldman lets us see all these sides of one of America's most complicated heroines, a woman who knew too well the hard choice between work and family. An irresistible and utterly timely novel."
— Margot Livesey, author of *Mercury*

"Feldman compellingly portrays the difficult choices confronting women living in a man's world. . . . This immersive, moving, and thought-provoking book is worthy of the intense discussions it's sure to spark." — *Booklist*, starred review

"How does a minimally educated, working class woman redirect the moral compass of an entire generation? Feldman shows us how in her masterful novel, *Terrible Virtue*. Passionate, driven, the Margaret Sanger of Feldman's imagination is every bit as complex as the world she was determined to enlighten."
— Mary Beth Keane, author of
Fever: A Novel of Typhoid Mary

"Compelling. . . . An excellent choice for book groups."
— *Library Journal*

"Margaret Sanger blazes to life in this riveting, powerful novel. Read *Terrible Virtue* once to learn about the woman whose work ultimately shaped Western culture, then read it again for Ellen Feldman's masterful storytelling. Fascinating and unforgettable." —Lynn Cullen, author of *Twain's End*

"A fascinating exploration of Margaret Sanger as a visionary tour de force who left a stream of public victories and private casualties in her wake. Birth control, sex, family, work, individual need, free love, the greater good—it's all here, historically grounded but as relevant today as it was then." —Elizabeth Graver, author of *The End of the Point*

PRAISE FOR *The Unwitting*

"A compelling story . . . of mystery, political intrigue, and forgiveness. Much of the fun comes from the literary cameos (think: Mary McCarthy, Richard Wright, and Robert Lowell), but it's the novel's haunting portrait of a marriage that make this Cold War novel so resonant for readers of any time period, including our own." —Oprah's Book of the Week

"Bold and original. . . . The originality of voice and thought [is] evident on every page . . . part love story, part mystery, and part political thriller. I would heartily recommend." —*All Things Considered*, NPR

PRAISE FOR *Scottsboro*

"A riveting drama. . . . Inspired and inspiring. . . . Ruby is a gem of a character, and belongs with the best of William Faulkner's, or Alice Walker's, women." —*San Francisco Chronicle*

"Powerful. . . . Feldman gets her history right and . . . the fictional characters are rendered in artful service to the novel's larger project" —*Atlanta Journal Constitution*

"A novel that is based on archival records, court records, and first-person accounts but that succeeds overwhelmingly as a work of imagination . . . distilled with great subtlety and wit, into a story worth retelling and remembering." —*Boston Globe*

"Spellbinding fiction. . . . Rich imagination, memorable characters, and elegant but restrained prose. . . . On par with Feldman's characterizations is her subtle reflection of reality. With a sure sense of storytelling, a deft hand at characterization, and a stylish and sensitive use of language, Feldman has created another affecting portrait of the past. And in so doing, her tale of racism and poverty, lies and hopelessness, brings an American disgrace to life with eloquence, intelligence, and passion."
—*Richmond Times Dispatch*

PRAISE FOR *Next to Love*

"A lustrous evocation of a stormy period in our past; highly recommended for lovers of World War II fiction."
—*Library Journal*, starred review

"An intimate look at how we can be dismantled and rebuilt by changing times." —*O, The Oprah Magazine*

TERRIBLE

VIRTUE

ALSO BY ELLEN FELDMAN

The Unwitting
Next to Love
Scottsboro
The Boy Who Loved Anne Frank
Lucy

HARPER ● PERENNIAL

NEW YORK ● LONDON ● TORONTO ● SYDNEY ● NEW DELHI ● AUCKLAND

TERRIBLE

VIRTUE

A NOVEL

ELLEN

FELDMAN

A hardcover edition of this book was published in 2016
by HarperCollins Publishers.

P.S.™ is a trademark of HarperCollins Publishers.

HarperCollins books may be purchased for educational, business, or sales pro-
motional use. For information, please e-mail the Special Markets Department at
SPsales@harpercollins.com.

Terrible Virtue is a work of historical fiction. Apart from the well-known actual
people, events, and locales that figure in the narrative, all names, characters,
places, and incidents are the products of the author's imagination or are used
fictitiously. Any resemblance to current events or locales, or to living persons, is
entirely coincidental.

FIRST HARPER PERENNIAL EDITION PUBLISHED 2017.

Designed by William Ruoto

Library of Congress Cataloging-in-Publication Data has been applied for.

ISBN: 978-0-06-240756-6 (pbk.)

17 18 19 20 21   OV/LSC   10 9 8 7 6 5 4 3 2 1

For

Laurie Blackburn

and

Fred Allen

and again and always

for Stephen

It is only rebel woman, when she gets out of the habits imposed on her by bourgeois convention, who can do some deed of terrible virtue.

—MARGARET SANGER, 1914

TERRIBLE

VIRTUE

Prologue

ALL MY LIFE people have been asking me the same question. Margaret, they say, Maggie, Marge, Peg, Darling from the society ladies, Dear from those less swell, and you can tell from the way they say it that they can't decide whether to disapprove or envy, or maybe they disapprove because they envy. What made you do it, they ask. What made you sacrifice everything, husband, children, a normal life—whatever that's supposed to be—for the cause? Once, a friend who was a convert to Freudian theories agreed to fund my magazine, *The Woman Rebel*, if I'd go into treatment to find out my real motives for wanting to publish it. I did not have to go into psychoanalysis to know my motives. And it was not a sacrifice. I never told them that. Honesty is not the best policy, no matter what some of those good women who ask the question stitch on their samplers. Instead, I told them about Sadie Sachs.

Sadie's story silenced them. It was a heartbreaker. And it was true, I always added, because that's something else people said about me all my life, that I embellished the facts, made myths about myself, in a word, lied. Even J.J. accused me of it.

"Tell the truth, Peg, there never was a Sadie Sachs."

I stood staring at him with the go-to-hell look in my eye. It made Bill back down, or fly into a rage. It made J.J. amorous.

"You're right," I said. "There never was *a* Sadie Sachs. There were thousands of them. Millions."

Including my mother. I didn't tell him that, but he understood. God, that man had a sweet sympathy.

My mother, hunched over a washtub full of husband-and-child-soiled shirts and socks and underwear; my mother, bent over a pot of soup stretched thin as water to feed thirteen greedy mouths; my mother, kneeling on a mud-streaked floor that no amount of elbow grease would ever get clean. My gaunt, God-whipped, digger-of-her-own-grave mother made me do it. And the women on the hill. The ones who were nothing like my mother. I could have killed them for that. But I loved them for it too. That's what made me do it. My mother, the women on the hill, and the howling gulf between.

And oh, yes, love. That made me do it too.

But there is another question, and that has come to me only here in this bleached white room of this prison they call a nursing home. Peggy is the one who asks it.

She creeps in, her small bare feet silent on the linoleum floor, unlike the rubber-soled whispers of the nurses or the clicking high heels of my granddaughters who come to visit, perches on the bed, and stares down at me with eyes as blue as the Caribbean and as merciless as the priests and politicians and prosecutors who fought me all my life.

May I ask you something, Mama? Her tone surprises me. There's a sweet shyness to it. I had expected her to be angry.

I tell her she can ask me anything, though my damaged heart pounds in my withered chest as I say it. I know what's coming.

If you could do it again, would you do it the same?

And even now, in this narrow loveless bed, in this sterile white room, faced with the memory I have spent my life trying not to remember, with the guilt I thought I had drowned in the well of life, I cannot give her an answer.

So perhaps the question of sacrifice is not irrelevant.

One

ONCE, ON A train going God knows where, to give still another speech, I awakened in the middle of the night nauseated. Oh, no, I thought, pregnant again. It didn't seem fair. I'd been so careful. Then I calculated the timing. I couldn't be pregnant. To calm myself, I raised the shade of the window above my berth and looked out. I was just in time to see the sign marking the station fly by. CORNING. Even after all those years, merely passing through the town could make me sick to my stomach.

I can't remember a time that I didn't dream of escape. When the neighborhood brats made fun of me, I told myself I'd show them someday. When Miss Graves drove me out of school, I swore I'd never return. How old was I then? Fifteen? Sixteen?

I was so proud that morning, swinging along in my new baby-soft white kidskin gloves embroidered with tiny pink and blue forget-me-nots. Well, not exactly new. They were a hand-me-down from Mrs. Abbot by way of my sister Mary. But they had barely been worn. The Abbots were like that.

Mary worked for the Abbotts, who were related to the Houghtons, who owned Corning Glass, which owned the town of Corning. My mother said Mary was lucky to have such a good job. My father said the Abbotts were the lucky ones, because a girl with a less forgiving nature than Mary would have murdered them in their beds long ago for the paltry wages they paid and the advantage they took. Mary said nothing, but then she got to live on the hill, even if her room was high in the attic under the eaves where the water froze in winter and she boiled in summer.

I started out for school that morning, joining the friends I usually walked with, slowing down here and there to give others a chance to catch up. I wanted everyone to see my new gloves. And sure enough, one after the other, the girls oohed and aahed and asked where I'd got such beautiful gloves. A gift, I answered and tried to look mysterious. Brigit O'Mara begged to try them on. "Maybe later," I lied. I had no intention of letting her or anyone else get her hands on, or more accurately in, them.

The teacher noticed my gloves too. How could she miss them when my hand shot up to answer the first question?

"What fine gloves," Miss Graves said, and I turned my wrist this way and that to give everyone a better view. That would teach them to mock me.

"Are those forget-me-nots?" she asked.

I allowed myself a regal smile and admitted they were.

"I wonder where Margaret Higgins got such fine gloves," she said to the class.

I didn't know what she was up to, but the tone of her voice made me lower my hand.

"She said they were a gift," Brigit volunteered.

"A gift?" Miss Graves's dark eyebrows that went straight across her forehead in a single line shot up. "Now who would give Margaret Higgins such a handsome gift, I wonder."

"My sister Mary," I admitted. Now everyone would know they were charity from Mrs. Abbot.

"And where would Mary Higgins get such fine gloves to give to her little sister?" Miss Graves went on.

I waited for the ridicule about my secondhand dresses and shoes and hats.

"Do you think she made a pact with someone?"

The girls who were supposed to be my friends tittered. A boy hooted. Now I knew what was coming, and it was worse than a sneer about hand-me-downs.

My father was the town's freethinker. "Devil's children," other kids brayed as they chased us through the unpaved streets, dusty in fall, muddy in spring. "Devil's children." Sometimes I ran; others I stood my ground and took swings at them. When I fought back, I came home dress-torn, dirt-stained, and bloody, scandalizing my mother. Girls don't fight, she always said.

I was accustomed to the slurs in the streets, but not in school. At least not from a teacher.

I hid my hands beneath the desk.

"Do you think the Higgins girls made a pact with the devil for those fine gloves?"

She did not have to say any more. First the boys took up the cry, then some of the girls joined in.

"Devil's children! Devil's children!"

I put my gloved hands on the desk, pushed myself up out of the seat, started down the aisle, and slammed out of the classroom. As I burst through the front door into the schoolyard, the sun beat down on my shame, but I kept going, dodging buggies, pedestrians, a man on a bicycle.

"Slow down, Margaret Higgins," a woman called after me.

"Where's the fire?" the man on the bicycle shouted.

My hair flew in my face, and my breath came in gasps, but I wouldn't stop. I leapt over a log and came down hard on the balls of my feet. My ankle twisted in a carriage rut. Instinctively, my hands rose to break my fall, then, just as instinctively, went behind my back. My hip collided with a rock. Pain wrenched my shoulder. The side of my face hit the ground. But I'd saved the baby-soft white kid gloves with the pink and blue forget-me-nots.

I WAS NEVER going back to school. No one could make me. My parents didn't even try. My mother, heart sore for her two eldest daughters who had high school diplomas but neither husbands nor children, said she could use some help at home. My father was jubilant. He liked to say formal education was nothing but a tool to breed docility and instill capitalist claptrap. "I myself am an autodidact," he announced. "And you're a chip off the old block, Peg."

My older sisters had other ideas. Nan came home from Buffalo, where she worked as a secretary, Mary came down from the hill, and they took me into the fields, away from our parents, sat me down on a log, and had at me.

Mary: Do you want to spend the rest of your life in Corning?

Nan: Do you want to marry a boy who works in the glassworks and start having children, one a year, until you're old and worn out and have never seen anything of the world?

Do you want to turn into Mother?

Neither of them said that, but all three of us were thinking it. If there was one point on which the Higgins sisters agreed, it was that we were never going to marry.

"You have a good mind," Mary said.

"Don't waste it," Nan warned and held a brochure out to me. As I reached for it, I felt the twinge in my shoulder. I was still black and blue from my fall. The cover showed a big stone building. The words *Claverack College and Hudson River Institute, a co-educational boarding school in the Hudson Valley* ran beneath it.

I opened the brochure and began to read. *A special program for women offers training in moral, physical, and social development.*

"Mary and I will scrape together the tuition," Nan said.

"You'll work in the kitchen for your room and board," Mary added.

Ten days later, on a clement September evening, I went up the hill to say good-bye to Mary.

The sun hung low in the sky, pink as a skinned rabbit. Beneath a canopy of rustling leaves, I made my way down a wide street. Unlike the roads at the bottom of the hill, the ones where I ran from the cries of "devil's children," it was paved, so I couldn't kick up dust if I wanted to. The smells of half a dozen suppers, which Mary said were called dinners up here, just as dinners were called luncheons, drifted through the screens of the open windows. Voices rode the supper scents as if they were waves. I was of two minds about those voices. My father, the smooth-tongued village atheist with a bag full of incendiary opinions, the hard-drinking stonecutter whose handsome cemetery monuments the good Catholics of the town shunned like sin, made fun of them. Flat as the world before Columbus, he said, and hard as Plymouth Rock. I heard the want of music in those voices, but what they lacked in Irish lilt, they made up with an absence of blarney.

I passed porches two and three times the size of our parlor, with white wicker chairs, oiled-to-a-whisper swings, and fiery geraniums rising from stout pots and swinging in baskets. Grass soft as a carpet and green as dollar bills spilled down the yards all the way to the street.

On one of the greenback lawns a family was playing croquet. There were four of them, mother, father, girl, and boy. I knew no more children lurked in the house behind, though it looked big enough to accommodate a brood of eight or ten or a dozen. I knew it from the whiteness of their clothes, as immaculate as the conception fable the priest handed out to the parishioners at the bottom of the hill; and from the mother's serene smiling face as she swung her arms and the sound of the mallet making contact with the ball cracked the quiet air; and from the confident careless mirth that bubbled up from the children as the ball rolled through the wicket. I knew it from the way they seemed to float in the soft evening, light as dandelion seeds. The sight of that perfect quartet who had never scrapped for food or love or attention, who had never been humiliated before an entire class, who had never felt ashamed of anything, reached out and grabbed me like an arresting officer. And I was guilty as charged, of envy and pride and shame.

FEW THINGS IN life fail to disappoint. The beau who pursues you becomes the husband who won't let you out of his sight. The lover who writes letters so ardent that the paper scalds your fingertips becomes the stranger waiting on a station platform wearing an ill-fitting suit and a hangdog expression. The women who are supposed to be your friends do cruel imitations of you behind your back. But Claverack did not disappoint. Claverack and the movement.

I discovered that my sisters were right, I was smart. Miss Graves and the other teachers in Corning had kept the information a secret. I also found out that I was pretty. My mother was the one who'd kept that secret. At home, Ethel, the youngest of us girls and my mother's favorite, was the pretty one. But at Claverack the red tint in my brown hair made it titian, the green lights in my hazel eyes turned them emerald, and my pale complexion was milky.

Smart and pretty, however, were not enough. I hadn't forgotten the aura of that family on the hill. I struggled to shed the echoes of my father's brogue. I imitated the easy educated voices of the other students who lived on whatever hills dominated the landscapes of their hometowns. I mimicked the way they dressed and moved and even ate. No changing of hands to ferry the food from fork to mouth. I learned to play croquet. Yes, we played croquet at Claverack, just as they did on the hill. Day by day, I felt myself growing smoother. I was becoming a polished stone, glossy on the outside, hard at my core, where it counted. At the monthly assemblies, I orated on Susan B. Anthony, Elizabeth Cady Stanton, and the Woman Suffrage Amendment, in refined tones, of course.

No one seemed to mind that I had to work in the kitchen for my room and board. No one except me. I tried to hide my roughened hands in my pockets or the folds of my skirt. I scrubbed my face and neck and hair for fear of reeking of last night's meat and potatoes. All that lathering must have worked, because Cory Alberson was always saying that I smelled like roses or lilies or fresh-cut grass. Later he'd say I tasted like honey right out of a comb.

Cory, who came from the wilds of Long Island, was the most popular boy at Claverack. Girls adored him; boys admired him; faculty approved of him. But he was no stuffed shirt. If he had been, he never would have lured me out the dormitory window and down to the abandoned off-limits shed, night after night.

One evening in the shed he took his cunning mouth from mine, turned his back, and felt around in the tangle of clothing on the gritty floor. When he turned back, he was holding something in his hand. I couldn't make out what it was in the dim light filtering through the grimy window from a sliver of moon, so I asked. My father had always encouraged my curiosity.

"A French letter." He whispered the words into my mouth, then went back to opening the packet.

I watched in fascination as he put it on. If only there were more light. He finished and turned back to me, and I forgot his words in the eye-widening wonder of what we were doing. But later when our breathing had returned to normal, I suddenly knew this was how the women on the hill kept their houses empty and their husbands happy, their children loved and themselves young. Here was a real miracle, better than anything the church had dreamed up.

"You know, Peg," he said a few nights later as we were putting on our clothes, "this doesn't make any difference."

"This?"

"What we do here."

I didn't understand. As far as I was concerned, what we did in that shed made all the difference in the world. Those off-limits nights had turned the body I had barely known into an instrument of awe. The sheer physicality of myself stunned me. How could he think it changed nothing?

"I still want to marry you," he went on.

I had to laugh. If I were going to marry, I could imagine marrying for this, but only a fool would not marry because of it.

OUTSIDE THE DORMITORY, the January darkness had already fallen, but inside lights were bright and radiators hissed and clanked. Unlike the house at the bottom of the hill, Claverack had electricity, central heating, and indoor plumbing. The room simmered with warmth and the aromas of hair pomade, dusting powder, and the candied breath of a dozen chattering girls. It was a Thursday night. Many of us were packing to go home for the weekend. I wasn't going home. I seldom did. I was going to spend the weekend at my best friend Amelia Stuart's.

Miss Fletcher appeared in the doorway. The room went as silent as the night pressing against the windows. Miss Fletcher was the Reverend Dr. Flack's assistant in charge of female students, the dark angel who summoned girls to the headmaster's office for the delivery of moral lectures, the meting out of punishments, and, once since I'd been there, the announcement of a dismissal. But I wasn't worried. Miss Fletcher never came for me. I was too clever for her.

She stepped into the room and started down the aisle between the rows of beds, past Amelia, past Frannie Sawyer, past Charity Gaines, who did a fake swoon of relief behind Miss Fletcher's back. She stopped in front of me. I was sure she had made a mistake. Or perhaps she was going to ask me about one of the other girls. I wouldn't tell her anything. Loyalty is one of my strong suits.

"You're wanted in the Reverend Dr. Flack's office, Miss Higgins."

I still wasn't worried. The worst reprimand Dr. Flack had

ever given me was after a bunch of us had sneaked out to a dance. He'd said that I was a born leader and had to be careful where I led.

I took my coat and followed Miss Fletcher out into the frigid night, across the snowy campus, into the administration building, and down the hall to Dr. Flack's office.

Five words were all it took. He spoke them with appropriate solemnity.

"You are needed at home."

NOTHING HAD CHANGED, not the paint flaking off the front of the house, or the reek of yesterday's boiled cabbage, or the rancid smell of big ideas gone sour. Not the lean man with the shock of wavy red hair, the blue eyes that refused to see the world as it was, and the chiseled nose he might have sculpted for his own tombstone, though he was not the one who was dying. Not the emaciated woman, who looked twice his age, though she was two years younger, and had to stiffen her arm against the wall to keep from collapsing when she coughed.

"I'm sorry." The sentence came from my mother's mouth as abjectly as the blood she coughed up.

I started to say it didn't matter, but the words stuck in my throat.

My father put his arm around my mother's shoulders and looked at her with eyes bleached as pale as his old work shirt. I wanted to gouge them. "She'll be back to her old self in no time."

Her old self, I wanted to scream. What is that? A woman who doesn't have to prop herself against the wall when she coughs, but can bring up the blood she spits into her crimson-stained handkerchief without support? A wife who never had a chance to recover from the last childbirth before taking to her bed for the next? A girl who sped from youth to old age with no stop between? But he didn't notice that. He loved her too much, if you could call that cavalier sex-fueled sentiment love.

"All she needs is a dose of good Irish whisky," he insisted.

Good Irish whisky was his all-purpose cure. He wasn't entirely wrong about its powers. It cured all his ills.

I slipped into my mother's scuffed newspaper-lined shoes. They pinched and rubbed my skin raw, but there was no point in crying out at the pain. Mary lived at the top of the hill. Nan was in Buffalo. The older boys were away all day in the glass factory; the younger boys and Ethel were in school. My father heard nothing but the roar of grief in his ears and the soothing clink of bottle against glass.

The winter-shortened days passed in an endless round of man-centered chores. My mother asked for little. Later, I'd occasionally regret that I hadn't made peace with her during those last months. No, *peace* is the wrong word. My mother had no animus against me. Birthing and nursing and cooking and cleaning for a family of eleven children had left no time for complicated emotions, and if she finally had the leisure to ruminate, she didn't have the inclination. Poor Anne Higgins, as the neighborhood women called her, as if the adjectival pity were part of her name, loved all her children. That was what infuriated me. I wanted her to admit her regrets. I wanted her to say that if she'd had her choice, as the women on the hill did, if my father believed in French letters as fervently as he did in the single tax and socialism, she would not have spent her life populating the world and cleaning up after it. Like the priest who had taken to visiting when my father was not home, I wanted her to confess.

But if my mother feared for her sins, she recognized no mistakes. All she saw was the eleven children God had given her, because He could have taken them as easily as the two who died in infancy and the five who perished in her womb. She could resent her children no more than she could blame the husband she loved with a brimstone-courting carnal passion or begrudge the priest who cultivated her soul.

"Look what they've done to you," I shouted one day, gesturing at the cramped room so furiously that my hand hit the wall.

She just smiled, a beatific worn-out Madonna who didn't mind being in a stable as long as she was off her feet for a while.

Do I sound harsh? Having your life wrenched away from you does that. But there was another side to those last months with my mother. Every now and then, I'd let the laundry go unironed or put off starting the supper and spend a quarter of an hour reading to her, or curling her hair after I shampooed it, or, best of all, talking to her, not about the marriage and motherhood I faulted her for, but about the youth she'd never had time to tell me about. I sat beside that drawn gray woman, saw a flaming-haired girl who defied her family for love, and felt a kinship I never had before. She'd once been a firebrand, not for a cause but for my father. She was still a romantic. And the more she reminisced about her youth, the more we reversed roles. She became the child, I the mother. I know now that's not unusual, but I was young at the time and found it strange, and not unfulfilling. In some inexplicable way, caring for my mother soothed the sting of her neglect.

She died on Good Friday. By then, the ground had begun to thaw enough for the men to shovel the dirt with easy practiced strokes. My father insisted she had waited intentionally, out of consideration for the gravediggers, out of complicity with her

God. He had even let the priest into the house to administer last rites. He would deny her nothing, now that it was too late.

Nan arrived from Buffalo for the funeral. Mary came down from the hill with a box of black gloves that Mrs. Abbott had donated to make our mourning more respectable. Beneath the pair that fit me, my hand was still bruised from the attempt to make my mother confess.

We stood at the grave, an even dozen of us. We stood like vultures around carrion. We had picked her clean. My father and brothers, down to the youngest, bowed their heads and held their hands clasped in front of them, like codpieces. My sisters and I did not bend our necks quite so low. Gradually my father began to sway, like a sapling in the wind, but the air was calm, and he was no sapling. He was tall and wiry tough, and drunk.

The priest went on for some time. He finally had the devil and the devil's children captive. And we endured, as we would have endured a dozen Hail Marys or pebbles in our shoes to remind us of Christ's sacrifice for our sins.

Mortal bodies, he intoned. *Resurrection*, he sang.

I will not beat in my head. I *will not*. I *will not*.

Two

A ND I DID not. Thanks to Mary and Nan, again, I made another escape. They scraped together the money for me to enroll in the nurses' training program at White Plains Hospital. I swore that this time nothing would stop me. And nothing did, until a lingering cold and fever sent me to one of the staff doctors.

Tuberculosis, he said, and the world went quiet around me. Pregnancy exacerbated the condition, he continued. I must never marry. I laughed at that, a dry rustling sound in my throat. I intended to emulate my older sisters, who swore they would never marry, not Ethel, my younger sister, who, desperate to get out from under my father or maybe only to claim something of her own in the chaotic world that was the Higgins household, had run off with the Byrne boy. She was already pregnant. Her recklessness strengthened my resolve. I had my mother's disease. I would not succumb to her fate. The hospital was my only hope. But now that was endangered too. How could I go on nursing if I was sick myself? I asked the doctor if I could continue my training.

He sat staring at me for what seemed like forever.

"I assume you've heard of Florence Nightingale," he said finally.

I had to smile at that, though I had no idea where the comment was leading.

"Throughout her life, she has had to take to her bed with various symptoms of illness. But she's still alive and, as the saying goes, kicking. More to the point, she has saved millions of other lives. You're a good nurse, Miss Higgins. The world needs good nurses. Take the same care of yourself as you do of your patients and everything will be fine."

Who was I to argue with a staff doctor and Florence Nightingale?

I doubled my determination.

The training program was grueling for girls in good health, murderous for a student who was not, and trying to hide it. For eighteen hours a day I sat in classes, ran up and down dark staircases—the dilapidated mansion-turned-hospital had neither electricity nor running water—emptied bedpans, made beds, and changed dressings. Not all the work was menial. I helped deliver babies, assisted at surgeries, attended deathbeds, and sat in on postmortems. But I was no Florence Nightingale. The smell of diseased flesh made me retch, and the sight of blood turned my knees to water. Nonetheless, I hid my weaknesses and whispered *I will not* under my breath. And again I did not, until the night of the spring dance at the Manhattan Eye and Ear Infirmary.

Bill Sanger erupted into the ballroom full of cautious physicians in conventional suits and buttoned-up minds with a roll of architectural plans under his arm and a head full of subversive ideas beneath an artist's mane of curly black hair. He had dark brooding eyes, a hawk's nose, thin lips that sat in judgment of the world, and, God help me, a cleft in his chin. Still, I did not have to marry him.

He hadn't come to dance. He was delivering the architectural plans to one of the doctors. But the moment he spotted my flaming hair and my skin like marble waiting to be sculpted, or so he told me, he put down the plans, crossed the room, and cut through the circle of doctors to get to me.

What did we dance to that night? The Turkey Trot and Bunny Hug hadn't yet come along. Did we waltz? I can't recall. All I can remember is the sensation of man and woman. We might as well have been in a jungle clearing, pounding out a primitive mating ritual. Later I discovered that Bill had less sexual experience than I did, but experience was beside the point. As my brother who became a university football coach would have said, Bill was a natural, as unstoppable, fearless, and stupid as nature. And in the weeks after we met, I became his match and his mate. Sex beat in my head *I will, I will, I will.* Still, I did not have to marry him.

The sex was inexorable, but it was also a challenge. Bill lived with his parents. I roomed in the nurses' dormitory. In those days, only the rich had automobiles. But we were resourceful. In fields shrouded in darkness or carpeted with moonlight, he spread his coat and we undid buttons and hooks and ties until we struck the gold of bare flesh. When it rained, we stood under the shelter of a tree and fumbled through layers of clothing. Occasionally if a house was dark, we risked a barn or garage. The danger turned up the heat. Still, I did not have to marry him.

·}{ · }{·

THE SKY WAS leaden that afternoon, and the air ached with an impending thunderstorm. That was why I had put on

Nan's ugly blue hand-me-down dress. I didn't want to ruin anything nicer. As if the unflattering dress were not bad enough, my adrenal glands, the seat of my tuberculosis, were acting up, and I was running a low fever. I didn't have to pinch my cheeks for color, but I was hot-eyed and drawn. Funny that when I recall that day, I always remember how awful I looked.

We had planned to take a walk before I went on duty, but Bill arrived with a hired horse and buggy and announced he had a minister waiting.

"Waiting for what?" I asked, as he helped me up to the carriage. I wasn't being coquettish, at least not entirely. We'd talked about marriage. At least he had. But Bill's parents were observant Jews. I'd been raised in the Catholic Church, or just outside it. Why had he lined up a minister?

"To marry us, of course."

I told him I couldn't possibly get married that afternoon. I went on duty in two hours. Note the coyness. I didn't say I wouldn't elope with him, only that I didn't have time to elope with him that afternoon.

"It's now or never, Peg. I'm not going to wait around to have my heart broken."

The conversation was getting interesting.

"I don't believe in marriage," I said.

His laugh was shrewd. The sound frightened me. Was it possible he knew something about me I didn't?

I tried a more practical tack. "They'll drum me out of the training program."

"You don't need the training program. You won't have to work. I'm going to take care of you."

"I don't want to be taken care of."

He laughed again. Now I was getting angry.

"Of course you do. All women do."

"I'm not like other women," I said, though even as I spoke, I felt a pull as powerful as a rip tide. No more running up and down dark cold stairwells, no more retching at the sight of wounds and incisions and blood, no more exhaustion, no more struggle, no more fear, no more loneliness. *I will not,* I repeated in my head, but the voice was puny.

Did he sense my vacillation at that moment? He pressed his leg against mine. I felt the heat through his trousers and the ugly blue dress. It ratcheted up the temperature of the steamy afternoon.

"Please, Peg." His breath caught in his throat, and I imagined I heard the death rattle of a man being strangled by love.

"Yes," I answered, as my mother and my grandmother and even my little sister had before me.

FOR YEARS, PEOPLE speculated about why I married Bill Sanger. I often wondered myself. Some said I was looking for a father. I could have told them that the one I had, overbearing, underprotective, huge of spirit, small of accomplishment, was more than enough, thank you. Others said I wanted security. Though Bill had the soul of an artist, he worked as a draftsman at McKim, Mead & White. But even then I must have sensed that he was not cut out for life in an office. Still others insisted I was thumbing my nose at the church. But though Bill had been raised as a Jew, he believed only in art, social justice, love, and sex. His sex upended the world. His love filled the hole my childhood had carved out of me. Maybe that was the reason I married him.

·⊰ · ⊱·

I TOLD NO one except my family about the elopement. I was sure I could keep the nurses' training program from finding out. Perhaps that was another reason I married Bill, to break silly rules and defy foolish prejudices. My marital status would have no effect on my nursing ability.

He took a room in a boardinghouse on Christopher Street. I escaped there whenever I wasn't on duty. We no longer had to lie in fields, or huddle under trees, or risk being arrested for public indecency, though when the Sixth Avenue Elevated rumbled past our window, we sometimes scandalized the passengers.

The small room at the top of that down-at-its-heels house simmered with sex and love and one other joy. In the crowded, raucous house in Corning, sleeping, eating, and washing elbow to elbow with my ten siblings, I'd been chronically and deeply lonely. Now, suddenly, I was no longer alone. On the street, we walked arm in arm. At concerts and lectures, we leaned toward each other. At rallies, our voices rose in unison and our hands pumped the air in rhythm as we demanded justice. Then we'd stroll home and climb the steep steps that sagged to one side, breathless with the ascent and the anticipation of what we knew we'd find at the top, each other, ourselves. We roiled around the room, unbuttoning, unlacing, tugging at each other's clothes, shedding our own, until finally there was no boundary between us, and eyes wide because we wanted to see as well as touch and feel and smell and taste, we turned the world inside out. And sometimes, afterward, when we lay entangled and contented, I wondered why I'd fought marriage.

Then Bill began to talk about children. Night after night,

morning after morning, as the stench of summer steamed up from the street, as the first chill of autumn made me pull the covers around us, as the aroma of chestnuts roasting over trash cans made my mouth water, we went round and round. The discussion twisted and turned, but the line between us ran straight. Bill wanted them. I didn't.

He thought he understood my reluctance.

"I'm not talking about a brood of eleven or thirteen or even five," he explained. "I mean a child, born of love, welcomed with love, raised with love. As every child should be." He rolled over on his side and looked down at me. "As you never were, my poor darling."

He leaned down to kiss me. I turned my face away.

"I've managed to keep our marriage a secret from the training program," I reasoned, "but I'd never be able to hide a pregnancy."

"You'll be graduated before you begin to show."

He went on trying to persuade me. I continued to resist, though I never repeated the doctor's warning that pregnancy would exacerbate my tuberculosis. I refused to think of myself as a sick woman. I would not let others brand me as one.

"I just can't imagine your not having children," he said one Sunday morning. Outside, rain pelted the window and the lights of the Sixth Avenue El cars shone a jaundiced yellow as they rattled by, but inside, our room was dry and warm. "Childless women are, I don't know, somehow unfinished. No, not unfinished, unrealized. Like a painting that's technically perfect on the surface but lacks depth and feeling."

I thought of my sisters Mary and Nan. I didn't mean to, but I couldn't help myself.

"You're not like that, Peg. You're the most womanly woman I

know. You're the essence of womanhood. Not having children is a denial of that essence, as surely as not making love would be."

He rolled over to me. I reached for the bedside drawer where we kept the French letters. He took my hand and put it on his erection. I let him.

Three

I NEVER KNEW HOW the training program found out. Perhaps one of the other students spotted me coming out of the house on Christopher Street before I took the ring off the third finger of my left hand. Perhaps a doctor or nurse overheard me throwing up morning after morning. I stood in the small closet, retching over the bedpan, sweat from the fever and the nausea running down my sides, and raged against my body for betraying me, and this alien creature for taking over my life, and myself for my weakness, though I wasn't sure whether I meant weakness for giving in to Bill or to my morning sickness.

My glands grew more inflamed, as the doctor had predicted. Bill took care of me, as he'd promised. He sent me to Dr. Trudeau's famous sanitarium in upstate New York.

They stuffed me with milk and eggs and creosote capsules that made my mouth taste like a tar pit. They forced me to sit, robe-wrapped, on open porches for endless hours, then sent me on forced marches with other lungers, as they called themselves. I refused to use the word. Fevers made us blush, and a nurse with a skull's smile carved into her face called us her apple-cheeked darlings. Rotten to the core, she added under her breath. I balled my hands to keep from slapping her. The posture was becoming habitual. I missed Bill. I missed my old slender body. I missed freedom.

Days were long and stultifying. Nights were filled with cold sweats and terror. A week into my stay, a girl of about six or seven arrived, her eyes wide with fear, her thin arms clutching a teddy bear. The nurse with the death's-head smile wrestled the bear away from her and tossed it into the big metal drum where contaminated items were burned. A stuffed animal cannot be sterilized. The flames licked the thin wholesome atmosphere. The child stood staring, too frightened to cry.

Death hovered over the premises like a threat of bad weather. One day, the middle-aged woman in the room upstairs was there; the following, she was gone. A week later, the nice young man in the next cottage vanished. A few days after that, the little girl evaporated. No one mentioned the disappearances. The staff aired out the vacant rooms and changed the names on the row of mailboxes outside the great hall. The child might as well have gone up in smoke like her teddy bear. The woman and man might have vaporized into the health-giving air.

I had to save myself. One morning I sneaked out before dawn and made my way to the railroad depot. I hid until the train came in, then wired Bill from the first stop.

He was waiting at the Grand Central Terminal. I saw him as soon as I stepped down from the train. He towered above the crowd, his eyes raking the arriving passengers. He saw me and began to cut through the mob. I ran toward him. We embraced awkwardly around the child. His kiss tasted of life.

YEARS LATER, AFTER I became famous, the doctor who delivered Stuart wrote to ask whether my long and arduous ordeal had planted the seeds of my crusade. "It was a hard night for both of us," he concluded.

A hard night for both of us. Ah, doctors. Ah, men. They're such authorities on the hardship of childbirth. I, on the other hand, had been an expert on the subject since the day—how old was I? three? four?—when a neighborhood woman told me to go out and play and under no circumstances to come near the house again until I was called.

Her warning was pure incentive. I pulled a crate over to the window, stood on it, and peered in. My mother was thrashing on the rumpled bed, her face red and raw with pain, her hair matted, her mouth opened in a scream that shook the window. I was sure that she was on her way to heaven and I would never see her again.

She didn't go to heaven that time, or the time after, or all the times after that, but she grew increasingly distant. No, that's not fair. She wasn't distant, only harassed and driven and going down for the count.

I had learned about the agony of childbirth early, but until Stuart was born, I never knew the other side of it. When the doctor put him in my arms, flushed and furious at being dragged into this unforgiving world, I understood my mother's inability to regret. And later, when Bill berated me for neglecting the children, when Stuart talked about waiting for the ferry, when Peggy began to haunt my dreams, I would take out the memory of holding Stuart that first dawn and wonder how they could misunderstand me so completely. Surely, if I hadn't loved my firstborn, I would not have got pregnant again, and once more after that. I wanted a girl.

Having Peggy was a revelation. It wasn't that I loved her more than the boys, only differently. I whispered secrets I would

never tell anyone into the translucent pink seashell of her ear.
I murmured promises about her future. I knew her as I could
never know my sons.

BILL SANGER

You held our babies, and you understood. How hard is it to
love a helpless newborn, Peg? And a capacity for love was
something you always had. One might say a promiscuous
capacity. No, I take that back. You were my wife. You will always be my wife, despite the tawdry morass of disappointment and bitterness and heartbreak. But my enduring love
doesn't blind me. You're not blameless. Some things can be
laid at your door. Peggy can be laid at your door.

THOUGH I'D COME to motherhood reluctantly, I doted on the
children. But I didn't indulge them. Children crave rules as
much as they do love. I gave them plenty of both. I wasn't the
one who set fire to a house with three sleeping children in it.

WE MOVED TO Hastings-on-Hudson. The country would be better for the children. And Bill had decided to build me a dream
house. I didn't remember asking for a dream house, but what
woman in her right mind would turn one down? In the mean-
time, we were camping out in a rented cottage. Every evening he
took the 5:33 from the city, I left the children with the German
nurse and met him at the station, and we walked to the new
house. The theory was that the contractor would build during

the day and Bill would supervise at night. More often the contractor built during the day and Bill tore down at night.

That evening I stood in the unfinished living room watching him hack out a fireplace the contractor had just installed. During the past few months, he had gone after an arch that didn't soar in life as it did on paper, a staircase, and a wall. A dream house admits no imperfections.

I stood watching him, trying not to think of the mounting costs, just as I tried not to worry about the unpaid butcher's bill when he brought home opera tickets or a bouquet of hothouse flowers. Sometimes when I looked at him over the tickets or the flowers he held out to me, I saw my father coming up the dirt path to the house in Corning, carrying a new book on utopianism or a bottle of Irish whisky. But that was ridiculous. You couldn't compare a bottle of whisky to opera tickets. One was weakness, the other beauty. Nor could you put a dollar sign on art, Bill always said. That was why I hadn't argued about the rose window.

The rose window would be the glory of the house. It would sit at the top of the staircase and bathe our lives in radiance. He was making it himself, and I was helping. That was another reason I couldn't protest. The window would be a tangible expression of our love. Night after night, weekend after weekend, we leaded and welded the ruby petals until our fingers bled, and our eyes stung, and our tempers were as jagged as the shards of glass.

Meanwhile, the rented cottage was our way station. It was too cramped for our rambunctious family and too architecturally undistinguished for Bill's exacting taste, but we'd be moving on in no time. That was why I hadn't bothered to unpack all the boxes. And that was why that afternoon a few weeks after we moved in, I couldn't find the thermometer. I was furious at myself. What kind of a mother of three, what kind of a nurse, doesn't unpack the thermometer as soon as she sets foot in the house?

I rummaged through another box. It was hopeless. I went back to the children's room and laid my palm on Peggy's forehead. It was hot as bread just out of the oven. And there was something worse. She'd stopped crying. She wasn't even whimpering. She lay in the crib still as a cadaver.

I picked her up—it was like cradling a fire—carried her downstairs to the hall where the telephone was mounted, and lifted the earpiece off the wall. The operator came on the line. My mind went blank. I couldn't remember the doctor's number.

"I want Dr. Sherwood," I bleated into the phone.

Hastings was a small town. The operator said she'd connect me.

Dr. Sherwood's nurse told me he was with a patient.

"It's an emergency," I shouted.

"You can give me the symptoms, and I'll report them to the doctor." Her tone was intended to calm. I forced myself to describe Peggy's symptoms as coolly as I could.

She told me the doctor would call me back shortly.

"I'll hold on," I said.

I looked down at Peggy, hot and lifeless in my arms. A cold compress. Why hadn't I thought of a compress before I made the call? But I couldn't risk leaving the phone now. The nurse would return and find no one there. Her voice came back on the line, finally.

"Dr. Sherwood will be there in half an hour."

"Fifteen minutes," I begged. "Please. She's burning up."

Looking back at it now, I see those days in the hospital as a dress rehearsal. Keeping watch beside the crib. Listening to her labored breathing. Sponging her small body. No matter how gentle I was, she cringed and cried. The pain of being touched was too much for her.

Then, miraculously, her fever broke. Two months later, she was crawling and giggling and getting into everything; three, she began to walk. Shortly after that, Bill and I had the fight about the brace, the first fight about the brace.

For some reason I can't remember now—maybe one of the boys had a cold, maybe Bill had said he'd be late, maybe it was the maid's day off—I didn't meet Bill at the station to walk to the new house that night. Instead, he came straight home to the rented cottage. I was in the kitchen scrubbing a pot, so it must have been the maid's day off after all. I had burned the cocoa again. Somehow I always managed to. I'd resolve not to take my eyes off it for a minute, but then I'd pick up an article about working conditions in textile mills or infant mortality in urban slums or women being humiliated and harassed for marching for the vote, and the next thing I knew cocoa was boiling over onto the stove like an erupting volcano.

I was standing at the sink, scouring and gazing out the white-curtained window above it. The small garden in the backyard was going to seed. Mrs. Ferris, who lived next door, had said she'd be happy to show me how to ready it for winter, but I'd never got around to taking her up on the offer. I didn't have the patience to spend hours on my knees battling nature when workers were toiling under inhuman conditions and children were dying and women were being assaulted because they wanted to cast a ballot. Sometimes I thought how much easier life would be if I were like the other women on the street, child-obsessed, husband-dutiful, house and garden proud. The way my mother would have been if she'd had a house and garden to be proud of.

Sometimes, like my father, I raged at them for their indifference to the world's injustices.

I heard the front door open and close, the rattle of hangers in the front closet as Bill hung up his coat and took off his hat, and the sound of his shoes on the wide oak boards of the hall. He came into the kitchen carrying a bulky brown-paper-wrapped parcel. I glanced at it uneasily as he put it on the table. It was too oddly shaped to be a painting. Perhaps it was a piece of sculpture for the new house. Whatever it was, I was pretty sure we couldn't afford it.

He came up behind me at the sink and pressed himself against me. I leaned back into him. One hand cupped my breast, the other found its way beneath my skirt and petticoat and into my bloomers.

"Where are the children?" he murmured into my ear.

"Safe in bed."

I put down the pot and stood holding on to the sink, letting the pleasure overtake me. Then I turned to him. He unbuttoned his fly and lifted me onto the counter. It was some time before I noticed the package again. Then I asked him what it was.

"A brace."

I thought he was speaking architecturally. "What kind of a brace?"

"For Peggy's leg."

I tugged my clothing into place, walked to the table, and unwrapped the package. The device looked like something out of a medieval torture chamber, all hard metal and leather straps. I lifted it. It must have weighed seven or eight pounds. It did not belong on a child's leg. I saw Peggy dragging her encumbered limb like a wounded animal. I imagined her retreating into a corner, listless, miserable, fearful. I watched her spirit die.

"Peggy doesn't need a brace."

"The doctor says she does."

"The doctor says she does," I mimicked. "I could fill a book with the mistakes I've seen doctors make."

"You have to face it, Peg. That was infantile paralysis she had, not the flu."

"I say it was the flu, and I've nursed enough patients to know."

He stood staring at me for a moment. "I don't understand why you're so stubborn about this."

"Stubborn! I'm not the one who wants to put that"—I pointed to the contraption—"that thing on my daughter's perfectly healthy little leg."

He went on staring at me for another moment. "Is that what this is about?" he asked finally. "Your daughter—not ours but yours—and her perfection? Because anything less than perfect is impermissible. Anything less won't make up for your own childhood."

I stood staring back at him, my lover suddenly turned enemy. I never understood how that could happen so quickly. "This has nothing to do with my childhood," I said calmly, more calmly than his absurd accusation deserved.

"Let's just try the brace for a few days and see if it helps."

"Helps what?"

"Her limp."

"Her limp!" I wrestled my voice under control again. "Peggy does not have a limp. She has the normal—the perfectly normal—unsteadiness of a toddler learning to walk."

"The doctor—" he started again, but I didn't let him finish. I picked up the brace and, holding it away from me as if it were contaminated, crossed the kitchen to the back door.

"Where are you going?"

I didn't answer.

He started after me, but I was too fast for him. I slammed the door behind me.

It was only two blocks to the river. I ran the first block, then, when I was sure he wasn't after me, slowed down. Sometimes I think Bill was a little afraid of me.

A sliver of moon glowed dully through a thin scrim of clouds. The water flowed black and oily in the dim light. As I stood staring down at it, I felt the steel of the brace icy in my hand.

I wound my arm back the way my brothers had taught me when they'd deigned to play ball with me. The brace was heavy, but I put all my strength into it as I arced my arm forward, opened my hand, and let it fly. The splash broke the silence. A spray of phosphorescence exploded into the night. I went on standing there until the water went smooth again.

SIX WEEKS LATER, we welded the last pieces of glass into the rose window. Two days after that, on a snowy morning in December, we moved into the dream house. It wasn't quite finished, but who needs insulation when you have a rose window glowing at the top of the stairs? As I directed the movers—the sofa there, the end table there, the armoire upstairs—I tried to ignore the slushy footprints they tracked across the gleaming hardwood floor. Helga, the German maid, kept mopping.

They deposited the last boxes and left. The wind rattled the expensive windows Bill had insisted on installing, and beyond them snow swirled, but he cranked up the furnace, and we climbed the stairs to our new bedroom.

He closed the door behind us, and we stood grinning at each other. We had come a long way from moonlit fields, dripping trees, and borrowed barns and garages, but our desire was still as fierce and raw as it had been in the open air. We got into the big new bed and set about consecrating our dream house.

-ᄏ · Ӻ-

THE SHOUTS CRASHED into my sleep. *"Feuer! Feuer!"* the maid's voice rose from downstairs. I grabbed a robe and sprinted down the hall to Peggy's room. Bill was right behind me, heading for the boys across the hall. But I wasn't accustomed to the new house, and in the darkness I careened against one wall, banged into another, and stumbled on. Smoke blinded me. The crackling of flames was loud as thunder. My hands groped for the doorknob, found it, and pushed open the door. I could barely make out the crib in the smoky darkness. I grabbed Peggy and the bedclothes in a single movement and, hugging her to me with one arm, felt my way out of the room. Through the smoke, I made out Bill with a boy in each arm.

I retraced my way back down the unfamiliar hall to where the stairs should be and reached out a foot, praying there would be something beneath it. When I felt the first step, I pounded down. Flames leapt from the kitchen, licking their way along the hall. I buried Peggy's face against my chest and hurdled through the front door. My slippers sank into the snow. I began to run.

"Keep going," Bill shouted.

I heard the boys' terrified cries behind me. Peggy's screams seemed to come from my own throat. The wind-whipped fire roared above us. I hunched myself around her to shield her from the falling debris and kept running. A terrifying noise, like the world cracking open, split the night. Only when we were across the street, standing shivering in a neighbor's yard among a group of women with nightdresses hanging out of their coats and faces rosy with the reflection of the flames, did I turn to look back. A dazzling glass shower, red as blood, was still raining down.

When we went back the next morning, the shards of the rose window lay in the snow, the afterbirth of Bill's dream.

BILL AND I stood side by side in the sooty snow, watching the insurance investigator pick through the charred detritus of what was supposed to have been our future. Finally he made his way back to us, looked down, and nudged a piece of red glass with the toe of his boot, then looked up into the blindingly white winter sky. I glanced from him to Bill. Bill's face was as gray as the ash-dusted snow, but two circles of red burned in his cheeks. I've often wondered if he knew what was coming.

"The furnace pipes," the insurance man said.

Bill went on staring at him. The patches of red on his cheeks burned brighter.

"What about the furnace pipes?" I asked.

"There was no asbestos wrapping around them."

The three of us stood silent in the chill acrid air. The adjuster did not need to say anything more. Bill was too ashamed to speak. I was afraid that if I opened my mouth, the accusations would fly out. Or perhaps I feared I'd say something worse. I was, I suddenly realized, relieved to be free of the perfect house. Hope bounced above me in the winter morning like a child's balloon.

Four

WE PACKED THE few possessions we had salvaged and moved back to New York. We told people we wanted to be at the heart of the radical movement and the world of art. That was true. Ideas and isms raced through the city faster than the flames that had whipped through the Triangle Shirtwaist Factory. On street corners, labor leaders and anarchists and socialists climbed up on soapboxes and made the ground tremble beneath their feet. At the Armory, Cézanne and Seurat and *Nude Descending a Staircase* would soon stand the world on its head. But money was a problem too. We had overspent on the dream house. We were up to our ears in debt.

We took an apartment on West 135th Street. It was only a railroad flat with a parlor, kitchen, and bedrooms opening off a long hall, which the children loved chasing one another up and down, but the ceilings were high and the rooms light-filled. My mother-in-law moved in with us. Bill's father had recently died, and we felt responsible for her, but the arrangement also meant she could look after the children while I returned to work. I wasn't accredited as a registered nurse, but the Henry Street Settlement and other social organizations sent me out to fill in as a practical nurse. Sometimes my sister Ethel recommended me for jobs too.

Ethel had left her husband and children, come to New York to study nursing at Mount Sinai, and, unlike me, finished her training. But she managed to lose custody of her son and daughter in the bargain. The day she was served with the papers, she came to our apartment, weeping for her children, raging against her in-laws who'd taken them away, and spinning schemes to get them back.

That night I dreamed I'd lost my own children, not through a custody battle but through my own carelessness. They kept slipping out of my grasp or fading into the distance or getting lost. I awoke trembling, padded down the hall to the room where they slept, and stood listening to their breathing. I squinted into the darkness to make out their forms in the beds. I lifted the blanket that Stuart had kicked off and covered him. I adjusted the pillow that Grant had buried his face in so deeply I feared he'd suffocate. I laid my hand on Peggy's forehead checking for the fever I always feared would return. As I got back into bed, Bill turned to me and asked what was wrong.

"I was just checking on the children."

He smiled sleepily as he drew me to him. "And you were the woman who didn't want to be a mother."

·҂ · ҟ·

BILL HATED MY going back to work, especially when I had to get up out of a warm bed at odd hours for an emergency case or didn't get home from night duty until dawn. I never told him

how much I loved it. The cry of *The nurse is here! The nurse
is here!* ringing through the halls, up the stairs, and out the
windows to the neighboring buildings thrilled me. I was doing
something important.

We joined Local Number Five of the Socialist Party. I was
an anarchist by instinct, or at least experience. Growing up in
the middle of a family of eleven children had taught me all I
needed to know about sharing limited resources. I preferred personal freedom. But Bill persuaded me that as long as man had
to compete for food and shelter and other needs, individualism
was self-indulgence at best, a sure road to destruction at worst. I
remembered my poor hungry brothers vying for the last piece of
meat, when we had meat, and knew he was right.

Every night the headquarters of the local, which was above
a grocery store, erupted in volcanoes of Italian-, Russian-, Ger-
man-, Spanish-, and Yiddish-accented debates. Smaller gatherings in members' apartments were even more heated. At first I
was afraid to speak up. The men and women at those meetings
thought fast and talked even faster. Some had gone to jail for
their beliefs. One, John Reed, had gone to Harvard College to
discover his convictions. In the tenements I was a savior. Here I
was just a wife and mother with a seething but ill-defined rage
against injustice. I suppose that was how I came up with the
scheme to save the Lawrence strike. It was so obvious that you
didn't have to have an education to think of it. You only had to
have children. It was like the old chestnut that Big Bill Haywood, the notorious Wobbly leader who was there that night,
was always spouting about socialism. It was so clear and simple,
he liked to say, that no intellectual could understand it.

The night I spoke up started with the usual ritual of those evenings in cold-water flats and railroad apartments. As people arrived,

they dropped their loose change on a tray or in a bowl left out for the purpose. Later in the evening, when throats were dry from arguing and heads spinning with theories, two or three guests would take the kitty, head to the nearest grocery or saloon, and return with beer and sandwiches. Perhaps the beer did it. Without it I might not have had the courage to speak up. Not that I drank much that night or any other, at least at that stage of my life. Children of drunks rarely do, unless they're drunks themselves.

Silky-smooth John Reed with his Harvard accent and bristly Big Bill Haywood with his milky blind eye, which everyone assumed was the upshot of a labor scuffle but was really the result of a childhood accident, were arguing about how to keep the Lawrence, Massachusetts, textile strike going. The workers were disheartened, the weather was freezing, and the pickets were threatening to give up the fight and go back to work.

"It's the children," I said.

The two men went on arguing. Apparently my voice was not within their range of hearing.

"It's the children," I repeated, "not the bosses or the goons, who will break the strike."

Bill, not Big Bill but my Bill, was staring at me. He'd heard. "Listen," he shouted, "listen to Margaret. She has an excellent point."

As the noise died and people turned to me, my anger about the dream house and the brace and the dozens of other disappointments evaporated, and I remembered why I'd married him.

"It's one thing to march on a picket line," I began.

"What?" someone shouted.

"Speak up," Bill Haywood thundered.

"It's one thing to march on a picket line," I repeated in a voice I hadn't heard since I'd been on the Claverack debating team.

"Everyone in this room has put up with the cold and hunger and misery of that. It's something else to see your children's bellies swelling . . ." I thought of my children sleeping safely a few blocks away. My sister Ethel, who was there that night, caught my eye, but I looked away and went on. " . . . and hear their racking coughs, and watch them growing weaker every day."

"Margaret's right," John Reed called across the room.

"Only a mother could think of that," Big Bill shouted.

A few days later, I was part of a delegation that took the midnight train to Lawrence to bring back one hundred and nineteen sickly, malnourished, lice-ridden children, many barefoot and without coats or underwear in the depths of winter. Officials in Lawrence were so furious we barely got out with our lives. They used billy clubs to prevent a second delegation from taking another contingent.

Newspaper headlines blared the shame. Congress scheduled an inquiry and invited me down to Washington to testify. The nurse from New York, the papers called me. I am also a mother, I told them.

A photographer came to the apartment to get a picture of me with my own children. The boys were out playing, but I woke Peggy from her nap and dressed her in a smocked velvet dress that Bill's mother had made for her. I was wearing velvet that day too. I sat half turned to the camera with Peggy in my lap. Most children, awakened from a nap, would be fretful, but my daughter smiled to beat the band, waved to the photographer, then sat absolutely still when he told her to.

The photograph ran with a quote from me beneath it. "Until every mother cares for all children as she does for her own, there will be no social justice in the world."

Five

I WAS STANDING IN front of the hall mirror putting on my hat and thinking that being desired did more for a woman's complexion than cold cream. In the last few years, I'd tried half a dozen brands, but none of them had made me glow as I did tonight. A line I'd read somewhere floated through my mind. *It is as foolish to promise to love forever as to promise to live forever.* Not that I had stopped loving Bill.

Grant came barreling down the hall and stood behind me.

"Are you going out tonight, Mama?"

I sensed the cunning of an underage blackmailer.

"I am, my darling."

"Are you going to a shoshism meeting?"

I inserted the long pin into the crown of my hat and nodded at his reflection in the mirror. His small fists balled, ready to take on the world.

"I hate shoshism!"

"Maybe Grant has a point," Bill said. We had kissed the children, said good night to Bill's mother, and were on our way to the subway. "I certainly prefer my own family to Madame Pompadour de Dodge and her salon. It's a den of hypocrisy. They talk about socializing the means of production, but what they're really thinking about is appropriating someone else's wife."

I concentrated on lifting my evening dress an inch to keep from tripping on the steps down to the subway. I refused to argue with him about this.

Before Bill and I had eloped, we'd been in complete agreement on the nature of marriage. It was a stifling bourgeois institution, a form of legalized bondage that turned women into chattel. Ours would be a different kind of union, a melding of two equals based on love, mutual respect, and total freedom. We were committed to sexual equality. We believed that women as well as men had the right, the duty, to use their God-given bodies to live as fully as possible. In the abandoned shed with Cory Alberson, I'd known that instinctively. Since then, I'd read dozens of books, including works by the great Havelock Ellis, that proved it. The thwarting of passion, the suppression of the primal urge, injured not only the individual but society. Those convictions, not the minister's archaic words, had been our marriage vows that storm-threatened afternoon. But somehow in Hastings we'd lost our way. Living among a group of resolutely respectable young couples, we'd become conventional. Now, back in the city, moving among socialists, anarchists, and free-love advocates, gliding among men and women who believed that love was too precious ever to be denied, I was shedding my bourgeois camouflage. But Bill was still obsessed with fidelity. He didn't understand that love is not a limited resource but an exponential force. The more I lavished on others, the more I had to give him and the children and even poor Mrs. Berkowitz, whom the Henry Street Settlement had sent me to nurse back from an operation for what was commonly called woman's trouble.

The subway station was a cave of gleaming white tile deco-
rated with lavender street numbers. Bill slid two nickels to the
man in the booth, scooped up our tickets, put his hand on the
small of my back to guide me to the gate, then handed the tickets to the attendant, who dropped them into the glass ticket
chopper. It was all so smooth, an urban ballet. The subways
were one more reason I loved being back in the city. The speed
of the trains, the design of the stations, the sheer modernity of it
all was head-spinning. Imagine traveling more than a hundred
blocks in minutes.

A train rumbled in, the doors opened, and we stepped into
the car. It was crowded with men and women coming home
from work or going to a night job or heading out on the town. I
took the last empty seat. Bill hung on to the leather strap above
me. The train lurched out of the station and picked up speed,
but Bill refused to move on from the subject he was worrying.

"If revolution means promiscuity," he said as he swayed over
my head, "you can call me a conservative."

I pretended not to hear him above the noise of the train.

We climbed the steps and came up out of the subway at
Fourteenth Street. A horse-drawn streetcar clanged past. Above
the noise, a man dressed in black was haranguing the small
crowd that had gathered around him. It occurred to me that
black wasn't a color but an ideology. Anarchists wore black shirts
and trousers and caps as a statement of nihilism. Street preachers
dressed in black hats and suit jackets and throat-strangling ties
as signs of respectability and sobriety. This street-corner seducer
was working for God. He thumped his black Bible, and pointed
his finger at me in my satin dress and evening cape, and howled,
"Repent!" Hate twisted his mouth and glittered in his eyes, but
fear crouched in the faces of his band of followers. They were

terrified of ideas and art and freedom and sex, of the new and the unknown, of their own shadows and their own bodies, so they went creeping back to ancient times and old myths and a certainty no one could disprove because it was based on that syrupy-sounding word, *faith*. But if belief was so sweet, why was the man so full of hate? His predictions of my blood-soaked, fire-crisped everlasting future followed me east toward Mabel Dodge's house at 23 Fifth Avenue.

Mabel Dodge and I were nothing alike. Her "evenings" were written up in the newspaper. Her exploits were talked about all over town, and beyond. She had grown up with nursemaids and governesses, ponies, and dancing lessons for which she'd had dozens of pairs of white gloves like the ones that had got me in trouble back in Miss Graves's class. When she'd married, it had been to more money. But Mabel and I had two traits in common: a belief in radical ideas and a simmering restlessness neither of us could put a name to. That was why she had her evenings. That was why I went to them.

Mabel's salon was, like Mabel herself, a product of sheer imagination and fierce will. Who but an imaginative and willful woman would attempt suicide first by eating figs studded with shards of glass, as she told the story, then by taking laudanum, as a doctor verified? And all because she fell in love with a beautiful blond boy who looked as if he'd stepped out of one of the Renaissance paintings in her Medici villa in Florence and hired him as her chauffeur. At first everyone thought it was a case of unrequited love, but the beautiful blond boy had not rebuffed Mabel. It had been the other way around. At the last moment, Mabel had discovered she was too fastidious to sleep with the hired help, even if she had hired him for that purpose. Mabel Dodge was a cautionary tale for women in love and socialists the world over. Or perhaps she wasn't. Perhaps she was an inspiration, because despite shattered ideals (men she did not desire tried to take liberties with her) and broken hearts (men she desired insisted on taking their liberties with others) she seemed to be having an awfully good time of it.

"I used to collect dogs and glass and art," she liked to say, fixing her listener with heavy-lidded dark eyes. "Now I collect people. Important people."

Bill and I joined the stream of important and self-important people flowing into the apartment. The revolutionaries and artists went for the conversation and, because many of them were down and out, for the moment late in the evening when her butler threw open the doors and announced that supper was served. The more respectable guests went to mingle with the disreputable.

Mabel's apartment, like her life, was a protest against the stuffy conventional world into which she'd been born. In an era of dimly lit rooms dressed in dark colors, heavy fabrics, and murky paintings, her flat shone pure white. Even when the lights were dimmed, as they were at her evenings, the woodwork gleamed, and the silk hangings shimmered, and the bear rugs foamed like meringue. Need I add that Mabel, who stood at the door receiving her guests, wore a gown of radiant white?

"Good evening, how nice to see you," she murmured. "Good evening, thank you for coming." "Good evening, I hope you enjoy the talk." Except for those greetings, and equally impersonal good-byes as guests left, Mabel rarely spoke at her gatherings. That was why I was surprised when instead of releasing my hand, she leaned closer to whisper in my ear.

"John arrived wearing a face out of an El Greco painting." Mabel saw the world through an art collector's eyes. And like any serious collector, she hated to let go of anything once she got her hands on it. Several months earlier, she'd had an affair with John. "What did you do to the poor man?"

I tried for an enigmatic smile.

She started to say something else, but a small dark man with long greasy hair came rushing up and embraced her. "My little sister!" Hippolyte Havel cried in a shrill voice with a thick Russian accent. "My little goddamn bourgeois capitalist sister!"

Bill grimaced at me over Havel's patent-leather head. I smiled back. I would not let him ruin my evening.

We moved into the salon. In the center of the room, Big Bill Haywood, in a flannel shirt and corduroy jacket, was holding forth to a bouquet of pink and yellow and blue satin girls who blushed up at him with adoring faces. Emma Goldman, anarchist, rabble-rouser, and free-love advocate, was lecturing a dark Talmudic-looking boy who couldn't have been older than eighteen or nineteen. Her chubby finger poked his chest to emphasize her words, but he didn't seem to mind. Walter Lippmann, cofounder of *The New Republic*, was talking to Hutchins Hapgood, who liked to comb the Bowery looking for truth in the mouths of drunks. And John Rompapas—the Greek, as Bill called him—was leaning against a wall, his hungry black eyes measuring me.

Bill was still holding my arm. I shook off his hand and plunged into the room. As I did, Walter Lippmann moved to the center, held up his hands, and stood waiting for the conversation to quiet. It died by fits and starts. Since a guest who worked in a nightclub in Harlem had sung risqué songs at one of her gatherings, Mabel was careful to plan her evenings around a serious topic. Tonight, Lippmann announced, we would have a discussion of the labor movement. Big Bill Haywood would speak first.

A noise erupted in a corner of the room where a group of artists stood talking. My Bill had joined them. The sound might have been a sneeze, it might have been a snicker.

John Rompapas pulled himself up and away from the wall and began to make his way around the room.

Big Bill, a force of nature in front of a mob of workers, more thin-skinned in Mabel's salon full of artists, intellectuals, and slumming bourgeoisie, decided the noise had been a sneer. For Big Bill, the class war, like charity, began at home.

He swiveled his massive head and fixed the group with his good eye. "The first thing to understand is that the labor revolution will transform every aspect of the state."

John Rompapas came up behind me. I could feel his breath on my neck.

"Take art," Big Bill went on. "In the new order, art won't be above the masses. Artists won't be a chosen species."

Across the room, I saw my Bill's eyes narrow in anger. He admired Big Bill, but he was in thrall to art.

I felt John press close against my back. That afternoon, in the small room behind his bookstore, he had complained that I didn't love him. I did love him. I couldn't make love with someone I didn't love. But that didn't mean I would run off with him. It didn't even mean I had stopped loving Bill. Besides, I had the children to think of.

"Proletarian art is the art of the future," Big Bill proclaimed. "The state will see to it that everyone is an artist. The state will ensure that everyone has the leisure to paint or write or play the goddamn violin. Everyone will be an artist, and no one will be an *artiste*."

"They'll have the leisure," my Bill shouted, "but will they have the talent?"

My heart went out to him. It really did. But John was standing so close behind me, his chest pressed to my back, that his was the heart I felt beating.

"Perhaps we could move on from art to the woman question," Hutchins Hapgood suggested, like a policeman herding the crowd to safer ground, though only a man could think raising the woman question was pushing the discussion out of harm's way.

"Right," Emma Goldman cried. "Let's talk about equal pay for equal work."

I felt John's erection pressing against me.

Big Bill took a long swallow of his drink and handed the empty glass to one of the pastel satin girls, who danced off to refill it.

"Of course, socialism stands for equal pay for equal work," he pronounced. "But the measure is only a stopgap."

I leaned back against John. I would not run away with him, but I was willing to slip away with him for a while. We had done it at another of Mabel's evenings.

Big Bill took the fresh drink from the girl and drained half of it. "In the socialist state, women will not have to work at all. In the socialist state, women will not run a sewing machine, or toil in a mill, or mop the boss lady's floor. Their job will be to care for their children, as many as possible. Their job will be to raise a new breed of man, one who is truly free and equal to his fellow man."

John leaned over until his lips were against my ear. "Do I have to force you to run off?"

I took a step away from him. These blinkered men who thought women were nothing more than brood mares and love was a matter of absconding with the goods.

Six

FTER THAT NIGHT at Mabel's, I began to see the world
with different eyes. I continued to go to socialist meetings, strike-planning sessions, and Mabel's salon, but now when
I listened to the men arguing about socialism and communism
and anarchism, shouting one another down, banging their big
fists, swapping disparagements, I knew they were nothing more
than lost boys. Dialectic materialism, my foot. Dictatorship of
the proletarian, my eye. They thought they had the answers.
They didn't even know the questions. I didn't either, but at least
I was searching. I never dreamed I'd stumble on a clue delivering
a talk at a women's meeting of Socialist Local Number Five.

Anita Block, the head, asked me to fill in for a speaker who'd
fallen ill at the last moment. The subject was woman suffrage. I
told her I couldn't possibly get up in front of a crowd and lecture
on the ballot for women. I was in favor of it, of course, but I
wasn't an authority.

"You know enough," Anita said. "As for a crowd, you'll be
lucky if ten people show up."

Standing in the doorway to the cramped chilly room above
the grocery store, I counted seven. They sat in the rickety

chairs, bleary-eyed from a long day spent sewing piecework and making artificial flowers, bone-tired from cleaning other women's houses, lifeless as rag dolls. That they had come at all amazed me.

I stepped into the room. Heads turned. They eyed me warily. I walked to the lectern that had been set up. "Good evening." My voice came out arch and uncertain, a bad imitation of John Reed's tony Harvard accent with an undercurrent of shanty Irish.

Two of the women shifted in their chairs.

"I've come to talk to you about the ballot," I went on in that ridiculous accent I couldn't seem to shed.

One of the women yawned. Another, who looked sixty but was probably in her forties, blinked several times, as if she were fighting sleep. But the worst was a young girl sitting right in front of me. She was leaning forward eagerly, clearly hungry for information about the ballot. As I went on looking at her, I saw Peggy in fifteen years, curious, determined, alive to life's opportunities. That was when the idea came to me. I knew what these women wanted to hear, I knew what they needed to hear, and it wasn't a lecture on suffrage. The vote couldn't save them. Socialism couldn't change their lives. Only one thing would do that.

"However, I am not going to speak about the ballot. You all know it is our inalienable right to have a voice in making the laws we must obey. You all know there will be no justice in the world until women can vote side by side with their fathers, brothers, husbands, and sons. You know all that, but what do you know about . . ." I hesitated, debating the proper words, not because I was afraid to use them, but because I wanted to make it clear to them what I was going to talk about. " . . . women's health?"

A quickening of interest rustled through the room like silk.

"Women's health," I repeated the words. "It is a subject shrouded in mystery. A forbidden topic. Or so men tell us. But even the ballot is not as important to our well-being, our safety, our lives, and those of our children. I do not pretend to be an expert in the field, but as a nurse I do know something about the subject. And I would like to tell you what I know."

The young girl was leaning so far forward I was afraid she'd fall out of her chair. The skeptics were alert. The old-before-her-time woman was nodding her head vigorously.

I talked for almost an hour. I didn't impart any medical or specialized information. I merely explained the facts of life. It's shocking how few women are acquainted with them. They know about demanding husbands and agonizing deliveries and painful menstruation, but they understand little of the connection among those things.

Two days later, Anita turned up at the apartment. "I heard you gave quite a talk the other night."

I had sworn I wasn't going to apologize.

"They said it was the best talk they ever heard. The committee wants you to give another next week."

The following week close to a hundred women showed up. Word had spread. They crowded into the small headquarters above the shop and spilled out into the hall.

The talks were such a success that Anita asked me to write a series of articles for the *Call*, the New York socialist daily.

I started to say that I'd never written for a newspaper.

"We'll call it 'What Every Girl Should Know,'" she went on.

I'd grown up gleaning information from the whispers of

other girls, the teasing of boys, the jokes of older siblings, the unspoken words and veiled looks of my parents. Once again, I thought of Peggy. I told Anita I'd write the series.

Bill asked when I'd find the time. He never understood that for me, work, like love, was exponential. The more I did, the more I could do. He was just the opposite, but then he was an artist.

For the next month I sat beside dozing patients and taught a thirteen-year-old Peggy about menstruation, a seventeen-year-old Peggy about love, a twenty-four-year-old Peggy about childbirth, a twenty- and thirty- and even forty-year-old Peggy about how to avoid it. But I was careful. I wrote the last in veiled explanations and exhortations to demand more specific information. I wanted my voice heard, not censored, and I knew how close I was coming to that.

WHEN I HAD night duty, I picked up the paper on the way home in the morning and stood in front of the vendor reading my column on the street. On the days when I wasn't working and my column was running, Bill went out and brought the paper back to me before he went to work. On the morning the next-to-the-last piece was scheduled to run, I took the paper from him as soon as he walked in the door and turned to the woman's page. It was an expanse of white. At first I thought he'd picked up a bum copy. Then I realized.

A headline marched across the top.

WHAT EVERY GIRL SHOULD KNOW

Beneath it the white space was broken by seven bold black letters falling vertically.

N
O
T
H
I
N
G

By Order of
The Post-Office Department

What it should have read was by order of Anthony Comstock and his Society for the Suppression of Vice.

Anthony Comstock was a big brutal bully with a dirty little mind. Who else but a tyrant with a warped sex-obsessed brain would want to be the nation's censor? Thanks to a ridiculous woman-and-child-killing law he'd managed to ram through Congress, he had the power to open any piece of mail passing through the United States Postal Service and designate it lewd, lascivious, indecent, or obscene. And it wasn't only the postal system. He'd tried to remove nude models from the Art Students League. He was a philistine as well as a despot. He boasted that he'd destroyed one hundred and sixty tons of literature, convicted enough men and women to fill sixty-one railroad coaches, and driven Madame Restell—an abortionist, yes, but one who provided safe procedures—to suicide. It wasn't only Madame Restell. He bragged that thanks to him, a grand total of fifteen individuals had taken their own lives. He would not drive me to that extreme. He spurred me to action. A few weeks after Comstock murdered my articles in the *Call*, I gave birth to Sadie Sachs.

I could have named her Rachael or Rifka or Teresa or Maria or Mary or Brigit or Anna. She could as easily have married Mr. Caniglio or Mr. Reilly or Mr. Zilkowski. As long as she had an identity. Human nature likes a clear narrative line. No one wants to hear about scores of women mutilating themselves with a variety of sharp instruments, and poisoning themselves with old wives' remedies, and bleeding to death at the hands of quacks. People want a woman with a name and a face and three small motherless children sobbing their hearts out. So I gave them Sadie Sachs. Her story might not have been factual, but it was true.

I LIFTED MY skirt several inches and stepped carefully as I made my way down Grand Street. My stomach still churned at the stench, though I should have been used to it by now. I averted my eyes from the carcass of a dead horse.

They came for streets paved with gold. What they found was streets and sidewalks and alleys and courtyards strewn with the garbage of too many people living too close together. There was nowhere else to dispose of the detritus of their grim lives. Out the window went old meat bones, rotten vegetables, dead rats, dead cats, and human excrement because the single bathroom that served two floors of the tenement was backed up. If they had an old newspaper, they wrapped the filth. If they didn't, so much the worse. I had known poverty at the bottom of the hill, but this was a more primitive hell, a jungle where men slaved for a few cents a day, then came home to take out their frustration with tongue-lashings and beatings and sex; where women berated and cursed and slapped the children whom they'd suffered and almost died to bring into the world; where people cheated their neighbors, stole from their friends, and swindled their relatives just off the boat. How else could they survive? Surely a world so vicious and bereft of love could not give birth to new life, but it teemed with it.

I did not have to search for the number of the tenement. I had been there every day for the past two weeks since the Henry Street Settlement had assigned me to the case. I climbed past two girls, about seven or eight, hunched together on the stoop. They looked like sisters with their dark eyes sunken in shadows, waxy pallor, and lank unwashed hair. I thought of my daughter with her mop of shining white-gold hair, safe and sunny in the scrubbed apartment uptown.

Still, these two wan undernourished waifs were the lucky ones. They could sit on the stoop in the spring sunshine, even if the spring sunshine stank like a sewer. Most of the neighborhood children were upstairs in rancid flats or behind the locked fire doors of sweatshops, sewing buttons or stitching hatbands or twining wire stems on artificial flowers.

The girls watched me pass without curiosity. By now I was a familiar presence in the tenement, though when I'd first arrived, within minutes the women had begun drifting out of their kitchens. It was the same in every building. The ones who were not behind in the rent, or had been paid for their piecework recently, or had found a new boarder waylaid me with gifts of cakes and jellies and gefilte fish. The ones who were broke brought only their questions. They asked about coughs, stomach ailments, rashes, sores, bites, broken bones, diarrhea, and constipation—their children's, their husbands', and their own. Then, after I answered them, they had one more question.

"Please," they whispered. "Tell me the secret. Tell me how to keep from having another baby."

I told them what I knew. They found the information unhelpful. Condoms or French letters were legal only to stop the spread of disease, and then only for men. They were also expensive. There was no law against coitus interruptus, except the law of human nature.

They shook their heads and asked again. They wanted the real method, the one the rich ladies uptown used to keep their families small.

I told them about pessaries, and added that only a woman with money and an accommodating private physician who was willing to skirt the law was likely to get her hands on one.

There must be something else, they insisted. A few thought their kitchen gifts insufficient and offered bribes. When I refused the money and swore I had no more information, some grew angry. Most became despondent. Withdrawal and French letters or rubbers or whatever you chose to call them, if you could get your hands on them, depended on the man, and the women knew that when it came to sex, even the most dependable were not.

I pushed open the door to the tenement and stepped from the blinding yellow morning into darkness. A cobweb brushed my face. Dead roaches crackled beneath my shoes. I couldn't understand the society women who relished their work in the tenements and settlement houses. I found it sinister, despite my warm welcome. But then those women walked the slums like tourists.

A girl about the same age as the two on the stoop opened the door to my knock. She was as sad-eyed and hollow-cheeked as they, but every now and then in the past two weeks, I'd made her giggle. Her giggle could be as infectious as Peggy's. I wondered how long it would take life to beat the laughter out of her.

Two younger children squatted on the floor playing with a pot and a pan. The woman who would become Sadie Sachs was leaning over a metal tub, working a piece of faded cloth against a washboard. The doctor had told her to stay in bed for at least another week, but if you have three small children and a good husband—for this husband was one of the good ones—and pride, you cannot stay in bed when you have strength to stand on your feet, no matter what the doctor says.

The woman took her hands out of the tub and dried them on her apron. I asked how she was feeling. She said she was fine, and without being told sat in a chair and opened her shirtwaist. I listened to her heart, counted her pulse, and checked her breathing, and all the time I was measuring her vital signs, her mouth kept moving. At first I thought she was praying, though on earlier visits she hadn't seemed religious. Then I realized. She wasn't praying, she was working up to a question. She was working up to *the* question.

"Mrs. Sanger," she said as she began buttoning her shirtwaist, "a thing like I just had, I can't go through again."

"No, you can't. You mustn't."

She grabbed my hand in both of hers. "Then tell me, please, to keep from having the babies, what can I do?"

I told her what she, or rather her husband, could do, and as I spoke, I watched the shadow of hopelessness spread across her face, dark and ugly as the hemorrhagic rash from the septicemia she'd got inserting a knitting needle into her vagina. I had treated the rash, but there was nothing I could do for this.

THE BOYS HAD left for school, Bill had gone off to work, and my mother-in-law was in the kitchen begging Peggy to finish her oatmeal. My daughter was a picky eater. I confess to a secret pride in her fastidiousness and in the fact that she'd never known the hunger I had. The sound of the telephone we'd installed so the Henry Street Settlement, doctors, and social workers could call me for nursing assignments rattled the silence. I crossed the room to the far wall and lifted the earpiece out of the holder. In a jumble of Yiddish and English, a male voice cried and pleaded for help from Mrs. Sanger and God. I didn't recognize the voice, but I knew the panic. Finally I made out the name. It was the husband of the young woman who'd used a knitting needle, the most recent young woman who'd used a knitting needle, the man who would become Jake Sachs.

I raced to the subway, snatched the ticket from the clerk, flung it at the man behind the ticket chopper, and slid into the car just as the doors were closing. When the train reached Canal Street, I leapt off, raced up the steps, and ran all the way to the tenement. I was still too late. This time she had used a button-hook.

As time went on, I embellished the story, nothing substantial, only a few details. When I told it—and I told it again and again, to small groups and large audiences, in New York, across the country, and around the world—the family lived on the fifth floor, and the time was the dog days of August. That was why the husband, the three small children, and I had to lug blocks of ice, bags of food, and medications up the dark, filthy, sweltering staircase.

I added one more detail. I had Bill to thank for that. If it hadn't been for him, I never would have been in the shop that specialized in art books that afternoon, and I wouldn't have seen the doctor. He was sitting in one of the easy chairs, studying a book of Courbet paintings. It was open to a nude, one of the nudes that the critics had called pornographic. No, not studying it, lost in it. But gradually he must have sensed he was being watched, because he looked up, and when he saw me, he did what any respectable middle-aged doctor would do. He turned the page and pretended not to know the nurse who had caught him in the act. That was when I came up with what the man who is writing my biography calls the telling detail.

In the story as I told it from then on, Sadie didn't ask me the crucial question, she asked the doctor.

"Please, Doctor, tell me. To keep from having the babies, what can I do?"

The doctor stood looking down at Sadie. He was not a bad man, I was always careful to say. He had an avuncular bedside manner and an admirable patience with overdue bills. But he was a doctor and a man. He had saved Sadie's life, for a while, but he couldn't imagine Sadie's life.

"So, young lady, you want to have your cake and eat it too," I had the doctor say.

Sadie went on looking up at him with her old eyes. "Not for me the cake, Doctor, for Jake."

The doctor laughed. "What can you do?" he said. "I'll tell you what you can do. You can tell Jake to sleep on the roof."

Not a woman who heard the story doubted the words I put in the doctor's mouth.

THE NIGHT I gave birth to Sadie Sachs, I sat up in the dark front parlor staring out the window at the uncaring city. Sadie had given me a way to state the problem, but she hadn't brought me any closer to a solution.

"Come to bed, Peg," Bill called from down the hall.

I pretended not to hear him.

"Peg," he called twice more.

I didn't answer.

I heard the bed creak, the sound of his slippers whispering down the hall, the cry of protest from the spot where the floorboards squeaked.

"Are you all right?"

"I'm fine," I said without turning to look at him. "I'm just thinking."

He crossed the room, sat beside me on the sofa, traced the line of my jaw with his thumb, and started to turn my face to his. I pulled away.

"It's lonely in there," he said.

"I'm trying to work something out."

"You can work it out in the morning. Come to bed." He took my hand and placed it on the fly of his pajamas.

I pulled my hand away. "This is important."

He took my hand and put it on him again. "What could be more important than this?"

I pulled my hand away again.

"Peg, what's happening to you?"

"I told you, I'm trying to think."

He sat staring at me as if I were a stranger he couldn't place.

"I'll be in soon," I said in the same voice I used to reassure the children that there were no bogeymen under the bed or ghosts outside the window. He was no more reassured than they were. He stood and made his way down the hall to the bedroom without a word.

Years later I wrote Bill a letter to be mailed after my death. The contents weren't entirely truthful. I told him his love and passion and sex had beautified my life, and that much was accurate, but I also said that without him I would not have had the courage to do what I did. We both knew that was a lie. Nothing could have kept me from my work. Nothing did keep me from my work, but I won't talk about that. Nonetheless, I wanted to make amends. I'd hurt him too much.

He never got the letter. He died before I did. Stuart and Grant didn't tell me. I suppose they meant well. Spare Mother the pain. Peggy was the one who broke the news. I didn't tell the boys that. My sons are men of science, doctors of medicine. They believe only what they can see and touch. But I'm getting ahead of myself.

After Bill went back to bed that night, I turned to the windows again. Here and there an isolated rectangle of light burned a hole in the darkness. I sat thinking about all the women in all the apartments; some, like Sadie, lying wide-eyed in the darkness, their minds racing for ways to stave off or end another pregnancy that their bodies and budgets and sanity couldn't afford; others spread silent and terrified beneath an angry or drunken or vengeful man; and still others, intoxicated by the wonder of a man's body, and their own, unmindful, for the moment, of the consequences. We were trapped, by men, and by ourselves.

I didn't know how long the whimpers from the children's room had been building before I noticed them, but when I did, I hurried down the hall, scooped up Peggy, and carried her back to the parlor. I didn't want her waking the boys or her grandmother.

"Did you have a bad dream, my darling?" I crooned into her ear.

A hiccup interrupted the whimpers. Her arms were a vise around my throat.

I sat on the sofa with her in my lap. She nestled her head into the hollow between my shoulder and neck. The whimpers began to subside. Her thumb found its way to her mouth. She sucked contentedly.

I thought of my own childhood terrors that had gone unrecognized and unsoothed. Suddenly I was furious. At my father's cavalier irresponsibility; at my mother's fecklessness and, despite the fact that she had wrecked her health and sacrificed her life to us, selfishness; at a society that would let children enter the world unwanted and unloved.

But this was the twentieth century. If trains could race beneath the city eating up time as they went, if man could soar like a bird in a heavier-than-air machine, if scientists could harness electricity to run irons and gramophones and floor sweepers, surely mankind, or womankind, could find a way to prevent pregnancy and make abortion unnecessary.

As the lights began to go on in the windows across the way and shadows struggled toward another day, I made up my mind. I'd had enough of treating the symptoms of the disease. I was determined to find the cure. I would give up nursing and devote myself to contraception. I would free women from their biological shackles. I would liberate love from its consequences. And I would make sure that every child entered the world desired and cherished.

Seven

DESPITE MY RESOLUTION to stop treating the symptoms and look for the cure, I continued to accept the occasional nursing assignment. We needed the money. But most mornings I left Peggy with my mother-in-law, walked the boys to school, and took the subway down to Forty-Second Street to the new public library, where I spent the day reading, taking notes, and following a chain of references from one book to the next. The process was slow and frustrating. What little information existed was veiled in euphemisms and hidden in puritanical ellipses.

I tried interviewing doctors I knew. Most refused to talk about the subject. The ones who would talk often knew less than I did. A few didn't even understand the difference between contraception and abortion. The medical school libraries weren't much more helpful. Nonetheless, I struggled on. Day by day, my index cards mounted and my knowledge grew, but as June melted into July, the city became increasingly unbearable, and finally dangerous.

Polio lurked everywhere, especially in wait for the young. Finally it moved into our building. One twilight evening, a girl of about seven or eight, who lived on the floor below us, was jumping rope on the sidewalk, despite the heat; the next morning I looked out the window to see her mother following a stretcher to a waiting ambulance. I had to get the children out of the city. Peggy had had the flu, not polio, no matter what Bill and the doctor said, but she might not be so lucky a second time.

I decided to take the children to Provincetown, a small Portuguese fishing village on the tip of Cape Cod. Half the people we knew would be there, including Big Bill Haywood and John Reed and Eugene O'Neill, to name only a few. They were going to write and paint and put on plays, to organize causes and argue and fall in and out of love. Later, Bill would accuse me of having an affair with Gene O'Neill that summer, and I'd become indignant. That summer I was mad about Walter Roberts, a lanky man with a long morose face and an irresistibly lopsided smile, while Gene was head over heels in love with Louise Bryant, who was living with John Reed. That was not to say the fresh air, sunshine, and sea would not be good for the children. Bill had to stay in town to work, but he'd manage to come up on weekends. The trip from New York on the side-wheelers of the Fall River Line was long, and the train ride worse, boiling when the windows were closed, dangerous when they were open and cinders flew in to bite and blind, but he insisted it was worth the trouble and discomfort to see the children and me. I could even continue my research. Each week I'd take the steamer to Boston and use the library there for a day or two while Ethel, who missed her own children, would stay with mine.

WE CAME DOWN the gangplank and stood on the pier blinking against the glare of the sun that beat down on our straw hats, hit the water, and bounced back at us. I raised my hand to shade my eyes and looked toward the town. Between the two main streets that followed the curve of the bay, a tangle of small gardens rioted in color. Stuart, Grant, and Peggy were hopping from one foot to the other, pulling on Ethel and me, and giving off sparks of excitement. I calmed them down for long enough to load our things on a wagon, and we started for the rented cottage. Big Bill, who'd found it for us, said it was so close to the water that high tide practically lapped at the door. He hadn't exaggerated.

As the days and weeks passed, the children thrived. Stuart roamed the rocks and fished and seemed to be growing up overnight. Grant came home with pockets full of colored shells, sea-smoothed stones, and tiny crabs. Peggy ran on the beach, her blond hair gleaming in the sunlight, her chubby brown legs steady beneath her.

"I told you she didn't need a brace," I said to Bill when he arrived for the weekend.

"She still has the limp, Peg."

The man was impossible.

She even learned to swim.

The light hit the bay and splintered like the facets of a diamond as her small water-lightened body floated in my outstretched arms. At first she flailed, but little by little, as I counted, she began to kick her legs and move her arms in rhythm.

I took one hand away. She kept paddling. I removed the other.

"I'm swimming!" she shouted when she realized I'd let go of her. "I'm swimming!"

She swam a short distance away from me, the water streaking off her sleek brown skin, her red bathing suit flashing like a buoy, then circled and returned, once, twice, a third time. I stood waist-deep in the water, laughing at her excitement, marveling at her fearlessness, rejoicing that each time she went a little farther away, and each time she came back to me.

That evening, exhausted from the sun and sea and effort, she fell asleep against my shoulder as we sat in the porch swing. I carried her into the house and tucked her into her bed. As I stood looking down at her, her mouth curled into a smile, and I knew that in her dreams, she was still afloat. And I was there with her.

I had never known such blissful times with my children. That was why I couldn't understand the fuss Stuart made about an unimportant incident.

ETHEL BYRNE

It wasn't unimportant to him, Marg. I was his aunt, not his mother, but I could see that. Of course, I spent more time with the children that summer. I'm not casting stones. A woman who has lost her children to her in-laws in a custody battle isn't exactly in a position to. (Have you noticed that we never talk about the choices we made? I got my nursing degree but lost my children. You never finished training but still have yours, as well as my daughter, come to think of it. Olive adores you. But I don't suppose we ever will talk about it. Sometimes it's easier to save the world than ourselves.)

Nonetheless, once you told Stuart he could meet the *Dorothy Bradford* at the dock, you should have made it your business to be on the steamer. The least you could have done after you missed it was take the train later in the day.

I told him you must have got caught up in your research. My excuse turned out to be true, though try explaining to a ten-year-old boy that his mother came across a reference to an Egyptian condom, not an herb or plant or lemon, which were common contraceptives in ancient times, but a condom, the earliest she'd ever heard of. The other excuse wasn't any better. Mother overslept, because after a dinner to celebrate her discovery, she was up all night making love with Walter Roberts, whom your father calls the Eagle, because he's a reporter for the *Brooklyn Eagle* and because the eagle is a bird of prey. That's a lot for a ten-year-old boy to digest.

I stood on the porch watching him stride down the dunes toward town that day, an intrepid explorer in his mind's eye, then went back into the house to make lunch for Grant and Peggy. I remember, because I forgot to cut the crusts off Peggy's sandwich, and you know how she was about that. She raised hell. That was your fault. You spoiled her rotten. You could go off and leave her for a year—I know, I know, that came later, and you had no choice—but when you were with her, you couldn't say no to her smallest whim.

When two o'clock turned to three and three to four, and Stuart wasn't back, with or without you, I began to worry. Finally I put Grant and Peggy in the wagon and started for town.

Half a block away from the Cape Cod Steamship Pier, I could see it was deserted except for the Waiting Woman. You remember her. Day after day, night after night, she stood, staring out to sea. People said she had spent so much of her life scanning the horizon for fathers and brothers and husbands and sons who'd never returned that she couldn't turn her back on the water. I'd never spoken to her, few people in town ventured to, but that day I did. I asked her if she'd seen a boy. "Ten years old. Blond hair. He was wearing khaki shorts and a white shirt." I was describing half the boys in town, outside the Portuguese community.

"The one who was waiting for his ma?" I was surprised. Her voice sounded ordinary, not even rusty from lack of use.

"That's the one."

"He's a good waiter. Set half the afternoon."

I asked if she knew where he'd gone.

"Railroad depot. I told him might as well stay here. Harbor's where the boats come in." She pronounced it haabor. "Harbor's where they come home."

By this time Grant and Peggy had climbed out of the wagon and refused to get back in. On the way down the pier, Peggy tripped on the uneven planking—she really was unsteady on her feet—fell, and started to cry. I picked her up. She squirmed against me. "Mama," she whined. "I want my mama." Grant hung on to my skirt, heavy as an anchor. We dragged our way toward Pilgrim Monument.

I saw him from halfway down Bradford Street, his shirt white against the dark green paint of the bench, his brown legs swinging above the platform, his face staring down the track, just as the Waiting Woman watched out to sea.

"She wasn't on the boat," he said, when we reached the bench. The words came out flat and even, as if any emotion would lead to tears. "So I came here to meet the train."

I told him that was very smart of him.

"But she wasn't on the train neither."

I didn't correct him, though I bet you would have.

Peggy cried all the way back to the house. Grant sulked.

But Stuart was stoic. He didn't say a word. He just kept his eyes on the sea. If you had seen him, Marg, you would have understood why he makes so much of it. If you had seen him, he would have broken your heart, because there's one thing I know about you. You love your children. That's why you ought to be more careful. You don't want to end up like me. Or do you?

Eight

I WAS SITTING AT the dining table in the apartment on 135th Street, organizing the notes from my summer research, when I heard Bill's key in the lock. Time must have got away from me. It often did when I was working. I glanced at the watch pinned to my shirtwaist. It was only a little after three. It wasn't late, he was early.

When I looked up again, he was standing in the archway. Something about his smile made me uncomfortable.

"You're home early. Are you sick?"

"Change the vowel. Not sick, sacked. The august firm of McKim, Mead & White no longer requires my services."

"No!"

The smile grew wider and more malevolent. "Yes."

"But you're the best draftsman they have."

"Apparently they don't think so."

"It's because of your socialist connections. We always knew you were working for the enemy."

His mother came down the hall from the kitchen. Voices traveled in that apartment. "It's because you're a Jew," she said.

He looked from one of us to the other, and the grin became feral. "The two are not mutually exclusive."

Three evenings later, he returned from God knew where—since he'd been fired, I didn't like to ask what he did with his time—and stood in the archway again. His smile was different, but I didn't like it any better. It reminded me of the grin my father used to wear when he returned home to tell us how he'd bested the town's devout believers, capitalist dupes, and spineless followers in a philosophical argument.

"The august firm of McKim, Mead, etcetera, etcetera, and so forth doesn't know it, but they gave us a blessing in disguise. We're free!"

"Free?" I wasn't arguing. I just didn't understand what he meant. We still had three children. We still had to feed and clothe and shelter them. The only thing we were suddenly free of was a regular paycheck.

"To go to Paris. You say the Europeans are light-years ahead of us in contraception. You'll do your research, I'll paint, and the children will learn French. We'll all learn French. *Bonjour. Comment allez-vous? Voulez-vous coucher avec moi?* Think of it, Peg, it will be a fresh start."

He seemed to be growing taller, broader, more handsome as he spoke. I remembered again why I'd married him. I stood, crossed the room, and put my arms around him.

"A new start in Paris," I agreed.

"Without the Greek or the Eagle."

Why did he always have to ruin things?

A FREEZING FLAT four floors up on the Boulevard Saint-Michel, even one across from the Luxembourg Gardens where the children could play, turned out to be no place for a new start. We shivered in flannel underwear, suffered from chilblains, and grew more short-tempered each day. The children were not chattering in French. They were sulking in silence. The situation was hardest on Peggy. She barely recovered from one cold before she succumbed to the next. She lay on her small cot either gray and listless with the cold or flushed and burning with a fever. Later, when Bill tried to blame me, I'd remind him that Paris had been his idea.

Two and a half months after we arrived, I told Bill I was ready to return home. We had another row about it. He insisted he painted better in Paris. I pointed out he had few enough canvases to prove the point.

"I'm sorry. It's just that you seemed to get more done in New York."

"New York! That hellhole of free love and promiscuity. That's what you can't wait to return to?"

I went into the bedroom, where I kept my research, found a map I'd discovered a few weeks earlier, and carried it back to him. It was a representation by gradations of shading of the incidence of prostitution in the various arrondissements.

I held it out to him. "New York is a hellhole of promiscuity? Take a look at this. Not a single arrondissement is white."

He didn't even glance at it. The door slammed behind him.

When he returned several hours later, he was carrying a bouquet of camellias. They weren't roses, but I still tried not to think of how much they cost. We ended up in bed. We always ended up in bed after an argument. But the sex never changed anything. The next day I booked passage for the children and me on the SS *New York*.

BILL STOOD ON the pier crying. His image was wavy through the tears streaming down my own face. Beside me on the deck the children were weeping too, though they weren't sure why.

They didn't want to leave their father, but they were overjoyed to be going home, and a boat was an adventure.

Tugs inched the ship away from the dock. The horn sounded a cry that sent a shiver down my spine. Engines rumbled. Black water churned around the hull. One after another the streamers from ship to shore snapped. I felt the breaks as if in my own body. How could I be leaving Bill? I was miserable. I was leaving Bill. I was free!

BILL SANGER

I can't recall the train ride back to Paris. My mind had shut down, my body gone numb from the pain of your leaving. I walked from the Gare Saint-Lazare to the flat. I was trying to tire myself, though I knew the effort was hopeless. I'd never be able to sleep without you beside me.

The concierge let me into the dark sour-smelling hallway. She asked where Madame was. I turned my face away. I was ashamed to have her see the tears. I know I shouldn't tell you this. My weakness only feeds your disgust.

I climbed the stairs to the flat and stood outside it. The key hung useless in my hand. I couldn't lift my arm. I didn't have the heart to unlock the door. I didn't have the courage to walk into that apartment, drained of the children's voices, empty of you, unoccupied by love, that word we never stop arguing about. I should have gone with you, but I couldn't return to the world you were making for yourself. Does that make me a coward? I felt like one. My cravenness shadowed my steps back down the stairs and out into the street.

The café around the corner glowed in the cold night. Normally my eye would have been trying to memorize the effect of the light spilling through the window and over the wet cobblestones. I barely noticed it. Still, the café was better than that empty room.

I was a few feet away from the door when a woman in a frayed coat with gaudily rouged cheeks fell in step beside me. She called me monsieur, and asked if I was lonely, and promised solace. I didn't want that kind of solace, not now, not when you used to urge me to sleep with other women. You prided yourself on your lack of jealousy. I twisted in the cold wind of your indifference. You didn't leave a man much, Peg. But here's the worst part of it. By some cruel cosmic joke of God, in whom I don't believe, or nature, I still love and want you.

I WAS AS happy to be going home as the children were, though I wasn't sure what I was going to do when I got there. The French were, as I'd told Bill, ahead of us in contraception, and I'd learned a great deal during my stay, but the knowledge would get me nowhere without a strategy. It wasn't enough to teach a handful of desperate women specific methods. I needed to overthrow archaic laws, reshape public opinion, and enlighten, or at least outsmart, the men in power who were determined to keep us in chains. But how? Should I break the laws in order to win judgments in the courts or lobby legislators to write new laws? Should the issue be free speech or women's rights or public health, which was just beginning to garner attention? The possibilities raced around in my head as the ship steamed toward New York and shipboard life, oblivious to the problem, went on about me.

The voyage was calm for a winter crossing, and the children and I linked arms and circled the deck while the ship rolled gently beneath our feet and the wind hurried us down the starboard side and fought us up the port, or vice versa when we went in the other direction.

They ate at an early children's sitting, and I ate alone in the dining room at the second sitting. I was seated next to a man who wore handsome silk ties and expensive suits that were soft to the touch. He carried a silver cigarette case engraved with his initials and told me he'd never known a socialist before. You bet, I wanted to say. But as we sat side by side at meals, and danced across the polished floor of the main saloon, and promenaded the deck arm in arm after I'd put the children to bed, I sensed that my radical ideas titillated him almost as much as my physical closeness. He invited me to his cabin. I went.

I was not sorry afterward, though he wanted me to be. He wanted me to creep around in darkness, clutching my clothes to hide my bare flesh, begging for reassurance that the incident was not what it appeared to be. He didn't like my strutting naked in the unsparing electric light. He bridled at the sound of my heels clicking jauntily down the passage away from his cabin, back to my own. He hated my joy, my lack of shame—oh, how those upstanding men love shame—my independence. But he found them irresistible too. For the rest of the crossing, he couldn't stay away from me.

His prurient small-mindedness gave me the idea. It slapped me in the face as fresh as the wind as I came around the stern of the ship during a solitary walk on the next-to-the-last night at sea and sent me hurrying down to the ship's library. I would start by banishing shame.

I tugged off my gloves, took a sheet of stationery and a pen, and began to write.

The Woman Rebel

I leaned back and looked at the words. No one who saw them on the cover of a magazine could mistake the contents. I sat up to the desk and began to write again.

No Gods: No Masters

It was the old Wobbly slogan, but it fit.
Now I couldn't stop.

A woman's duty: To look the whole world in the face with a go-to-hell look in her eyes, to have an ideal, to speak and act in defiance of convention.

I had found the means of my mission. I would publish a magazine that spoke to and for downtrodden women everywhere. I would rouse them to mutiny against the forces that enslaved them. I would give them the tools to choose when to fulfill the supreme function of motherhood. And I did think it was supreme, as long as it was of our own volition. I would do all that, and one more thing. By sending the magazine through the mails, I would challenge Comstock's absurd and pernicious law.

Nine

WALTER, AKA THE Eagle, was waiting for us on the pier. He hugged the boys, held Peggy high in the air, embraced me, and asked how Paris had been.

"I hate Paris," Peggy answered before I could.

I found an apartment on Post Avenue near Dyckman Street. It was so far uptown that the Broadway subway streaked out from underground into fresh air to reach it. The country atmosphere would be good for the children, the rent was cheap, and I could use the dining room as an office.

Now all I had to do was raise money to publish my magazine. I started my appeal with Theodore Schroeder, a free-speech lawyer who was known to support radical causes. We met at the Liberal Club on MacDougal Street on a surprisingly mild evening in the middle of a January thaw. The window in front of the two Morris chairs where we sat facing each other was open a few inches, and I could smell the onions wafting up from Polly's restaurant next door. Hippolyte Havel, the patent-leather-haired Russian revolutionary from Mabel's evenings who was Polly's lover and the cook, insisted that if onions were as expensive as caviar, the world would call them a delicacy.

I told Ted about my idea for the magazine, the people who had promised to contribute articles, and the other financial backers. The last was a bit premature. No one had yet written a check, but I was sure they would.

He took a handkerchief from his pocket, removed his glasses, wiped first one lens and then the other, put them back on, and sat staring at me with owlish intensity. "Tell me, Margaret, have you ever been psychoanalyzed?"

I tried not to show my impatience. Since Freud had come to America to give a series of lectures four years earlier, Ted had been in thrall to the doctor's theories. He believed in psychoanalysis the way my mother had believed in the virgin birth.

"No, but if you'd like to write an article about your experience, I'd be happy to run it in the magazine." I wouldn't be happy, but I'd do more than that for five hundred dollars, or even three or two.

"I wasn't speaking about me. I was thinking of you and your motives for wanting to start this magazine."

"My motives? Look around you. Tenements bursting with sick starving children. Hospital wards and graveyards full of women desperate not to have another baby. Abortionists thriving. Those are my motives."

"On the surface, yes, but I think it goes deeper than that. It always does. If you go into psychoanalysis for three months, I'll give you money for your magazine . . ." He hesitated.

I waited.

" . . . providing you still want to publish it at the end of that time," he said with a smile that was too smug by half.

"You think I won't?"

"I'm certain you won't."

It was maddening. While I was fighting for women's lives,

he was worrying about my childhood fears and sexual fantasies. You see, I had read some Freud, or at least articles about his theories.

"I don't have three months. I've got to start publishing this magazine."

"What are you afraid of finding out?"

"I'm not afraid of finding out anything. I just refuse to waste time lying on a couch, talking about my dreams, while women and children are suffering and dying. I won't do it, Ted. I can't."

He shook his head. "You're a stubborn woman, Margaret."

I gave him a smile that stopped just this side of flirtatious. "No one ever made a revolution by being reasonable."

He laughed. For a serious lawyer and passionate Freudian, he had a surprisingly boisterous laugh. It rolled through the room and out into the mild night. He shook his head again. That was when I knew he was going to give me the money, though he couldn't resist making a comment about the unexamined life when he did. He was wrong. I knew exactly what I was up to.

WORD OF THE magazine spread quickly. The main thrust would be contraception, but I wanted pieces on other subjects as well. Friends and colleagues offered to write articles on everything from strikes and child labor to Mary Wollstonecraft and Cleopatra. Emma Goldman agreed to contribute an essay on marriage as a degenerate institution. I couldn't decide whether her choice of subject matter was fitting or bizarre. The U.S. government called Emma the most dangerous woman in America. Crowds flocked to hear her speak—no, not speak, harangue. She had faced down police harassment and stood up to death threats, but she was no match for a man named Ben Reitman with his honeyed words and brutal emotional battering. He broke her heart every chance she gave him. And they weren't even married. It broke my heart too, and turned my stomach. Much as I loved love, I couldn't imagine sacrificing myself to it. I certainly would never let a flimflam philanderer like Ben Reitman work me over as Emma did.

I was ambivalent about running her piece in the first issue for another reason as well. Emma's followers liked to point out that she had been advocating family limitation years before I came on the scene. I wanted to tell them so had Plato and Aristotle and those Egyptians from the Boston Public Library. Besides, for Emma, contraception was only one of a patchwork of socialist ideas. For me it was the cornerstone. Emma didn't even have a proper name for it. Family limitation was a drab negative description. I came up with a battle cry, though I never claimed I did it alone. I know how to give credit when credit is due, no matter what people say.

We were sitting around the dining table that served as my desk. Ethel was there. She and Rob Parker had arrived late, wearing the faintly unkempt look of people who have just tumbled out of bed. Rob, a bespectacled and bookish-looking man with a slight limp, the result of childhood polio, wrote drama criticism and anything else that magazines would pay him for and his social conscience would permit. Walter Roberts, aka the Eagle, had brought sandwiches and a pitcher of beer from the local delicatessen. Kitty Marion had arrived with a bunch of violets that had seen better days. She said she'd rescued them from a trash can. Kitty had enjoyed a small success on the London stage and still looked the part with her dark luxuriant pompadour and creamy skin, but she was serious about suffrage and contraception and a variety of feminist causes. A few others were crowded around the table.

We had gathered to talk about the magazine, but I was brooding about the movement. "We have to find a new name for what we're after," I told them. "Family limitation sounds like a Victorian lady reclining on a chaise. It isn't even an accurate description. I don't want to limit women to one or two children, like the French plan. I want a world of complete freedom where every woman can choose for herself how many children to have or even whether to have them at all."

"Voluntary parenthood," Walter suggested.

"Voluntary motherhood," Kitty said, her British accent gliding over the middle syllable of voluntary.

"The new motherhood."

"The new generation."

"Constructive generation."

Each suggestion led to another, but none was right.

"The point is that women must have control of their own bodies," I explained. "Without control, we're slaves, to nature, to society, to men."

"Control," Rob repeated. "That's good. How about family control?"

"Population control," someone else suggested.

"Birth rate control," Kitty said.

I felt as if someone had just walked fingers down my spine. "Drop the rate."

"What?" Kitty asked.

"Birth control," I said.

So perhaps I did come up with it after all.

I STOOD IN the small printshop as the first issue of *The Woman Rebel* rolled off the press. The noise was thunderous. The room reeked of paper, molten lead, and machine oil. I hadn't inhaled anything so heady since I'd held my freshly bathed and powered babies in my arms.

The printer handed me the first page. My statement marched across it.

Is there any reason why women should not receive clean, harmless, scientific knowledge on how to prevent conception? Everybody is aware that the old, stupid fallacy that such knowledge will cause a girl to enter into prostitution has long been shattered. As is well known, a law exists forbidding the imparting of information on this subject, the penalty being several years imprisonment. Is it not time to defy this law? And what fitter place could be found than in the pages of THE WOMAN REBEL?

The idea I'd hatched the night I'd given birth to Sadie Sachs was on the march.

WE BEGAN MAILING the issue the next day. Various radical groups, labor unions, and progressive individuals had already subscribed. One year cost a dollar; six months, fifty cents.

Two weeks later the letter arrived. The return address on the envelope was OFFICE OF THE POSTMASTER, U.S. POST OFFICE. Once again, it should have read Anthony Comstock.

I'd known it was coming, but it still caught me off guard. In the past weeks, I'd got carried away by the excitement of publication. That and my father's example had lured me into thinking I just might get away with it. He had thumbed his nose at authority and suffered no hardships, except the self-inflicted ones. What I hadn't realized was that no one cared how a penniless Irish stonecutter ranted in his cups, but men in power were not about to let a woman with a cause use the United States mails to incite other women and some men to action.

I tore the envelope open. The letter was brief.

Dear Madam:

In accordance with advice from the Assistant Attorney General for the Post Office Department, you are informed that the publication entitled "The Woman Rebel," for March 1914, is unmailable under the provisions of Section 211 of the Criminal Code.

E. M. Morgan, Postmaster

The letter made it clear. If I kept publishing and mailing the magazine—and nothing would stop me from that—I'd get my day in court.

The next morning, on my way to the subway, a headline in the *Sun* caught my eye.

"WOMAN REBEL"
BARRED FROM MAILS

I'd been prepared for legal harassment but not free publicity. I put down a penny, picked up a copy of the paper, and stood reading it while people hurried around me.

Too bad. The case should be reversed. They should be barred from her and spelled differently.

The cheap play on words disgusted me. The letter from the post office had been infuriating. This was humiliating. For women all over the country, the issue was a matter of life and death. For the editors of the *Sun*, it was a wink of the eye, an elbow in the ribs, a dirty joke. I crumpled the newspaper and threw it in a trash basket.

We posted the next issue in batches. Alone or in groups of two or three, we fanned out to mailboxes and chutes all over town, dropping a single issue here, five there, a dozen around the corner. I had a variety of friends and colleagues who stayed with the children, but sometimes when no one was available, I took them with me. The boys were demons, racing up and down streets, flinging the mailings into the boxes on the fly. Sometimes, I'd lift Peggy up and let her drop one or two magazines into the slot. I laughed as I heard the whoosh of insurrection sent on its way, and she giggled with me, two women rebels in cahoots. We also mailed some copies wrapped in other magazines and newspapers inside envelopes. It was an old socialist trick.

Life had never been so thrilling. Dawn often found me still clutching the last few copies, tramping up one avenue and down the next. I worked long hours with little sleep, intermittent meals, and no money, and loved every minute of it. Late at night or early in the morning, I fell into bed, footsore, bone weary, exhilarated. Muscles still tense from physical exertion, nerves still humming with the buzz of subversion, I was too tired to sleep, but not to make love. Sex took on a new intensity. It was the physical and spiritual component of our political creed. To deny it would have been cowardly.

Nonetheless, I had to be careful. I was prepared to be charged with sending so-called pornography through the mails, but I couldn't afford to have my cause sullied by personal scandal.

I knew from Bill's letters that there was gossip. He'd start out by praising my work, then suddenly change gears, accusing me of infidelity and various men of stealing my affections, as if he owned them.

He wasn't the only one who was suspicious. Sometimes when I looked out the window of the apartment, I saw strange men lingering across the street. I knew without asking that they were Anthony Comstock's henchmen. Only men obsessed with and deprived of sex could look that furtive while smoking a cigar and pretending to read a newspaper.

IT WAS ALMOST eleven when a knock came on the door of the apartment. The sound was so soft that I wasn't sure I'd heard it. Then it came again, only a little louder. The children were asleep, and I wasn't expecting anyone. I walked to the window and pushed the curtain aside an inch. The stooge was still standing under the lamp across the street, smoking a cigar. Why did they think cigars were a good cover?

I went to the door and opened it. The man standing in the hall was tall with wide shoulders, a head of thick fair hair beneath a cheap-looking homburg, and an unnervingly handsome face. The face was vaguely familiar. It took me a moment to remember that he had been a member of Socialist Local Number Five when Bill and I had belonged. Bill had always maintained that he was in love with me, but that he was no threat because he was so stupid. Isn't it odd that men can fall for a pretty face no matter how dumb, but women are supposed to be more high-minded. I invited him in.

"Thank you, Mrs. Sanger, but what I have to say won't take long." He glanced around the empty hall, then back at me and blinked nervously. Whatever he was here for, he was having second thoughts about it.

I said I hadn't seen him in some time.

"I work at the post office now." He took a handkerchief from his pocket and mopped his upper lip, which was covered with a film of sweat, though the spring evening was cool. "I can't afford socialist meetings, not with a wife and five little ones to support."

So that was it. He wanted contraceptive information. No wonder he looked so furtive.

"I shouldn't be here now," he went on, "but I heard something down at the post office that I thought you'd want to know." He glanced around the hall again. "An order came down from the top today. From now on, we're supposed to hold all second- and third-class mail, magazines, and newspapers in wrappers up to the light to make sure another piece of mail isn't enclosed." He hesitated. "Some of the men asked what we were looking for. 'A rag called *The Woman Rebel*,' the supervisor said. 'It's been declared obscene, but the bitch—'" His face flamed. "Excuse me . . . the lady . . . 'who edits it, name of Mrs. Margaret Sanger, has been trying to fool us by mailing her filth camouflaged in respectable newspapers and magazines.' I just thought you'd want to know," he repeated.

I said I was very glad to know and thanked him. He started down the hall, but I called him back.

"There's a man standing across the street. I'm sure he's one of Comstock's stooges. When you get downstairs, take the service entrance in the back. It leads to an alley that comes out around the corner. If he doesn't see you leave, he'll think you're a tenant. We don't want him suspecting that you came to see me, though I'm grateful you did."

He smiled, and though he still looked frightened, he no longer looked miserable.

I STOPPED WASTING my time trying to hide copies of the magazine.

In the July issue, I ran an article called "Are Preventive Means Injurious?" and another titled "The Marriage Bed." If the number of letters that flooded in was any indication, our mailings were getting through. It was only a matter of time until Comstock upped the ante.

·⹋ · ⹌·

THE ELECTRIC FAN set behind a block of ice was no match for the August morning. When the bell rang, I moved to the door slowly, like a swimmer churning through water.

Two men, one burly, one slight, stood in my doorway sweating. Half-moon-shaped stains hung from the armpits of their jackets. Their detachable shirt collars looked as if they'd come through the wringer of a washing machine. The burly one asked if I was Mrs. Margaret Sanger. I said I was. He pushed past me into the apartment. His sidekick followed.

They looked around the room as if they expected to find evidence of something. Then the burly one asked if I was the editor and publisher of a magazine called *The Woman Rebel*. He smirked when he said it. Again I admitted I was. He held out a legal-looking document. There was nothing I could do but take it.

I opened the seal and stood reading. A grand jury had indicted me on nine counts.

"A maximum sentence of forty-five years in the penitentiary," the fat one gloated.

The number made me shiver in the summer heat. I'd been looking forward to a chance to state my case in court. I'd known I might have to serve time in jail. Emma Goldman, Big Bill Haywood, Elizabeth Gurley Flynn, and half the people in my world had been locked up at one time or another for good causes. But not for forty-five years.

After they left, I sat at the dining table staring at the indictment, gazing into the future. I saw my children huddled in the bleak visitors' room of a state prison, the boys refusing to speak, Peggy clinging to Ethel in fear. I saw them growing older, bodies elongating, faces taking definition, while I shriveled into an old woman and faded into the distance, out of their lives.

But as I went on sitting there, three other children crept into my consciousness, only they weren't children but undersized adults, made old before their time by the misery and deprivation of life in a Grand Street tenement. Those were the children who persuaded me. I could not give up the fight for all children, even if it meant losing my own.

But I was being melodramatic. The post office had tried to silence me. The courts, if they carried through on this, would give me an opportunity to be heard. But they wouldn't carry through. That was the point. They didn't want me to speak, because they knew that all across the country, women, and many men, were eager to listen. They didn't want to make a martyr of a respectable woman either. And they did think I was respectable, despite Mr. Comstock's henchmen lurking across the street. Respectable and sympathetic. I was a mother alone with three small photogenic children. When reporters came to interview me, as they occasionally did, Stuart and Grant greeted them at the door, took their hats, and sat politely while the newsmen fired questions at me and I fired back. Peggy had an uncanny ability to spot the softhearted among them, climb into their laps, and wind her arms around their necks. She had my instincts for sizing up people. No judge, politician, or government official in his right mind would send the decent mother of those three winning, well-behaved children to the penitentiary for forty-five years. Society wouldn't stand for it.

Ten

THE MORNING OF the arraignment I put on a severe black dress with a starched white collar and a small black hat trimmed with a demure veil.

"What the well-dressed nun is wearing this season," Ethel said when she came to pick me up.

She could joke, but I knew what I was doing. Ted Schroeder, who had given up on getting me into psychoanalysis but was still devoted to good causes, had warned that Judge Hazel, who would preside at my arraignment, was the father of nine. It was no accident that I had turned up on his docket.

Most of the morning was gone by the time the clerk called the case of the *People versus Margaret Sanger*. The phrasing gave me a moment's pause. I was outnumbered.

I rose, approached the bench with eyes lowered, the docile young lady my mother had wanted me to be, and stood listening as the prosecutor read the charges. When he finished, the judge leaned forward and peered down at me. From under lowered lashes, I looked up at him. My magazine could provoke. I would seduce.

"She doesn't look like a bomb thrower or assassin to me," he said to the district attorney, then brought his gavel down and postponed the case until the fall term.

I had been right. No judge in his right mind would make a martyr of me.

THOUGH *THE WOMAN REBEL* hadn't yet run any specific information on contraception, it had urged readers to ask for it. Bags of letters arrived demanding it. I began work on a pamphlet describing the various methods of birth control. Friends warned against it. Bill wrote from Paris urging caution. I was already under indictment, they pointed out. My case had been postponed, I explained.

I wrote the booklet "Family Limitation" in a white heat, like my father on a bender. Months of research poured out. The myth of the safe period. The practice of coitus interruptus. The use of condoms. The pessary, the sponge, and vaginal suppositories. I covered it all in only sixteen pages in language simple enough for a child, or at least young people stirred by sex, and any uneducated adult to understand.

The hard part was finding someone to produce it. Twenty printers turned me down. I'm not exaggerating. I kept a list. A few said it was too smutty. Most said it was too dangerous. Men who'd risked prison for running off calls for strikes and incitements to violence would not touch a pamphlet about women's bodies. One called it a Sing Sing job. Finally a brawny Russian labor organizer who operated a linotype across the river in New Jersey agreed to do the job after hours. I never asked him how many children he had, but I was willing to bet it was a full house.

Word of the pamphlet had already spread through the socialist and anarchist grapevine. Women—and men too—wrote asking for copies. Radical groups and labor organizations requested bulk deliveries to distribute to workers in the mills and mines and factories. When people couldn't get hold of a printed version, they copied someone else's by hand. There were also typed bootleg versions. I imagined secretaries and typewriters, their hands hovering over the keys, one eye on the door, working in deserted offices as the windows grew dark in the evening or as the sun came up in the morning.

-)(·)(-

THE BOYS HAD left for school, Peggy was with the woman downstairs who took care of her these days—now that Bill was gone, so was his mother, but Peggy was such a winning child that I never had difficulty finding people to look after her while I worked—and the dining room sat silent and peaceful in the October morning. Crimson and purple and yellow leaves pressed against the windows turning them to stained glass. Sunlight slanted across the paper-littered table. I basked in it as I wrote a letter to the editor of *Metropolitan Magazine* in answer to an article by Theodore Roosevelt urging women, of good American stock of course, to have at least six children. No, shaming women of good American stock who dared to have fewer than six children.

The telephone shattered the silence. I stood, crossed the room, and took the earpiece off the wall. The voice on the other end of the line asked if he was speaking to Mrs. Margaret Sanger. I told him he was. He said he was calling from the district attorney's office.

"You have a court hearing tomorrow morning at nine, Mrs. Sanger."

"But I was given no warning."

"The court must have notified your lawyer." The voice wasn't unkind, merely businesslike.

I didn't tell him that I hadn't got around to hiring a lawyer. I'd been too busy writing, printing, and distributing "Family Limitation." And I was still toying with the idea of representing myself, though Ted Schroeder warned it would be dangerous for me and detrimental to the cause. If I slipped up in any way, I would have no grounds for appeal. If the court ruled against me, I would set an unfortunate precedent. But I had no intention of slipping up.

I told the voice on the other end of the line that I would be there.

I PUT ON the same black dress with the starched white collar and the same hat with the demure veil, part superstition, part calculation.

Once again, the clerk called the case of the *People versus Margaret Sanger*, but this time I didn't feel outnumbered. I walked to the front of the room, stood before the bench, and looked up through lowered lashes. The judge screwed up his features as if he smelled something unpleasant.

"Where is your lawyer, Mrs. Sanger?"

"I didn't think one was necessary to plead for a postponement." I let the shyest hint of a smile play around my mouth.

The judge's scowl deepened. "I expect you back in court after the noon recess, Mrs. Sanger. With a lawyer." His gavel came down with a bang intended to make me jump. I managed not to give him the satisfaction.

I called Ted Schroeder. He didn't say he'd told me so. He instructed me to stay where I was.

"J. J. Goldstein will be there in half an hour, forty-five minutes at the outside."

"J.J.?"

"Jonah J. Goldstein. If he'll take the case. His Tammany connections won't like him defending a birth controller."

"You're sending me a Tammany lawyer?"

"He cut his teeth with Lillian Wald at the Henry Street Settlement and Mary Simkhovitch at Greenwich House."

"Ah, the grandes dames who do the feather-dusting of welfare work. Aren't you afraid I'll shock him?"

"I'm hanging up now, Margaret. Try to get the chip off your shoulder before J.J. gets there. And try to believe me when I tell you that Anthony Comstock is not playing games. Nine counts. Forty-five years."

Jonah J. Goldstein did not take half an hour. Twenty minutes later he came barreling down the marble corridor of the courthouse, a short powerhouse of a man with wide shoulders and deep-set black eyes sunk in dark smudges that spoke of long hours of work or years of unhealthy living or both. His suit coat was too broad for him and his trousers too long. The man had obviously never heard of a tailor. His hat was too big too, and sat low on his forehead. When he took it off to introduce himself, his eyes flashed with impatience at this headstrong woman who insisted on tangling with the law. I disliked him on sight.

JONAH J. GOLDSTEIN

You didn't dislike me, Peg. You just didn't know what to make of me. It wasn't only the clothes. That came from growing up poor. You should have known that. You learn to get your money's worth, or at least as much fabric as possible. It was me, the poor Jewish boy on the make for a big chance. You knew from the get-go I wasn't one of those smooth opera- tors, the ones who buzzed around you, writing you flowery love letters and poetry, finding a dozen different highfalutin ways to say they were crazy about you. I used to be sorry I wasn't one of those Joes, but now I know if I had been, you wouldn't have given me the time of day. Why would you want a second-rate imitation when you had the real thing with those socialist parlor snakes at home and later that gang in England, the Wantley circle? Someday someone is going to write a real biography of you—not a whitewash like the one by this Lader fellow, who can't see straight for being so crazy about you—and I can see the index now. Sanger, Margaret, love affairs, see Brodie, Hugh; Child, Harold; de Selincourt, Hugh; Ellis, Havelock; MacDonald, Angus; Mylius, Edward; Portet, Lorenzo; Roberts, Walter; Rompapas, John; Wells, H. G.; Williams, William; and so on for a couple of pages.

The real surprise is that the world never caught on. When it came to public relations, something that didn't have a name in those days, you were a pro. You waged a revolution dressed in prim black dresses with prudish white collars. You slept with whomever you pleased whenever you pleased and had every- one believing you were a devoted mother, alone in the world, struggling to bring up your children on your own. Sometimes when I went to one of your talks, I had to laugh. *You mean that delicate little lady with the soft voice is Margaret Sanger, the birth control rebel?* they asked one another incredulously. If they had only known.

Don't get me wrong. I'm not criticizing you for the mas- querade. You had to dissemble. Women would have pilloried you if they'd learned the truth. Men would have done worse. They don't like having their sexual prerogatives usurped. But I didn't mind it. I loved it. And you. I think I knew it that first day, even if you didn't. But you know what? I have a feeling you did. You just don't like to admit it, because then you'd have to admit you made a mistake, in the beginning, and at the end.

I STARTED TO tell J. J. Goldstein what had happened in court that morning. He cut me off.

"You never should have gone in without a lawyer."

"Last time the judge gave me a postponement. He said I didn't look like a bomb thrower."

He stared at me for a moment. "You don't," he said finally. "But courts don't convict on appearance. At least not only on appearance. If the request comes in the proper form from a lawyer, the judge will grant a postponement. I guarantee it."

"You guarantee it?"

He grinned. I was shocked. How had this short Jewish know-it-all come by that irresistible lock-up-your-daughters smile?

"You'd prefer maybe a lawyer who's scared of his own shadow?" He took my arm and started toward the courtroom. "Come on, Mrs. Sanger. Let's get you sprung."

J. J. Goldstein did not get me sprung. He approached the bench, half swagger, half deference. He used the proper language requesting a month's stay in the case of the *People versus Margaret Sanger*. The judge barely let him finish.

"Request denied."

J. J. Goldstein requested a two-week stay in the case of the *People versus Margaret Sanger*.

"Denied." The judge looked from J. J. Goldstein to me. "Mrs. Sanger will appear in court tomorrow morning at nine o'clock." This time the sound of wood hitting wood as he brought down the gavel succeeded in making me jump.

Outside the courtroom, J. J. Goldstein said we could discuss the case over a cup of coffee. He looked at me from under the wide brim of that ridiculous hat. "On second thought, you need a drink."

We went to a restaurant around the corner from the courthouse. It was all cut velvet and fringed swags. The headwaiter greeted him warmly. I don't know why I was surprised. Ted had said he had Tammany connections. The real puzzle was why he would risk them to defend me.

"The way I see it," he said after we were seated at a table and he'd ordered a sherry for me and a whisky for him, "you plead guilty, and I get you off with a year. Probably less." He sat staring at me for a moment. "Definitely less. I guarantee it."

"You guaranteed you could get me a postponement."

"You want to cry over spilled milk or you want to beat this? The DA might even settle for a fine. All you have to do is admit your guilt and seem contrite. The clothes are fine, but the act doesn't cut the mustard."

"What do you mean, the act? You think I'm not serious about this?"

He flashed the dangerous smile again. "I think you're dead serious. I just don't want the judge to think it. Stop looking him in the eye."

He was right. The moment the judge had denied the postponement, I'd dropped the docile-young-lady façade.

"And stop acting as if you're smarter than every man in the courtroom. For all I know you are, but don't let it show. Turn on the charm. You bamboozle the judge, I'll plead you guilty to satisfy the DA, and we'll have you out of there with a fine. Your political friends will be happy to pay it."

"I can't plead guilty."

"Why not? You are. You sent those magazines through the mail."

"I set out to prove the law is unjust. Pleading guilty will only validate it."

He sat looking at me. His manner was all elbows, but his eyes gave away the hole in his heart.

"The way I hear it," he went on, "you got three kids."

"What does that have to do with anything?"

"Where's their father?" His voice was even.

"In Paris."

"Divorced?"

"Not yet." The answer surprised me. I hadn't quite made up my mind about a divorce.

He straightened his shoulders inside that too-roomy suit coat. "So who's going to take care of the kids while you go to jail to prove a point?"

"I'll manage."

"Mrs. Sanger, they're not just whistling Dixie in there. You saw the DA and the judge. They're out to make an example of you."

"That's the first good news I've heard all day."

"In other words, you've got your heart set on being a martyr."

"I have my heart set on undoing an unjust and dangerous law."

There was nothing more to say, though that didn't stop him from trying to persuade me. Finally he gave up, and we said good-bye on the street in front of the restaurant. He told me to call him if I changed my mind and wanted to plead guilty. I said I wasn't likely to.

"Then what are you going to do?"

"I'm not sure."

He took a card from his pocket, pressed it into my hand, and held on for a second longer than necessary. I didn't pull away.

"Okay, you win. Call me if you decide to plead not guilty. I'm in either way."

"You're in? This isn't a poker game, Mr. Goldstein. For women all over the country it's a matter of life and death."

His gaze was level. "I didn't know that, you think I'd be here? I was marching in suffrage parades when I was only a kid. Just because I want you to plead guilty doesn't mean I don't believe in your cause. Give me a call whatever you decide."

I told him I would, but I was certain I wouldn't.

THE SUBWAY STREAKED out of the tunnel into a crimson sunset bleeding down the western sky. I walked home from the station through the sounds of women calling children to supper, and girls skipping rope, and boys shouting *ollie ollie umphrey*.

The telephone was ringing as I opened the door to the apartment. I walked past it. It stopped. There was a moment of silence; then it began to ring again. The noise jangled my nerves. It would only get worse as word of my hearing spread. More and more people would call. Ethel would return with the children. They'd want attention. She'd demand to hear everything that had happened. I had to think, but I couldn't do it here.

I went into the bedroom, took a suitcase from under the bed, and began tossing things into it. Only when I snapped the locks and lifted it did I realize I'd packed far too much for one night, but the phone was ringing again, and Ethel would be back with the children any minute. I scrawled her a note and hurried down the steps to the street. The heavy suitcase banged against my thigh all the way to the subway.

I got off at Thirty-Fourth Street. There was bound to be a cheap hotel for commercial travelers in the area. I walked past two and entered the third on pure whim. As I signed the register, the desk clerk eyed me suspiciously. I was a woman alone. I must be up to no good. The disapproval on the bellhop's face said he was sure of it. He led me to a small, sparsely furnished room. The bed was narrow, a Gideon Bible stood on the table, and the single electric lightbulb permitted no illusions. The only distraction was a copy of the morning paper that fell out of my carrying case as I tossed it on the bed. The headline stared up at me from the floor.

LONDON HEARS THAT ANTWERP HAS FALLEN;
CITY AFLAME UNDER RAIN OF GERMAN SHELLS;
FRENCH CAPTURE 1600 GERMANS NEAR ROYE

I sat in the single straight-backed chair and stared at the words. Four months earlier, a young man dreaming of Serbian nationalism, as if declaring nationhood would improve the lot of the downtrodden of his country or any other, had shot an Austrian archduke, and overnight the world had gone mad with war fever. Even in America, which was officially neutral, the papers ran black with the news of battles fought by men, and heroism shown by men, and death suffered by men. I'd be lucky to get an inch of space and a few lines of print about women's battles against unwanted pregnancies, and women's heroism raising children they could neither feed nor clothe, and women's death in childbirth and the attempts to prevent it. As I sat staring down at the paper splattered with war news as gory as blood, I knew one thing for certain. There is no such thing as a martyr without an audience.

I telephoned Ethel to tell her I was leaving for Canada and ask her to take care of the children. I thought for a moment of going back to say good-bye to them, but what good would it do? The boys would turn away in anger, Peggy would cling to me, and I'd lose the will to leave. No, it was better this way. I'd explain when they were older.

STUART SANGER

Disappearing acts were your style, Mother. You vanished and you made others go missing. I'm talking about Father. I know Peggy wasn't your fault, at least not entirely.

What good would saying good-bye have done, you ask. At least we would have known you'd gone somewhere and not vanished like something in a magician's act. Didn't you remember how terrifying you found those disappearances at the sanitarium? You were an adult, and those people were strangers. We were children, and you were our mother. Peggy cried constantly. *Mama* was the word she squeezed out through the sobs. Grant stopped talking. I got into fights, the bigger and meaner the other boy, the better. But that was all right. You'd explain it to us later.

You had a peculiar view of childhood. What did you tell that reporter? I was away at school when the interview ran, but I remember reading it. "Young children are by nature selfish. It isn't good to indulge them." That's one thing you can't be accused of.

Don't misunderstand me. I'm not blaming you for my failings. The drinking and the depression are my weaknesses. I own up to them. My psychiatrist says I'm too hard on myself. I told him I take after my mother.

But in all fairness, when it came to neglect, you studied at the feet of masters. Your father spent his last dollar on a banquet for a visiting freethinker while the rest of you struggled to silence your protesting stomachs. Your mother was so busy having babies that she had no time to care for children. It must have been especially painful for you, wedged in the middle of the brood, between the firstborns who managed to grab a few grains of attention before the supply ran out and the babies whom it fell to you to care for. I suppose your parents gave you a kind of reflexive love, but like the food, there just wasn't enough to go around. Do you realize the only story you ever told us about your childhood, other than the one about the dinner for the visiting freethinker, was that macabre tale of the time your father took you to the cemetery in the middle of the night to stand guard while he dug up your little brother's body—an illegal as well as a ghoulish act—to make a plaster of Paris mask of the dead baby's face to comfort your mother? What a cruel thing to do to a child. But you didn't see it that way. You were so proud that he'd singled you out to be his partner in that morbid crime. You were so grateful for the crumbs of attention. That's why I don't hold you responsible, at least not entirely. You were desperate for love. Who isn't? But here's what I can't understand. Why did you have to spend your life racing around the world looking for it when the three of us, four before we left Father, were so eager to give it to you?

I refuse to believe it was only sex. I know you would never put the words *only* and *sex* together. My Margaret came home from her last visit to you and announced, "Grandmother says a person should have sexual intercourse three times a day, like a square meal." Sometimes I wonder how you found the time to change the world with all that hopping in and out of bed. Not something a son particularly wants to know about his mother. You think I'm a prude, but you're wrong. I don't object to the sex, though the way you went about it strikes me as awfully grim and mechanical. I won't ask you where was the love, because I know your answer. You couldn't make love with someone you didn't love. But that's a pretty promiscuous definition of a serious emotional state.

People got hurt, Mother.

Eleven

IN CANADA, MY socialist friends and friends of friends took
me in but warned that it would be dangerous to stay for
long. I might be spotted. The authorities might ask for extra-
dition. Europe would be safer. And in Europe I could continue
my work.

Three weeks after I arrived, I sailed from Montreal on the
RMS *Virginian*, a woman alone and therefore, once again, sus-
pect. And no one even knew about the fake passport. It listed me
as Bertha Watson. I'd chosen the name because a woman called
Bertha Watson couldn't possibly be anyone of interest, let alone
an outlaw, but now I regretted it. I didn't like masquerading as
dowdy.

I wasn't the only anxious passenger. Fear enveloped the ship,
thick and viscous as the Atlantic fog. Passengers were constantly
imagining they spotted German U-boats. Rumor had it that
the hold was a powder keg packed with munitions for England.
There was another terror as well. Our course took us through
the waters where the *Titanic* had gone down two and a half
years earlier. A more recent disaster was even more chilling. Less
than a year before, the *Empress of Ireland* had sunk in the St.

Lawrence River with a greater loss of life, but more people had heard of the *Titanic* disaster because of all the presailing hoopla about how big the ship was, and how fast, and how unsinkable.

As bad as the fear was, my homesickness was worse. No, not homesickness, childsickness. I ached for my babies. Everywhere I looked, I saw their faces. The boys' voices carried on the wind. Peggy's giggles haunted me, though Bill, who'd returned from Paris, had written to me in care of the friends in Montreal that she cried constantly. I wanted to tell him that was because of the brace he'd put on her leg, not her mother's absence.

THE SHIP MADE landfall, and I sailed through customs as the dowdy Bertha Watson, then made my way to London. The train was cold and damp. It was good preparation for the city. Rain streamed down the buildings, raced along the gutters, and settled in my bones and glands. My childsickness grew worse.

I found a cheerless room on the top floor of 67 Torrington Square, just behind the British Museum. The building smelled of boiled sprouts and unwashed bodies. Use of the bath cost extra. So did the coal heater in my room. It devoured the confusing currency at a breakneck rate. The money my Canadian friends had scraped together was running out.

I took a job waiting tables in a tearoom. Jail would have been better. At least behind bars I would have been making a statement. Here, I was merely a woman alone and broke, trying to hide my rage behind a respectful smile as patrons complained that the water wasn't hot enough and their scones were taking too long to arrive at the table. My American accent didn't help. The city was war mad, and I was personally responsible for America's refusal to get into the fight. As a socialist, I'd always

thought patriotism was one more trick of the ruling class to sub-
jugate the downtrodden, but the more those tea-swilling women
complained of American cowardice, the more American I felt.

The cold and damp grew worse. Sometimes I felt as if I would
never be warm again. Others I burned with fever. As I lay in bed
at three a.m. staring at the water-stained ceiling, as I cracked the
ice in the pitcher each morning to wash my face and brush my
teeth, as I huddled blanket-wrapped in front of the cold heater
each evening, I heard my children pleading with me to come
home. I had never been lonelier.

My friends in Canada had given me letters of introduction to Charles and Bessie Drysdale of the Malthusian League,
but I'd been reluctant to write to them. From what I'd read
and heard, the Malthusians were in favor of contraceptives for
the bourgeoisie but didn't give a hoot about the working class.
I could imagine what they'd make of an uneducated socialist outlaw who was determined to unshackle the poor from
their biological chains. But finally, desperate, I wrote to the
Drysdales. They wrote back immediately, inviting me to tea.
One thing led to another. They took me to lectures and meetings. They introduced me to other people. The children still
importuned me to come home during the day and stalked my
dreams at night, but I was less lonely. Sufficient funds arrived
from socialist friends in New York to allow me to quit my job
and return to my research. Work was a godsend. It filled the
time and some of the emptiness.

One morning I came down the stairs, careful not to trip on
the torn carpet runner, and found an envelope on the hall table.
Mrs. Margaret Sanger was written on the front, *Mr. Havelock
Ellis* on the back flap. My new friends had promised to tell
him about me, but I hadn't expected to hear from him. He was

renowned. It was said that Freud kept an inscribed photograph of him on his examining-room wall.

I tore open the envelope.

Dear Mrs. Sanger,

Will you do me the honor of coming to tea on December 22?

He went on to give me the address, 14 Dover Mansions in Brixton on the other side of the Thames, and detailed instructions for getting there from my boardinghouse. Most people left me to find my way around the city on my own, but here was one of the great thinkers and writers of our era taking the time to give me directions. I was still in awe of him, but I was also touched.

THE BUS SMELLED of wet wool permeated with coal smoke. Around me, cockney voices rose and fell. Everyone was carrying parcels, some of them already wrapped for Christmas and Boxing Day. The war seemed far away. The Zeppelin raids that would terrify the population as the fighting dragged on hadn't yet begun. People said the Kaiser was reluctant to endanger his relatives. The idea infuriated me. He could turn laborers and miners and farmers into cannon fodder, but he didn't want to harm a hair on his royal cousins' heads. I rubbed the fogged-over window with my gloved hand to get a glimpse of the street. I didn't want to miss my stop.

By the time I stepped down from the bus, I was overcome with shyness and self-doubt. My accent was wrong, my education was wanting, and I couldn't get over the feeling that I was out of my depth. A few years ago, I'd been afraid to speak up among the New York socialists. A few weeks ago, I'd been reluctant to write to my new Malthusian friends. But Havelock Ellis was beyond all of them. I was terrified to meet him. And I wouldn't have given up the chance for the world.

I found the address easily. Rain stained the drab redbrick façade of the building black. A police station sat grim and forbidding on the ground floor. He hadn't mentioned that. Traveling on a fake passport encourages paranoia.

I started up the stairs. On the third landing, a card engraved with the name MR. HAVELOCK ELLIS was mounted in a brass holder. I lifted the knocker and tapped it against the door. It opened immediately, almost as if he'd been lurking on the other side of it.

How do I describe my first sight of the man who would become the inspiration, the guide, the love of my life? His head was massive, as if it had to be larger than that of mere mortals to hold all his wisdom. His mane of white hair foamed over his bold features like a breaking wave. His white beard was worthy of an Old Testament prophet, his smile that of an angel. No, not an angel, a saint. Then he spoke. I was shocked. The voice of this powerfully built man was high and reedy, squeaky as a boy's in the throes of puberty. He reached out, took my hand, and drew me into the room. I forgot his unfortunate voice. I don't think I ever noticed it again.

A jumble of books, magazines, newspapers, and writing pads covered every surface. Paintings crowded the walls. I recognized a Matisse close by an old master whose provenance I didn't know but whose beauty I couldn't miss. A coal fire glowed in the hearth. He lit two candles on the mantel. Our shadows sprang up on the opposite wall.

He helped me off with my coat, and we sat at either end of

a sofa. A moment of silence embarrassed the room. I had heard he hated small talk. That was all right. I was too awed to make any. Then he asked about the indictment that had brought me to London. I answered. The words began to spill out. Neither of us could stop them. Here is a partial list, in no particular order, of the topics we discussed that first afternoon. Shakespeare, Shaw, travel writing, art criticism, the criminal mind, censorship, Fabianism, socialism, anarchism, the ballot for women, social hygiene, convention, hypocrisy, marriage. He explained that he and his wife lived apart most of the time. He found the arrangement more conducive to happiness. Contraception. He said that in his experience—he was speaking of his training as a medical doctor, not his personal life, he assured me—*karezza* was the best method of contraception and dismissed my contention that only a sexually sophisticated man could manage to postpone his orgasm until the woman was satisfied, then ejaculate outside the vagina. He spoke of his book *Sexual Inversion*. It had been acclaimed for its candor and tolerance—he saw no shame in any sexual act and danger in repression—and pilloried for the same traits. After that experience, he'd decided to publish abroad rather than battle the British legal system and recommended that I do the same, bypassing puritanical America for the Continent. "You must concentrate on your work, not litigation."

We stopped talking only when he excused himself to make tea and returned a few minutes later with a tray laden with pots of tea and hot water, cups, saucers, and scones and cakes.

"I am my own charwoman," he announced as he put the tray on the table in front of the sofa. "I would rather be able to lay a proper fire, market, and cook than write an essay."

They were the only words he spoke that afternoon that I didn't believe.

Etiquette dictated that I stay for an hour. The clock on the mantel chimed. We went on talking. It chimed again, and again after that. I'd arrived at three. I left at a little after nine.

I apologized.

His beatific smile spilled over me like sunlight. "Scandalous, isn't it."

We agreed to meet the next day at the British Museum. He was going to supervise my course of inquiry.

"You read too promiscuously," he said.

I walked all the way home. I couldn't bear to board a stuffy bus packed with mundane humanity, not after I had spent an afternoon and evening locked in conversation with a god. It wasn't only that he understood and elevated sex. It was that he articulated the convictions I'd known instinctively all my life.

I lay awake for a long time that night. My mind raced with ideas. Fragments of conversation ricocheted around in my head. In half consciousness, I had an erotic encounter with the great man and woke from it tense and disappointed.

I got out of bed, wrapped myself in the blanket, crossed to the window, and stood staring out into the night. Havelock had said we would celebrate Boxing Day together. He liked it better than Christmas, because traditionally it was the day the servants had off from their work to return to their families with boxes of food and gifts. The custom had intrigued me, but suddenly the thought gave way to self-reproach. I had never been apart from the children at Christmas. I hadn't realized it until now, but then I hadn't thought of the children all day.

NINE DAYS LATER, on New Year's Eve, exactly a year after the children and I had left Bill in Paris, bells tolled, horns sounded, and people cheered in the streets, while in the hushed privacy of Havelock's flat, he blushed—a grown man of fifty-six who was unafraid to write about the most forbidden sexual acts blushed!—as he leaned in to kiss me.

"I cannot promise you an erection, my dear rebel, but I can assure you of pleasure."

I will not go into the details of that evening, though many people would love to know. I'm aware of the gossip that swirls around Havelock's sexual prowess. But I refuse to cater to prurient interests. Suffice it to say that Havelock gave me the pleasure he promised. And I returned it in kind.

Twelve

W E BECAME INSEPARABLE. Each morning we met outside the British Museum, made our way to neighboring desks, and got down to work. He supervised my research; he also gave me the education in the arts and sciences that fate—or perhaps only my impetuousness—had cheated me of.

At midday, one of us would lean over and place a hand on the other's arm. Then the one still working would slip bookmarks into various volumes, tidy notes, and stand. Together we left the building and walked a few blocks to our favorite tearoom.

One day as we were getting ready to leave, he whispered that he was taking me to the Monico in Piccadilly for lunch. From the black scowl the man at the next desk gave us, you would have thought Havelock had shouted.

"And tomorrow I'll take you to Claridge's for tea," I joked as we came out of the building. I'd never been to the Monico, but I'd heard enough about it to know that it was outrageously expensive and dazzlingly vulgar. The building was a labyrinth of marble staircases, gilded ornamentation, frock-coated maître d's, and a small army of musicians wandering through a winter garden, beer cellar, and maze of private dining rooms, every foot of which was multiplied by miles of mirrors. Even if we could have afforded it, we would not have set foot in it.

"I know," Havelock said, "the place is dreadful, but it's Hugh de Selincourt's favorite restaurant, and we're supposed to be celebrating his finishing the third book in his trilogy. Still, I can't quite face lunch alone with him—he's so exhausting—so I'm taking you along. Besides, he wants to meet you."

"How does he know about me?"

He patted my hand, which was tucked in his arm. "Because, dear rebel, I simply cannot stop talking about you."

Later, when he would erase my name from his autobiography for fear of offending his wife, to whom he had talked about me incessantly—an American nurse, he called me in the book, as if I were nothing more than a nationality and a profession—that extravagance of praise would come home to wound me. But at the time I was flattered. A great man, one of the greatest of our time, was besotted with me. As I was with him, though I was beginning to put my infatuation in perspective. Havelock would always be the love of my life—he was, as I said, my intellectual touchstone, my inspiration, my ideal—but he lacked the romance I longed for.

I spotted Hugh de Selincourt halfway across the grill room, and not because he stood as he saw us coming. He was the handsomest man in the room. He was probably the handsomest man in all the rooms of the restaurant that day or any day. He had soft brown eyes set far apart, a narrow aristocratic nose, a wide sensual mouth, and wavy fair hair that begged a woman to run her fingers through it. From the way he embraced me with those eyes, I had the feeling he knew my hands were itching. His suit, stiff collar, and luxuriant silk tie screamed patrician, but beneath the well-tailored camouflage I sensed a sleek primitive animal on the prowl. I have never known a man who lived so easily in his body.

Lunch was breathtaking. I don't mean the food, though that was more exotic than anything I was accustomed to. Hugh insisted on ordering for all of us—oysters, partridges, and of course champagne—and I couldn't help wondering where the money was coming from. Was he heir to a fabulous fortune or simply splurging every penny the publisher had paid him for the books which Havelock, the least judgmental of men in sexual matters, had made sound like pornography? On the way to the restaurant he'd said *A Child's Guide to Vice* would be a more accurate title for the trilogy.

But it was the conversation that really dazzled, though I couldn't remember a word of it later. The champagne didn't cloud my memory; the heady experience of sitting between those two brilliant men while they vied for my attention, competed for my smile, and preened for me shamelessly did.

As we said good-bye outside the restaurant, Hugh insisted that I must come down to Wantley, his house in Sussex, for a weekend.

"You'll bring her, won't you, Ellis?"

Havelock looked off into the distance and said that he didn't have time for weekends in the country.

"Then you must come without the King," Hugh insisted.

Havelock turned back and stood staring down at me. The experience was eerily familiar. I had lived through it dozens of times with Bill. So even the great Havelock Ellis was not immune to jealousy, no matter what he wrote and lectured. And my reaction was the same as it had been with Bill. His possessiveness made me only more eager to go.

The following Saturday morning, I took the train to Sussex

and fell in love, not with a man but with a world. The property itself, which had once belonged to Shelley's father, though Shelley had never lived there, was a rolling patchwork of green fields, gardens, and orchards. Hugh called it the loveliest spot in England. His wife, Janet, said it was a place of childhood. I thought it was better than childhood, at least better than my childhood.

But the enchantment went beyond the verdant landscape and the old stone cottage where Hugh lived with Janet and their daughter, Bridget, Janet's lover Harold Child, and a variety of writers, painters, musicians, and like-minded souls who came and went at will. The allure lay in the poetry and music and art that filled the rooms, the love freely given, the pleasure guiltlessly taken. This was the world I'd read about in Havelock's books and argued about at Greenwich Village parties. This was where I belonged.

One afternoon a few weeks later I stepped down from the train into the embrace of a soft mist rising from the fields. At Wantley, even the weather was erotic. Hugh was waiting for me on the platform. We shook hands. Our little group always behaved impeccably in town. The formal gesture made us grin like naughty children. He opened the door of the roadster for me. I climbed in. As soon as we'd left the village behind, he pulled off the road.

After dinner with Janet and Harold and the other guests, he led me to the small tower bedroom that was mine when I visited, placed me in the center, and told me, no, dared me, not to move. I stood still as a statue while he unhooked and untied and unfastened me.

Later, we sent up such a racket that Janet and Harold joined us. How could so much love be called licentious?

My only disappointment was that Havelock refused to set foot on the property. His recalcitrance was inexplicable. They called him the King. His books were their bibles. But he was adamant.

HAVELOCK ELLIS

My books were their justification. And you were wasting time you should have been devoting to your work, cavorting with a bunch of second-rate poseurs who played at art and turned serious ideas into simplistic excuses to indulge their appetites. It pained me to see you squandering yourself that way. It distressed me to see how that world was changing you.

When you came to my flat that December afternoon, I'd thought we were in perfect accord. Oh, at first I was nervous, more nervous than you. That was why the door opened so quickly. I was lurking behind it, as you guessed. I am not a social animal, dear rebel. By now you know that. I'm wary of meeting new people. But everyone kept telling me that I had to meet this young American firebrand. And the moment I drew you into my flat and we began to talk, I knew they were right. I was besotted. Later you told me that you wrote in your journal that night, "I have never felt about any other person as I do about Havelock Ellis." At the same time, I was writing in my journal, "I have rarely known a more charming and congenial companion and I have never found one so swiftly."

My feelings deepened as we worked side by side in the museum. You were eager to learn, quick to understand, devoted, but never docile. I was twenty years your senior, but you made me feel like a boy again. And then I took you to lunch with Hugh. I knew that he'd set out to seduce you and that you'd be too curious to resist. I was prepared for you to surrender to the sexual attraction—the body is not nearly so intimate as the mind—but I thought you'd see through the artistic and intellectual pretensions. I thought I'd taught you better.

His novels, if you can call them that, are trash. *One Little Boy* isn't a perceptive exploration of adolescent awakening, as you seemed to think or at least as you told him, but a prurient exercise in masturbation. As you know, I have no prejudice against the act, only its masquerade as artistic expression. And how could you take seriously a grown man who spends half his life playing and writing about cricket? You saw him as an aesthete without practical or materialistic interests. I knew him to be a foolish boy who compensated for his banal mind and execrable writing with childish sports and compulsive fornication. He was nothing more than a sexual athlete. I said that once, saw the smile you tried to hide, and knew what you were thinking. Hugh practiced the techniques I could only write about. Perhaps that was true. I know I am not a great lover. But you always said I gave you pleasure. Nonetheless, I wasn't jealous. You know I don't believe in jealousy. I was disappointed. Hugh de Selincourt wasn't worthy of you, Margaret. The betrayal wasn't in the sex, it was in the mediocrity.

I WAS MAKING great strides under Havelock's guidance, but my knowledge was still theoretical. I needed practical experience, and for that I had to go to Holland, which was far ahead of other countries in disseminating contraceptives to the general population.

Friends warned against traveling to the Continent while the war was on, but I told them my work couldn't wait, and besides, Holland was neutral. When Havelock realized I would not be deterred, he gave me letters of introduction to Dr. Johannes Rutgers in The Hague and Dr. Aletta Jacobs in Amsterdam.

As it turned out, I'd been a bit too cavalier. The voyage took three times as long as expected because the ship kept changing course to avoid U-boats. Nonetheless, I arrived in The Hague overdue but safe.

I could not have asked for a better teacher than Dr. Rutgers. He took me under his wing and taught me about the practicalities of running a birth control clinic. After working with him for three weeks, I went off to learn what I could from Dr. Jacobs.

I arrived in Amsterdam on a blustery morning. The wind whipped up small whitecaps in the canals and rattled the signs over the shops, and a cold sun glinted off the water. I went straight to the hotel. As I signed the register, the clerk behind the desk handed me an envelope. I turned it over and saw that it was from Dr. Jacobs. How gracious of her to answer my letter telling her of my arrival, I thought, as I slit open the envelope.

The letter was written in English. I did not need a translator.

Dear Mrs. Sanger,

I will not see you and refuse to have anything to do with you or your studies. There is no room for the layman in the clinical science of contraception. Only professionals, who have the knowledge, skill, and training, have the right and the duty to pursue this critical field.

Sincerely,
Dr. Aletta Jacobs

Sometimes I think my sex is less than generous to its own.

BACK IN LONDON, under the aegis of women's rights groups, I visited slums, factories, and dockyards; gave lectures; and, thanks to Dr. Rutgers's training, held demonstration clinics for workers' wives. One evening I spoke at Fabian Hall. Standing before an audience of more than a hundred, I couldn't help thinking, if only my father could see me now. He had ranted radicalism in dark taverns and on open country roads. I lectured on it at the Fabian Society. He wouldn't even mind that I was doing it on English soil. George Bernard Shaw had been one of the founding Fabians.

FOG HUNG FROM the streetlamps and steamed up from the gutters. The lights of carriages and autos cut through it for a foot or two, then died. I made my way along the street carefully, trying to think of my success at Fabian Hall a few nights earlier and not to brood about the letter from Bill I'd received that day. I had written to him that our life together was over and I wanted a separation. He had written back about Peggy.

She is disconsolate without you. She cries all the time. I believe in your cause. You know that. But I won't let you sacrifice the children to it. Come home, Peg. We need you.

I was walking with my head down, my mind worrying the problem in frustrating circles. I had to see my children. I couldn't take the chance. A forty-five-year sentence still hung over my head.

Suddenly I found myself standing in a pool of yellow light. I looked up. The glow poured out of Albert Hall, pierced the fog, and illuminated the crowd moving inside. A concert wouldn't take my mind off the children, nothing could do that, but it might soothe. Perhaps it would even make me feel closer to them. Sometimes, if I thought about Peggy with all my concentration, I felt as if I were in communication with her.

I joined the crowd flowing into the hall. A few were in evening dress, but many were not. I would not be out of place. No sign indicated the evening's program, but I didn't care what it was. Beethoven or Bach, Mozart or Vivaldi, any music would serve.

I bought a ticket, made my way into the auditorium, and took a seat. Then I saw the sign on the stage. IF THE LOVE OF THE WORLD IS IN YOU, THE LOVE OF THE LORD IS NOT. I had stumbled into some sort of religious meeting.

I stood and started to make my way out to the aisle, then changed my mind and sat again. I was familiar with Catholic dogma, but this was another breed of intolerance. I might as well know the enemy.

A young woman—she couldn't have been older than seventeen or eighteen—stepped onto the stage and crossed to the

podium. She had masses of red-gold hair and a corn-fed full-
ness of body, but she moved with feline grace. I wasn't imagining her sensuousness. I knew it from the way the man sitting
beside me crossed and uncrossed his legs, then put his hand
over his crotch.

She was carrying what appeared to be a Bible. She stood
silent for a moment, then introduced herself as Sister Aimee
Semple McPherson. Around me, a murmur of disappointment
went from mouth to mouth. Apparently this was not the person
they'd come to hear.

She explained that she had been asked to speak at the last
moment and had prepared nothing. A snake-oil saleswoman's
line if ever I heard one.

"I will rely on the Lord for guidance." She held the Bible over
her head with both hands, then lowered it to the lectern and let
it fall open.

She began to speak. I had no idea what she was talking about.
Old Testament prophets and palmerworms and cankerworms
and locusts. But I knew what she was selling. Sex. She was whipping herself and the audience into a white heat.

I glanced around me. The symptoms were so classic they
might have come from one of Havelock's books. Flared nostrils, flushed cheeks, and eyes wide as startled animals'. The
man beside me crossed and uncrossed his legs again. Then
the responses started. The hallelujahs and amens and I-am-
saveds and Sister-Aimee-has-saved-mes grew louder and more
abandoned. Here was all of the power of sex with none of the
beauty. The girl up on the stage shouting and slithering and
burning with hysteria made a mockery of my lecture to the
Fabian Society. I had gloated over a hundred people willing to
hear an honest reasoned discussion of sex and contraception.

She packed Albert Hall with nine thousand hypocrites taking their pleasure on the sly.

The feeling of defeat followed me back to Torrington Square like a confidence man whispering blandishments in my ear. Why can't you be like other women? Why can't you be satisfied with a home and husband and children? Why can't you stop trying to save the world and save yourself and your children? Give up.

FOR THE NEXT few days, I flirted with the possibility. The weather turned unusually clear and clement, and I wandered St. James's and Green and Hyde Parks, imagining myself as a different woman, cared for, cosseted, content with my three children around me. But it was no good. My crusade wasn't a choice I had made; it was a calling, like the vocation of the nuns I had known in my childhood. I might fall short of success, just as they might not attain perfect faith, but we had to continue the struggle. So I was back where I'd started with my children on one side of the Atlantic and me on the other.

THE IDEA CAME to me a few days later as Havelock and I were walking to our usual tearoom near the British Museum. The weather had turned nasty again, and black umbrellas bobbed like corks in the April mist. Cold and wet and sooty as the city was that afternoon, it had captured my heart. If only I could bring Peggy over. The boys were happy in boarding school, and I didn't want to disrupt their lives, but Peggy belonged with me. The problem was getting her here. A five-year-old cannot cross the Atlantic alone, especially in wartime.

Havelock had the solution. When the war broke out, travelers had panicked, but now passenger liners, even German and British passenger liners, were considered safe, and people were sailing again. His wife was returning from a speaking engagement in America at the end of the month. She had already booked passage on the *Lusitania*. She could bring Peggy over.

Thirteen

I FOUGHT THROUGH THE crowd outside the Cunard office. The mob pushed and snarled and elbowed one another. Fear does that to people.

I was still clutching the newspaper with its pitiless headline.

LUSITANIA SUNK BY SUBMARINE, PROBABLY 1200 DEAD
TWICE TORPEDOED OFF IRISH COAST; SINKS IN 15 MINUTES

Inside, the walls were hung with posters of Cunard liners sailing placid waters. The images did nothing to calm the hysteria. A glass case housing a model of a Cunard ship crashed to the floor. Splinters flew. A woman held a handkerchief to her face. A man let the blood drip. The crowd crunched over the shards of glass, battling to get to the front desk, where officials stood with lists of survivors.

A woman shouted a name. One of the men behind the desk ran a finger down the pages he was holding.

"Not yet received." His voice wasn't unkind, merely exhausted.

"It must be there," the woman insisted. "Have you got the spelling right?"

The man ignored her and searched for another name that someone had called out.

I fought my way to the desk. "Margaret Sanger." My own name sounded strange in my ears. If only it had been mine; if only I could change places with Peggy.

The man looked down at the list again. "Not yet received," he repeated.

Perhaps Edith Ellis had registered her as Peggy rather than Margaret.

"Peggy Sanger," I shouted above the din.

This time the man merely shook his head.

"But she's only five," I insisted, as if age had anything to do with it, as if there were any logic to disaster.

The man turned away to another mother or father or wife or husband. There were hundreds of us, surging back and forth in the damp room that steamed with overheated bodies and terror.

At two in the morning, another man appeared behind the desk and called for quiet. I heard the hush fall as suddenly and completely as if I had gone deaf.

"A list of the dead and missing has been completed," he announced and began to read the names. A woman moaned. A man pounded his hand against a wall. Someone fainted.

The list was alphabetical. He got to the E's swiftly. Edith Ellis was not on the list. Surely if Edith had found her way into a lifeboat, she would have taken Peggy with her.

His voice droned on through the F's and G's and H's. Why didn't she have my last name? Higgins would have come sooner. He reached the S's. Neither Margaret nor Peggy Sanger was listed among the missing and dead.

My relief made me dizzy. I put a hand on the glass case of a ship model to steady myself.

HAVELOCK WAS WAITING for me in the sour-smelling parlor of 67 Torrington Square. He held out his hand. The yellow telegram paper looked brown in the dim light.

I knew without reading what it said. The list the man had read had been incomplete. Peggy was dead.

Havelock inched the cable closer to me. I took it between thumb and forefinger.

```
GERMAN AD IN NEW YORK WORLD WARNED AGAINST
SAILING ON BRITISH SHIP STOP BOOKED PASSAGE ON
AMERICAN LINER STOP DID NOT BRING PEGGY STOP
TOO MUCH RESPONSIBILITY DURING WAR STOP EDITH
```

Fourteen

I STOOD IN THE overcast October morning with the Hudson River at my back and Manhattan rising ahead. Iron wagon wheels and horses' hooves clattered over cobblestones. Automobile horns shrieked. Vendors hawked. The din was deafening. A man driving an ice wagon shouted, "Watch out, sister." I was home.

A month earlier I had received a letter from Jonah J. Goldstein. The climate of opinion was changing, he said. The words *birth control* no longer had to be whispered behind closed doors. Some of the more serious magazines like *Harper's Weekly* were running articles on the subject.

"If you're willing to take a chance and come home, Mrs. Sanger, I think we can strike a blow for the cause."

This time he hadn't guaranteed anything, but I'd booked passage that afternoon.

I picked up my suitcase now and began walking across Fourteenth Street. As I passed a newsstand, a headline jumped out at me from the cover of *Pictorial Review*.

WHAT SHALL WE DO ABOUT BIRTH CONTROL?

J. J. Goldstein had written that some of the more serious magazines were running articles, but I hadn't expected a glossy publication like *Pictorial Review*, filled with advice on how to make the latest-style hats, word a wedding invitation, and furnish a nursery, to take up the cause. I started walking again, more quickly now. I had no time to waste. I had to get back to work. But first I had to see my children.

BILL SANGER

You were in such a hurry, Peg, that you didn't even have time to visit your husband, who was serving thirty days in the Tombs for your cause. And don't tell me I wasn't your husband anymore. The law said we were still married, no matter how you carried on all over Europe. Don't tell me I was a fool to fall for the ploy that landed me in jail either. You would have too, if you'd seen the man.

I'd just gotten back from Paris—someone had to take care of the children—when he turned up at the studio I'd taken in the Village. He said we'd met a few years ago at Mabel Dodge's. I didn't remember him, but then I don't remember most of the characters from that den of iniquity. I believe Freud would call it repression. It's all too painful. I didn't let him in right away. I was trying to size him up. He didn't look like a policeman or one of Comstock's henchmen. He reminded me of the waiter at that café around the corner from our flat in Paris. You remember, the fellow I painted several times. But I still didn't open the door wide. I asked him what he wanted. He said his wife had tuberculosis, and the doctor had warned that another pregnancy would be fatal. He was desperate for a copy of "Family Limitation."

"I'm not a rich man, Mr. Sanger, but I'll pay anything you ask. What good is money in my pocket if my wife is in her grave?"

You're going to say I should have been suspicious of a tear-jerking line like that, but the day I become so hard-hearted that I can't sympathize with a husband's fear of losing his wife is the day I stop belonging to the human race. So I let him in and sold him a copy of the pamphlet.

A week later Comstock turned up at the studio with an arrest warrant. But here's the best part, Peg. Here's why I think the least you could have done was come to see me in prison. Comstock offered me a deal. He said if I told him where you were, he'd see I got off with a suspended sentence. I told him hell would freeze over before I told him anything.

At the sentencing, the judge gave me a choice between a one-hundred-and-fifty-dollar fine or thirty days in the Tombs. I took the thirty days. I figured it would be better publicity for the cause. But even that didn't get through to you, though it seems to have taken a toll on Comstock. Ten days after I began serving my sentence, he died of pneumonia. Some said it was brought on by my trial.

I don't know what else I can do for you, Peg, except give you the divorce you keep writing me about. Perhaps I would if I thought you meant it, but I know you don't. You couldn't, not after what we've been to each other.

If you don't care about me, think of the children. They can't go on this way, being bounced from pillar to post, a few weeks with Ethel, a month with friends in the Village, now boarding school. What kind of a mother puts a five-year-old child in a boarding school? Come home to us, Peg. I need you. We all need you.

. . .

PEGGY CAME RUNNING toward me down the dirt drive. I bent to scoop her up. Her arms went around my neck in a stranglehold. I couldn't imagine how I'd got along without her for a year.

"You're so big," I said, and she grinned and hugged me tighter.

Grant approached slowly, looking up at me from under a thick fringe of lashes.

"Hello, Mother," he said and held out his hand. I put Peggy down and shook his hand solemnly, then bent and hugged him to me. Beneath his thick winter coat, his muscles were so tight they felt as if they might snap. I went on hugging him. The muscles began to ease.

We started toward the old farmhouse-turned-school, Grant on one side, Peggy on the other. If only Stuart had been there, we'd be complete, but the freedom of a progressive school had proved too chaotic for him. Some children thrive on being able to show up when they want, stand or sit as they choose, read or paint, play games or work a loom when the mood moves them, but Stuart wasn't one of them. I'd had to take him out of the school in New Jersey and move him to a more conventional one on Long Island. I hated the idea of his sitting in a classroom all day, being forced to memorize and conform, but he was finally doing well in reading and arithmetic.

Peggy darted ahead, then circled back, steady on her legs. I'd always known she didn't need a brace, only an environment that encouraged her independence and let her run free.

I asked them to show me around. I knew Stelton only from the recommendations of friends like Will Durant, who'd helped establish it, though he'd left a year earlier to marry one of his students. There was a bit of a fuss about that. The girl had been only sixteen, but people said she made up in brilliance what she lacked in years.

In what must have once been the parlor of the farmhouse, a group of children, bundled up in coats and hats and mittens, sat at a table or sprawled on the floor, reading or drawing or simply thinking their own unfettered thoughts. Grant and Peggy led me into the kitchen. A small boy stood on a chair stirring a pot. Two other boys were throwing oranges and bananas against a wall. I tried not to look disapproving. Freedom was the watchword of the school. Only by giving children liberty could you raise adults who knew how to grasp it. Still, I hated waste.

"What an unusual game." I was careful to keep my voice neutral.

"It's not a game," Grant explained. "They're softening the fruit. Different grown-ups run the kitchen on different days. On Anyuta's day all we eat are raisins, nuts, and mushy fruit."

"We never get jelly sandwiches," Peggy said.

"I'm sure raisins, nuts, and fruits are very healthy. All the same, would you like to walk into town for lunch?" I wasn't subverting the regime, merely giving them a treat.

The tearoom was small, with three rough wooden tables, mismatched chairs, and limp red-and-white-checked curtains of questionable cleanliness. We were the only customers.

"Are you back for good, Mother?" Grant asked after I ordered hot chocolate and sandwiches, without the crusts on Peggy's.

"I am."

Peggy put down her cup of hot chocolate. It left a mustache of foam above her upper lip. "Can we come live with you?"

"Soon, my darling. But first I have important work to do. Besides, if you lived with me, you couldn't go to school here."

Her smile disappeared into the foam mustache.

"Aren't you happy here?"

"It's fine," Grant said before Peggy could answer.

"We have to go outside to pee," she said.

"The outhouse is okay," Grant insisted.

"It's always cold. We sleep in our coats. Last winter Grant's hair froze to the straw pillow."

"It didn't," Grant said.

"Did too. I saw it."

"A bit of cold won't kill you. When I was in London, I had to crack the ice in the pitcher every morning to wash. And I'm all the better for it."

Peggy looked dubious.

"I know how to set type," Grant said.

"That's wonderful! Much better than sitting in a stuffy classroom memorizing."

"There aren't any classrooms. After the morning meeting, we're allowed to go anywhere and do anything we want. Mostly me and Herbie play ball."

"Herbie and I," I said, though I was aware of the irony. I hadn't sent them to a modern school to learn grammar.

"Sometimes we run races. When the pond freezes again, we're going to go skating."

"Last year a boy fell through the ice," Peggy said.

"He was just playing at it. Anyway, one of the grown-ups pulled him out."

"I was scared," Peggy said.

I reached an arm around her and held her to me. She didn't feel as chubby as I remembered. "There's nothing to be frightened of. Mother is home and will never let anything bad happen to you. That's why I have to go back to work. To make the world safe for you."

"Why can't I go back to work with you?"

"When you're older," I said, and suddenly I saw it: Peggy grown, me still vital, working together. I tightened my grasp around her shoulders. "Hurry and grow up," I teased.

They fell silent on the walk back to the school, though neither of them let go of my hands. When we reached the dirt drive in front of the farmhouse, I stopped and turned to them. I hugged Grant first. His muscles felt tight as stretched rubber bands again. I bent and scooped up Peggy. She grabbed me in another stranglehold. When I put her down, I had to pry her arms from my neck.

She began to cry. I fought back my own tears. But Grant was a trooper. He took his little sister's hand.

"Don't cry, Peggy," I heard him say as he led her back to the house. "I'm still here."

GRANT SANGER

Were you really so blind that you didn't notice what was going on at that hellhole of a school, Mother, or did you just choose not to see? Did you think Peggy made up the story about my hair freezing to the straw pillow, or did you believe you were building our characters? As long as our souls and spirits were free, what did it matter if our minds were being neglected and our bodies punished? The main building had no heat. The dormitory was open-air. We ate and slept and went to the outhouse in our coats and hats and scarves and mittens. The only time I wasn't cold during the winter months was when I worked up a sweat running or playing outside. The food was some crazed utopian's idea of healthy. That meant we were hungry all the time. I could take it. I was older and stronger. I hadn't had polio as an infant. It was polio, Mother, not the flu. When are you going to admit it? Maybe that damn school had nothing to do with what happened. As a doctor, I can't prove cause and effect. But as a brother, I can tell you it was no place to send a little girl.

Fifteen

I TOOK A ROOM at the Hotel Rutledge on Lexington Avenue at Thirtieth Street. There was no time to hunt for an apartment. Then I called Jonah J. Goldstein to make an appointment. I'd planned to go to his office, but he said he'd come to the Rutledge. "You're still a wanted woman, Mrs. Sanger. I can't risk having the authorities pick you up before we notify them properly."

His knock on the door was brash.

I opened it. "Is this a raid, Mr. Goldstein?"

"I wanted to make sure you heard me."

I swung the door wider and glanced around the room. It couldn't have been more than fifteen by eighteen. "In case I was in the other wing, you mean?"

I moved aside. He stepped into the room and tossed his hat on the bed. I picked it up and put it on the desk.

His heavy eyebrows lifted in devilish arches. "Superstitious?"

"Tidy," I lied.

He took off his coat. Before he did, I noticed the fit. In the year I'd been away, he'd found a tailor. He put it on the bed. I let it lie. There was a single chair in the room. He took it. I perched on the side of the bed.

"We've got the DA on the run," he said. "He can't figure out how to pursue a case against you for demanding a discussion of contraception when half the respectable newspapers and magazines in the country are running articles on it. So he did the stupid thing and postponed the trial."

"Wonderful! The longer this drags on, the more publicity we get."

"You're a pistol, Mrs. Sanger. And incidentally, I think we've reached the Margaret and J.J. stage. Or better yet, Peg and Johnny."

"Johnny?"

"That's what the boys at Tammany call me. Some name for a boy who wanted to be a rabbi."

"You wanted to be a rabbi?"

"Had my heart set on it, until my brother told me it was a great racket. The word *racket* drove me straight to law school."

"It's a nice story, even if it isn't true."

"It's true. It just may not be factual. Isn't that the way you'd put it, Peg?"

·⊰ · ⊱·

IN THE NEXT few weeks, my initial dislike of J.J.—I couldn't call him Johnny; Johnny belonged to the boys at the bottom of the hill who'd chased me with shouts of "devil's children"— gradually turned to respect. We made a good team. I admired the twists and turns of his legal mind. He complimented me on my grasp of tactics and strategy. But the bond did not go beyond the professional. In court, he was a fighter. On social issues, he was a crusader. But in his heart, he was deeply conventional. My personal life would have shocked him. Wantley would have scandalized him. As we worked together in my small room at the Rutledge, I was intensely aware of his physical presence, but for the first time in my life, I fought an attraction. Bill had fooled me into thinking he was a free spirit. I wanted no more possessive, marriage-minded men in my life.

The district attorney postponed the trial a second time.

"Now he's cooked his goose," J.J. said.

He was right. The first postponement had called attention to the cause. The second had made it, and me, famous. By the time my hearing finally came up, reporters packed the courtroom. They even chronicled what I wore.

The accused was dressed in modish attire, a close-fitting suit of black broadcloth, patent leather pumps, white spats, and an English walking hat.

"Pip pip, cheerio, and all that," Ethel had said when she'd come to the hotel to pick me up.

"She'll have them cheering in the aisles," J.J. had predicted.

At the hearing, the district attorney asked the judge to drop all charges. "We are determined that Mrs. Sanger should not become a martyr. If we can help it."

"Lots of luck," J.J. muttered under his breath.

I was free.

THE DAY AFTER the hearing, I went out to New Jersey to see Grant and Peggy again. I explained the good news to them in terms a five- and six-year-old could understand.

"Now can we come live with you?" Peggy asked.

"Soon," I replied.

The answer broke my heart, but I had no choice. The movement was making progress. I had to press the advances I'd fought so hard for. I also had to take the battle to new territory. Now that the idea of contraception was becoming more respectable, its supporters had to be too. I already had the socialists and anarchists and other progressives in my corner. I had to win over the women of influence, the ones who could raise money and get things done.

I STOOD ON the stoop of a brownstone a few blocks south of the Hotel Rutledge under a washed winter sky. The house belonged to a maiden lady, an old-lace-and-smelling-salts term if ever I heard one, who had been born there some fifty years earlier and would probably die there in the not-too-distant future. She was one of those women who had made what I thought of as the choice—between feminism and life, between the vote and everything else, including men. Especially men. I called them the pink-tea ladies, women who cut the crusts off tea sandwiches, or had their maids do it for them. I knew I shouldn't let the shorn sandwiches bother me, but every time they arrived on a silver tray or china tea stand in one of those meetings I remembered supper in Corning. My mother and sisters and I had sat at the bottom of the table, below the salt, as I later learned it was called, and on lean nights the bread hadn't made it that far. Later, the trimmed sandwiches would bother me for another reason. Peggy had always been adamant about having the crusts cut off her bread.

I lifted the brass knocker in the shape of a hand holding a

bunch of grapes and let it fall against the door. A moment later, a maid in a gray uniform with a starched white apron opened it, took my coat, and led me down a dim hall. My eyes, still seared by winter brightness, adjusted slowly to the gloom.

The parlor she showed me into, a cave of thick velvet draperies, dark flocked wallpaper, and murky oil paintings of dour ancestors and melancholy landscapes, was no brighter. Ten or a dozen women—I didn't have time to count—sat erect and intimidating on horsehair-upholstered chairs and sofas. Every one of them had been raised never to let her shoulders graze the back of a chair. The hostess introduced me, and after I went around the room shaking hands, I took a seat, and we got down to business. A woman in a severe brown toque gave a report on the effort to organize women workers for the vote. It wasn't meeting with much success.

"Have you explained the importance of the ballot in simple language they can comprehend?" another woman asked.

"You must make them understand that woman suffrage is not only an inalienable right, it is the road to a better, more just world," a third suggested.

The discussion heated up.

"Explain that it will put an end to war. What woman would cast a vote to send her husband or son off to battle?"

"Tell them it will take children out of the factories and send them to school. What mother could sleep through the night while another mother's children slaved ten or twelve or fourteen hours a day over dangerous machinery?"

"It will save women from degradation."

At the last word, a shiver went through the room.

"Women will vote for equal pay for equal work, and their sisters will not have to take to the streets to support themselves."

"It will replace the tainted milk, contaminated bread, and spoiled produce of the cities with a safe food supply. Women know about marketing and preparation. Men know only about sitting down to a meal someone else has prepared."

And they thought socialists were dreamers.

Finally I couldn't take it anymore. "It's not that they don't understand. It's that they have more pressing problems on their minds."

"What could be more pressing than the ballot?"

"Mouths to feed." I was careful to keep my voice as tepid as the tea being poured.

"They should not have so many children."

The maid in the gray uniform and white apron held a silver tray with tea sandwiches out to me. I took one, raised it to my mouth, then lowered it to my saucer.

"They do not have them by choice."

The words hung in the musty air. The women averted their eyes from them.

"Self-restraint," someone whispered.

"The husbands are the ones who lack self-restraint," I whispered back.

"Perhaps they should not marry," the hostess suggested. "It is a small sacrifice for the greater welfare."

"Precisely," another woman agreed. "Our daughters and granddaughters will have the freedom to marry once we have won the vote."

I resisted the impulse to ask how these daughters and granddaughters would get themselves born.

"For these women, marriage is not a choice but an economic necessity," I explained. "Then, when they do marry, the children begin arriving, and each one makes the hardship worse."

A dozen pairs of eyes stared at me. To them hunger was a missed teatime; backbreaking work meant a long afternoon pruning rosebushes; and if they did have husbands who, after a few too many drinks, turned more amorous than they'd like, the men usually had the sense to take their attentions elsewhere.

"That's why contraception is so important."

I might as well have let a mangy dog into the parlor to push its snout into their innocent crotches.

"I do not understand how we got off on this subject," someone said.

"You're muddying the waters, Mrs. Sanger."

"You'll expose us to accusations of immorality."

"Men will use it as a way to silence us."

"Women who might support suffrage will be scandalized by this talk of . . . of . . . of this."

"You're asking for trouble," the hostess summed up.

I smiled politely. These women hadn't an inkling of how much trouble I was about to ask for.

A COLD WIND howled off the Hudson, down the cross streets, and out over the East River, but inside the ballroom of the Hotel Brevoort a tropical garden bloomed, fragrant with the bouquets of hothouse flowers on the white-linen-covered tables and the perfume of well-groomed ladies out on the town for a good cause. I was the good cause. The Committee of One Hundred, a tony group of society and club women, had decided to give a dinner to honor me. I had no intention of wasting the opportunity.

Most of the guests were women, not the bluestockings who believed in abstinence so their daughters and granddaughters could have the vote, but a more worldly breed. A few had brought their husbands. Several male doctors had come as well.

The speeches went on for too long, as those sorts of encomiums tend to. By the time I stood to deliver my remarks, a man in my line of vision was nodding off. The woman beside him opened her mouth in a cavernous yawn, then remembered herself and covered it with a hand weighed down by a wickedly big diamond.

I thanked the guests for coming. I told them how proud I was to be honored by them. I spoke about the injustice to hundreds, no, thousands, no, millions of our less fortunate sisters and their unwanted children, doomed to misery, illness, and death. I described the lines of women who queued up every Saturday, payday, for the five-dollar abortionist. I explained again, because it was shocking how few people knew it, that contraception was not abortion. Contraception was the tool that would make abortion unnecessary. I recounted the story of Sadie Sachs, but this time I left out the doctor's line about telling Jake to sleep on the roof. I needed the support of the physicians in the audience as well as their wives.

The dozing man's chin rested on his chest. The yawns had become contagious. Rings and bracelets on the hands trying to cover them flared around the room like fireflies.

"That is why I am asking fifty of you who are married women to sign this manifesto."

I held up a sheet of paper.

"I'm asking fifty of you to demand that information about birth control be made available to all married women, not only those of us who can afford private doctors, but those in tenements and slums who rely on social services. And . . . I am asking you to admit that you have used contraception yourselves."

The dozing man's eyes flew open. The woman next to him sat up. An intake of breath ran through the room like a gust of the wind coming off the Hudson.

I thanked them and took my seat.

Applause sputtered, then swelled to an ovation. People began pushing back their chairs, standing, and milling around. A line formed in front of the head table. One after another, the guests congratulated me, complimented me, and swore to support me. An inspiration, a triumph, a tour de force. There was so much excitement that I didn't get to look at the manifesto until the ballroom had emptied. I was studying it as J.J. came up carrying my coat.

"I figure we had between one fifty and two hundred people," he said. "Maybe thirty of them men. That still gives us a hefty margin."

I didn't say anything.

"So, how many signatures?"

I handed him the manifesto.

Six women had demanded the dissemination of birth control information. Three had admitted they'd used it.

"So much for my triumph," I said to J.J. as we made our way back to the Rutledge, our collars turned up against the cold, the wind whipping my coat around my ankles. "Every time I start to think I'm making progress, there's another setback."

"You're making progress."

"Of course. Now instead of throwing me in jail, they give dinners to honor me. Giving me a dinner is the easy part. It makes them feel progressive and high-minded and courageous. Putting themselves on the line is another story."

"Give them time."

"Tell that to a woman who's living in a cramped tenement

apartment, and whose husband is out of work or not even looking for work, and who's pregnant with her fifth or tenth or"—I
thought of my mother—"thirteenth child."

This time he didn't say anything. He merely took my hand
and tucked it in his coat pocket. I was surprised. We walked on
like that, the fingers of his left hand tangled with those of my
right in the warm nest of his coat. For an innocent connection,
it packed a powerful charge.

Half a block from the hotel, I took my hand from his pocket.
I was a married woman and the champion of a still-suspect
cause. The paltry number of signatures on the petitions was evidence of that.

In the elevator, we stood side by side, staring silently at the gray-
uniformed back of the operator. We were models of propriety, but
desire was flexing its unruly muscle in the pit of my stomach.

I stepped off the elevator, he followed, and we started down
the corridor with a prim slice of hotel-musty air between us.
When we reached my door, he opened it, and I stepped into the
room ahead of him and turned to face him. We stood that way
for a moment. I waited. That was new. I'd never waited before.
I'd never had to. And while I waited, I felt the attraction that
had been pulling me toward him since we'd left the dinner—for
longer than that, really—suddenly twist into anger. His caution
had awakened a similar response in me. I hated cautious people.

I said good night and closed the door.

JONAH J. GOLDSTEIN

You think it was easy not following you into your room that
night? I was punch-drunk with wanting you. But I knew more

about your life than you thought. Like Sherman through Georgia, you went through men. Sometimes I wonder why we all fell so hard. You were easy to look at, with that red hair and those green eyes, and you had a nice little shape, but face it, Peg, you didn't have the kind of beauty that stops traffic. You could be pigheaded and selfish, and your word wasn't exactly as reliable as the almanac. There was the sex, of course, but it couldn't have been only the sex. Men go to bed with women for sex, but they don't propose marriage to women for sex, and I'm not the only one who went down on one metaphorical knee more times than I like to remember. Sometimes I think it was because you didn't give a damn about any of us. We all played second banana to the movement. That's why you and I ended up eyeing each other across that no-man's-land of sex. I was crazy about you, but I wasn't suicidal.

Sixteen

SUDDENLY, ALL OVER America, women, and some men, wanted to hear me speak. I was delighted. I was terrified. As I walked to the podiums, I thought my knees would give out beneath me. It was fortunate that I didn't need notes, because my hands trembled too badly to hold them. I lived in fear that my voice would come out as a croak, and sometimes it did for the first few sentences. I told myself the stage fright would pass with practice. It didn't. I felt as sick to my stomach before my twentieth speech as I had before my first. Once or twice I attempted to begin with a witty comment or joke, but it always fell flat. Maybe that was why the public thought I had no sense of humor. I did, but not about birth control.

Later, looking back on those weeks and months of travel, I'd see them as one of those movie montages where a train comes speeding toward the audience while place-names whirl across the screen. Boston, Buffalo, Rochester, Cleveland, Detroit, Chicago, Denver, San Francisco, Seattle. The halls were packed. Five hundred, a thousand, two thousand—toffs and laborers, doctors and anarchists, club women and mothers of huge broods who smelled of laundry soap and baby spit-up. In Indianapolis, a woman stood up and quoted the biblical lines about suffering little children to come unto me. The audience booed her down. In St. Louis, the management bowed to threats from the Catholic Church and locked me out of a theater. I moved the meeting to a businessmen's club and drew larger crowds than either Taft or Roosevelt had. Not all religious groups opposed me. In Spokane, I spoke to a full house at a Unitarian church. In Los Angeles, I found copies of my pamphlet "Family Limitation" translated into Japanese and Spanish. In Portland, I was arrested along with several others, and when we refused bail and spent the night in jail, we set off demonstrations that made the national newspapers.

But despite the excitement of those meetings and the enthusiasm of my audiences, life on the road was bleak. I was tired all the time and feverish much of it. A hotel room for one is a lonely place. I missed my children. Sometimes, when I lay in the cold sheets of those narrow unloved beds, exhausted but unable to sleep, I switched on the electric light or turned up the gas lamp and read and reread their letters.

Dear Mother,

I received the marshmellows. Thank you very much.
Mother will you come down on Thanksgiving Day?
Now you put down in your engagement book, Nov. 28
Go down to see Grant. Answer soon.

Lots of love,
Grant

Dear Mother,

How are you? I am fine. When are you coming home?

Love,
Stuart

Peggy was too young to write. If only she hadn't been. I'd give a great deal now for a scrawled message from her.

Other letters poured in as well. Most of them went to New York, but sometimes I'd check into a hotel to find an envelope or five or ten waiting for me.

Dear Mrs. Sanger,

I have nine children, two died at birth,
and my husband is out of work. I will kill
myself before I have another child.

Dear Mrs. Sanger,

I am a churchgoing woman who tries to keep
a good clean home, and my husband is respected
in our town, but he will beat me if I get
pregnant again. He did the last time.

Dear Mrs. Sanger,

The doc says another baby will kill my wife.
I know I should stay away from her, but the
flesh is weak.

Then they all asked the same question, the one that had killed Sadie Sachs.

Other letters followed me across the country as well. Havelock wrote to his Dear Rebel. Hugh wrote to Darling Margaret. Walter Roberts wrote to his Dear One. Even Bill wrote to Peg,

My Sweetheart. The only one who didn't send letters was J.J. Occasionally I got a telegram from him about legal matters. I was relieved. Really I was. We were better off keeping our distance.

I covered hundreds of miles. The scenery changed, but the experience remained numbingly the same. Except for one talk in late October of 1915. I remember the timing because the incident occurred the evening before I was banned from speaking in Boston, and that's one night I will never forget.

But on the night I'm talking about, the night before Boston, I had finished my remarks and was answering the flood of questions that always followed. Suddenly, as I looked out at the audience, I saw Peggy in her favorite white nightgown with the yellow daises, floating above them. I closed my eyes to clear my vision. When I opened them, Peggy was still floating, but higher now, until she was level with the windows at the top of the auditorium. As I watched, a breeze sent her nightgown fluttering, and her small body drifted peacefully, oh, so peacefully, through the window and off into the darkening sky.

I chalked the vision up to exhaustion.

Seventeen

A WEEK AFTER THAT strange hallucination, a week I refuse to talk about, I locked myself in my room at the
Rutledge. Friends sent letters and cards. I barely glanced at them
before throwing them away—except for Emma Goldman's. For
some reason, I clung to that. "You must not blame yourself," she
wrote. "I cannot imagine anyone with your intelligence holding
herself responsible for something that could not possibly have
been in your power."

Others came in person. I refused to see them. Their pity
would make it real. I preferred my own version of events. I
inhabited a world where Stuart was getting along in his new
school, and Grant was flourishing at Stelton, and Peggy had
all the crustless jelly sandwiches she wanted. In that world, she
ran free, without a brace. In that world, we did everything together. We rode double-decker buses in London, and watched
the changing of the guard at Buckingham Palace, and fed the
waterfowl in St. James's Park. We collected shells and built sand
castles on the beach in Provincetown and ventured out into the
water, where I taught her to swim. I took her to the ballet and
museums and the library. As she grew older, she shadowed my

steps at rallies and strikes and speeches. The first time I'd held her in my arms, I'd sensed an attachment deeper than any I'd ever known. As time passed, she became my hope, my inspiration, the embodiment of my cause.

At the end of another week, I packed that world away for safekeeping—I knew I'd be coming back to it—washed my hair, put on a suit and hat, and faced myself in the mirror. The suit hung on me as if on a hanger. J.J. had arranged for the management to leave trays outside my door, but I'd barely touched them. My eyes were sunk in circles of darkness. The bones of my face were savagely sharp. I realized with a shock that I was squaring off with my mother's reflection. She had survived five miscarriages and two infant deaths. I would endure what I had to.

I telephoned J.J. I wasn't sure why. There were other people in the movement I could have called. Ethel had tried to see me a dozen times. But somehow I felt safer with J.J. He wasn't a part of my old life.

I asked how soon we could meet.

There was silence on the other end of the line.

"J.J., are you there?"

"Yes. Sure. I'm on my way."

Fifteen minutes later he knocked on my door. I opened it. The expression on his face was more telling than any mirror. I looked even worse than I'd thought, but for the first time in my life, I didn't care about my appearance.

He reached out to put a hand on my shoulder, then drew back, as if he were afraid to touch me.

I took his hand and drew him into the room. "I'm not a porcelain doll."

A porcelain doll. The doll with the painted china face I'd sent Peggy the previous Christmas. I'd bought it at Harrods and spent far too much money on it. The memory undid me. I could not go through with this after all. I did not have my mother's strength. I would send J.J. away, tear off my disguise of sanity, go back to bed, and hold my grief tight as a lover.

I thought of my mother again, of thousands of mothers. "It's time to get back to work," I said.

I WAS MORE in demand than ever. Reporters came to the Rutledge for interviews. Photographers snapped pictures. J.J. arranged for me to have a formal portrait taken with the boys. He thought it came out well. I hated it. Grant, wearing a Buster Brown suit, leans against me, his soft little-boy face above the floppy tie old with grief. Stuart stands at my side, his head tilted toward my shoulder, poised between a childish demand to be taken care of and a precocious offer to protect. The picture isn't even a photograph, it's a negative, not in the sense that black is white and white black, but because what matters is not the bodies in the frame but the empty space at its heart.

A few nights after I had the photograph taken, Bill showed up at the Rutledge. I hadn't seen him since I'd gone into hiding in my room. His strong features had somehow shriveled. All the force had seeped out of him.

"Aren't you going to invite me in?" He was still in the hall, and I was in the doorway with one hand on the frame, the other on the doorknob.

"I think it's better if you say whatever you want to say here."

"Is this what we've come to, Peg?"

"We'll only end up blaming each other. We don't seem to be able to stop blaming each other. That's why it's better if we're apart."

"It's not better for me. I love you."

"You have a strange way of showing it. Telling everyone what a bad mother I was."

He was silent for a moment, and when he spoke his voice was thick, as if he couldn't get his tongue around the words. "You weren't a bad mother. You aren't a bad mother," he corrected himself, "when you're with them. It's just that you're never with them. You're always off working and lecturing."

"And if I weren't off working and lecturing, who would support them?"

He flinched. I would have been sorry, if I'd had any sorrow to spare.

"Peg." He reached for me. I took a step back.

"Someone's coming," I said. It wasn't entirely a ruse. I'd heard the elevator doors open and close.

His face collapsed. "You're ice. Ice with a hole where your heart ought to be."

I wanted to scream at him not to talk about the hole where my heart ought to be. I managed to hold my tongue.

"You never gave a damn about me." His grief was curdling into anger. "I suppose there's a certain consolation in that. Ironic as it is. You didn't give a damn about me, but you don't give a damn about any of the others either." He was working himself up to a rage now. "Your affairs, your pathological promiscuity—"

"Is there a problem, Peg?"

At the sound of the voice, we both turned to see J.J. coming around the corner from the elevator.

"Bill was just leaving," I said.

Bill looked from J.J. to me and back. "All right, I'll go. But watch yourself, Mr. Goldstein. You think you're a smart lawyer, but you're no match for my wife. She'll eat you up and spit you out, and before you know it, this hardhearted, unnatural—"

J.J. took a step to my side. "Good night, Mr. Sanger."

Bill stood staring at J.J. I saw his hands ball into fists, then open, then close again.

"Go home," J.J. said quietly. His voice was kind but cool, and suddenly I understood the impulse that had made me telephone him when I'd decided to return to the world. I couldn't stand to be around Bill. It wasn't merely the backlog of bitterness and recrimination. It was the unbearable intimacy of shared agony. We tore at each other's wounds like animals. J.J. was a stranger to the hurt. He felt sympathy, but sympathy is not suffering. His distance from the pain was a kind of solace, and for the first time in my life, more than love, more than sex, I needed solace. That night I found it with J.J.

There was nothing romantic about our lovemaking. His hands were not practiced at hooks and laces. Mine were too impatient and tore a button off his fly. We did an awkward two-step to the bed. He was on top of me, then I was on top of him. We were too wild, too thrashingly eager. Then suddenly we stopped. He was on top of me again, and he put a hand on either side of my head, straightened his arms, as if he were doing a push-up, and held himself that way looking down at me. His eyes were like holes in the universe. I have never seen such darkness. I swam up into them.

Later, J.J. would say that sexually I was a revelation. I never told him that I could have said the same about him. I hadn't expected an accomplished lover. But when he raised himself on both arms and looked down at me, the world slowed. For a while, I could have sworn it stopped. There was nothing beyond the here and now and our two bodies hell-bent on pleasure. That was something else about J.J. It was just the two of us in bed that night. With Havelock and Hugh and the rest of the Wantley set, I'd always sensed a crowd. I don't mean the occasions when there really were other people in bed with us. I mean even alone with one man, I'd felt the hot breath of others upping the ante, the competition to give me more and better orgasms, the rivalry to postpone their own for longer, the drive to make me howl with pleasure as I never had before. I'm not complaining about any of that. I'm merely saying that it was nice being alone with J.J. and, for a minute or two, without my grief.

HE TOOK AN apartment on West Fourteenth Street for me, and for the boys when they were home from school. The building had lost its claim to respectability years earlier, though a set of lace curtains in the first-floor windows made a gallant stab at decorum and a couple of bright red geraniums strove for cheerfulness. The flat was on the fourth floor, a tiny bedroom with a window facing a brick wall and a larger square room with two windows, one facing the street, the other another brick wall. A tin bathtub, gas stove, and sink stood in one corner of the larger room.

"You can put a screen around those," J.J. said when he showed me the place.

He hired a woman from Harlem to come in and clean. I was too grateful to him for taking care of practical arrangements to notice that solace was inching toward domesticity.

Ethel liked the apartment so much that she took a smaller one, not much more than a room really, on the floor above. On the one below, a woman who wanted to sing lieder but performed ragtime in a music store on Broadway practiced scales at all hours. The building was louche, despite the lace curtains on the first floor, but that was the point. J.J. could stay the night rather than having to get up, put on his clothes, and go back to his own apartment, as he would have had to at the Rutledge or a more reputable establishment. Still, we had to be careful. He was a respectable attorney with political ambitions. I was a well-known activist for a still-questionable cause.

"We wouldn't have to worry if we were married," J.J. began saying.

"Why ruin things?" I always answered. "I like living in sin," I sometimes teased him.

"What about the boys?"

"You're wonderful with the boys," I said, though I knew that wasn't what he'd meant. "They're crazy about you."

It was true. He taught them the kinds of things boys were supposed to know and I didn't. Bill didn't seem to either, but then Bill wasn't around much. J.J. took them to ball games, and on outings to Surprise Lake with the Grand Street Boys, a group of youths he sponsored from the tenements, and to Coney Island in a Stutz Bearcat that belonged to a Tammany friend. One afternoon, he took them to the Lower East Side to buy Stuart his first pair of long pants. I'd promised to as soon as I had time, but I'd been so busy.

"Nice fit, right?" J.J. said while Stuart strutted around the living room in such high spirits that he knocked over the Japanese screen I'd put around sink and tub and stove.

That night J.J. brought up marriage again.

"I am married," I said. Bill still refused to give me a divorce or even a separation agreement.

"Have you even asked him for a divorce?"

"Every time I wrote from abroad."

"I mean more recently."

I hadn't. Much as I wanted to be free of Bill, he was my protection against another marriage. But J.J. kept harping on the subject. Finally I sent Bill an invitation to dinner. "You can see the boys and perhaps we can settle matters," I wrote.

He arrived with a dozen long-stemmed roses. There is something pitiful about a man in a shiny suit and frayed cuffs bearing roses.

The evening was not a success. Bill was overly hearty with the boys. They were too polite with him. I watched the three of them and thought how much easier we were when J.J. was there.

In the middle of dinner, Bill put down his knife and fork, laid his napkin on the table, and stood. "I can't." He stumbled out of the room as if he'd been drinking, though he hadn't.

The next day I got a letter from him. "Please don't invite me again. I sat across the table from you and still loved you so much I couldn't bear it."

That evening J.J. asked how the dinner had gone. I told him we'd never got around to discussing a divorce.

"Did you even bring it up?"

"He didn't give me a chance. He left in the middle of it." I didn't mention Bill's letter, but I didn't have to.

J.J. shook his head. "The poor bugger," he said and stopped talking about marriage. Maybe Bill's example had put him off. Or maybe he didn't stop, but I no longer heard him. I was too preoccupied.

Eighteen

I STOOD IN THE cool October dawn waiting. Ethel and little Fania, who had the fair-haired ethereal look of a nymph and the steel-nerved daring of a cat burglar, had gone home to snatch an hour or two of sleep, but I was too wound up to rest. The three of us had worked all night plastering the flyers on buildings and streetlamps and storefronts. Now they fluttered in the morning breeze.

MOTHERS!

Can you afford to have a large family?

Do you want any more children?

If not, why do you have them?

DO NOT KILL, DO NOT TAKE LIFE, BUT PREVENT

Safe, Harmless Information can be obtained of trained Nurses at

46 AMBOY STREET

NEAR PITKIN AVE.—BROOKLYN

Tell Your Friends and Neighbors. All Mothers Welcome.

A registration fee of 10 cents entitles any mother to this information.

מוטערס!

זייט איהר פערמעגליך צו האבען א גרויסע פאמיליע?

ווילט איהר האבען נאך קינדער?

רטינ ביוא, וואָרום האָט איהר זיי?

מערדערט ניט, נעהמט ניט קיין לעבען, ניו פערהיט זיך

זיכערע, אָנגשעדליכע אויסקינפּטע קענט איהר בעקומען פון ערפארענע נוירסעס אין

46 אמבאָי סטריט ניער פּיטקין עוועניו ברוקלין

מאכט דאס בעקאנט צו אייערע פריינד און שכנות. יעדער מוטער איז ווילקאמען

פיר 10 סענט איינשרייב-געלד זיינט איהר בערעכטיגט צו דיעזע אינפאָרמיישאן

MADRI!

Potete permettervi il lusso d'avere altri bambini?

Ne volete ancora?

Se non ne volete più, perché continuate a metterli al mondo?

NON UCCIDETE MA PREVENITE!

Informazioni sicure ed innocue saranno fornite da infermiere

autorizzate a

46 AMBOY STREET Near Pitkin Ave. Brooklyn

a cominciare dal 12 Ottobre. Avvertite le vostre amiche e vicine.

Tutte le madri sono ben accette. La tassa d'iscrizione di 10

cents da diritto a qualunque madre di ricevere consigli ed

informazioni gratis.

In Holland I had seen how well their clinics worked. Now, a year after I'd returned, I was ready to open one in America.

The sun inched above the tenements, splitting the street into light and shadow like a harlequin mask. I lingered on the shadowy side, waiting.

Across the street a man came down the steps of a tenement, a newspaper bulky with his lunch under his arm. His eyes were still half closed against the day ahead. He started down the street, glanced at a lamppost, and plodded on. Suddenly he stopped, turned back, and stood studying the poster for a moment. He shook his head and moved on.

A woman came down another stoop, dragging a carriage with one hand, holding a baby in her other arm, her body already a curve of exhaustion. She made her way along the street. The sign stopped her. She looked around to see if anyone was watching, then moved closer. As she stood reading, other men and women began coming out of paint-peeling doors and down cracked stoops. Several of the men glanced at the signs, but most kept going. The women stopped. Some read in silence. Others were noisier.

It's a joke.

Hochme.

It's trap.

Pulapka.

It's a miracle.

Miracolo.

I made my way down Amboy Street to Pitkin Avenue, past shabby storefronts and crumbling tenements. My own rented space on the corner was no better, but the crisp white curtains Fania had sewn hung in the plate-glass window, and Mr. Rabinowitz, the landlord, was sweeping the sidewalk in front of it. I was still grateful to him. In a city where property owners didn't hesitate to rent space for noisy bars, stinking cigar factories, and inhuman sweatshops, Mr. Rabinowitz was the only one who was willing to lease space to a nurse intending to collude against nature with a bunch of impoverished mothers. And at my trial the prosecution would accuse me of opening the clinic in Brownsville in order to wipe out the Jewish people. I could have told them that my children were half Jewish, but I didn't.

I had tried to find a doctor to run the clinic. Most of them knew less about contraception than I did, but the presence of a doctor, no matter how uninformed, would make the clinic more respectable, if still illegal. But the doctors I'd approached had been as squeamish as the landlords. And no self-respecting male doctor would work in a clinic started by a female. I'd finally found a woman doctor, but after Gouverneur Hospital hounded her off the staff for prescribing a pessary for a woman with severe tuberculosis, she'd got cold feet. So Ethel and I would run the clinic, and Fania Mindell and Elizabeth Stuyvesant would assist us. Two Irish nurses from the bottom of the hill, a Jewish girl from the Chicago slums who spoke three languages, and a social worker with a gold-plated Old New York name would man, or in this case woman, the first birth control clinic in the country. That's America for you, J.J. said.

I put my key in the lock, pushed open the door, and stepped inside. Even empty of people, the waiting area was crowded. A desk, filing cabinets, and chairs and benches cluttered the small space. Behind cheerful chintz curtains, also sewn by Fania, two private alcoves led to a tiny storeroom stacked with boxes of Mizpah pessaries. Ethel and I would not examine the women, though in The Hague under the tutelage of Dr. Rutgers I'd learned both to examine patients and to fit pessaries. But we were nurses, not doctors, and I was calculating the risk. Breaking the law to change it was one thing; antagonizing the medical profession, or rather antagonizing the medical profession even more than I already had, was another. That was why we would limit ourselves to explaining how pessaries worked and, if a woman didn't have the money to buy one at a pharmacy, slipping a box from the back room into a baby carriage or the tomatoes for the pasta sauce or the greens for the chicken soup.

I looked at my watch. It was a little after seven. I didn't have a chance to glance at it again until nine o'clock. By then the waiting room was full and a line snaked down the block. Women stood patiently, rocking baby carriages, quieting restive children who darted among them, casting uneasy glances at passersby. Surely this could not be kosher, they murmured to one another.

In the waiting room, Fania was taking down information on index cards and collecting ten-cent registration fees in English, Yiddish, Polish, and a few words of Italian supplemented with gestures. Elizabeth moved among the waiting women, comforting children, reassuring mothers, keeping track of who was next. Behind the curtains, Ethel and I explained and demonstrated with pictures and models. Occasionally, we called in Fania to translate, and Elizabeth filled in behind the desk. We were each doing our job, like Mr. Ford's new assembly line, and the product we were manufacturing was hope.

I took an index card from Fania, called the name on it, and held aside the curtain to the alcove. A woman left a small boy in the care of a slightly larger girl, who could not have been older than four. As she entered the alcove, she ducked her head with a birdlike motion, then glanced up at me briefly. Fear roosted in her eyes.

I asked if she spoke English. She nodded. I wouldn't need Fania. I gestured her to one of the two chairs, took the other, and began to explain about the Mizpah pessary.

"It was designed for prolapsed uteruses."

Her face was blank as a peeled potato.

Taking the open book from the table, I showed her a diagram of a Mizpah pessary supporting a prolapsed uterus. She stared at it and shook her head. I wasn't sure whether the gesture indicated distaste or lack of understanding.

"It also works to prevent babies," I went on slowly, enunciating every word. I picked up the model and a pessary and demonstrated how to insert it. "If you use it every time with your husband, it will keep you . . . safe. You won't get pregnant."

She looked from the model to me, her eyes wide with wonder. "No more babies?"

"Not if you use it every time. It has to be every time. No matter how tired you are. No matter how much of a hurry he's in."

Her pursed mouth unzipped into a smile as wide as the open spaces that were only rumors in the teeming neighborhood where she lived.

It went on that way all day, and the next, and the one after that. Word of the clinic spread through the infested tenements of Brownsville and beyond like an epidemic. Occasionally a well-heeled woman, or perhaps two finding courage in numbers, showed up. In those days, social workers spoke of the deserving poor. I said we would treat even the undeserving rich.

Ethel was against the idea. "Let them go to their private doctors."

"Let them eat cake," I answered. "Better yet, let them have three or four or six more children. By then, they'll be the deserving poor, and we can treat them."

But the real question was when we would be raided. We all knew it was only a matter of time. That was the point. Only by getting myself arrested could I make my case in court.

THE WOMAN WORE a startled expression, as if she didn't know how she'd ended up in a ramshackle clinic in a shabby corner of Brooklyn. Ethel took one look at her coat, which clearly had not come off a pushcart, and her fashionable hat stuck with a long red feather, and whispered to me, "Finally, the police."

"She's too frightened," I whispered back.

"Wouldn't you be if you were a police decoy in enemy territory?"

I ushered the woman into the alcove, directed her to a seat, and took the other chair. We sat knee to knee in the cramped windowless space. She had taken off her gloves and wore, next to her wedding band, a small diamond engagement ring on her soft well-cared-for hands. She was not a policewoman. I was sure of it.

I looked down at the index card Fania had handed me. Mrs. Horace McAllister was twenty-three years old and had no children. Surely a policewoman would pretend to have at least five or six.

I asked the basic questions about her health, then moved on to her marriage. We always spoke of marriage, as if sex could not take place outside of it.

"What should I do if someone comes in who isn't married?" Fania had asked when we'd opened.

"Send for a minister," I'd answered, because I hadn't made up my mind what to do. It would be unconscionable to turn away unmarried women. It would be asking for trouble, more trouble, to treat them. I had talked it over with J.J. I wanted a test case that would persuade people, not alienate them.

Mrs. McAllister kept her eyes on her lap as she squeezed out the answers to my questions. Finally I took out the Mizpah pessary. Her eyes widened in alarm. This was no policewoman.

"That's not why I'm here."

"You didn't come for contraceptive information?"

She shook her head.

"You know what contraception is, don't you?"

"A sin against nature."

"Who told you that?"

"I read it. Mother gave me a book. It's by a physician. Dr. Henry Guernsey. He says preventions to conception are one of the greatest crimes of the present age."

"I'm familiar with Dr. Guernsey's book, and if he knew anything about women's health, and children's, he wouldn't make such a reckless statement."

"But isn't it a sin not to let nature take its course?"

"Is it a sin to treat an infection? Or remove an appendix that's about to burst?" I looked down at her long fingers twisted tight as a knot in her lap. "Or trim your nails? All of those are preventions to nature taking its course."

She raised her eyes. "I never thought of it that way."

"Now you can."

"But I want babies."

"Are you having trouble conceiving?" I thought of all the self-proclaimed nice girls I'd known in my life. "You have had sexual relations with your husband, haven't you?"

She dropped her eyes again and nodded.

"Did your mother or a doctor or anyone give you any instruction about the sexual side of marriage?"

"Mother said I was never to dress or undress in front of my husband. If there was no dressing room or closet, I was to turn out the light."

"That's Victorian prudery, not sexual information."

"No, she said it was a well-known fact. It would be too . . . stimulating."

"For your husband?"

"Of course."

"What about for you?"

She let out a small soft moan of despair that I couldn't make sense of.

"Did she tell you anything else?"

"She gave me Dr. Guernsey's book."

"Which does not have a single word about the sexual act. Only a lot of pieties about Christian love, and men having to tame their sexual drive, while women have no drive at all, unless they're fallen women. What I don't understand is if we don't like sex, why are we always trying to ruin men by luring them into it?"

A tear slid down her face and made a dark spot on her navy serge skirt.

"Does the act of love trouble you?"

"Not the actual act," she mumbled to her lap.

"Is there some other aspect of lovemaking that bothers you?"

She barely nodded.

I thought of Havelock. "Nothing that gives two people pleasure is wrong."

She didn't answer.

"Does your husband give you pleasure?"

"That's the problem."

"That he gives you pleasure?" Now I was completely lost.

"That I forget myself when he does. I move around. My husband says I . . . thrash . . . and . . ." Her voice trailed off again.

"Yes?"

"I make noises. I can't help myself. I try not to, but I can't help myself."

"Your response is perfectly natural."

"That's not what he says. He says he never heard of a nice girl behaving like that."

"He's wrong."

She shook her head. "Dr. Guernsey says the same thing. You just admitted it. You said only fallen women like that part of marriage. Nice girls just put up with it because it's their duty. And they want babies."

"I wasn't serious about what you call fallen women. I was trying to show you how illogical Dr. Guernsey and his ilk are. Women do enjoy the sexual act. They don't just put up with it as a wifely duty."

"But I don't want to enjoy it. Not if it makes my husband angry."

"Angry?"

"He says he always thought I was a nice girl. That's why he married me. To ennoble him. To keep him from giving in to his bestial nature. But now he finds out I'm a thousand times worse than he is."

"What you are is a fortunate woman. You should rejoice in your responses. So should he."

"He can't."

"You mean he won't because of his bourgeois prejudices." I hadn't meant to say that. This was a medical clinic, not a socialist rally.

"I mean he can't." She dropped her eyes again. "He finds me so disgusting that . . . that he can't go on."

"You mean he loses his erection?"

She nodded.

"There's a book I could recommend for him. Havelock Ellis—"

"Oh, no! He'd be furious if he knew I told anyone."

"Then what do you want me to do?"

"Give me something to make me stop liking it."

In all the years I had been nursing, I'd never wanted to shake a patient.

"Mrs. McAllister, there is nothing I can give you. And if there were, I wouldn't."

"He'll leave me." Now she was crying openly.

I took a pen and a piece of paper, wrote Havelock's name and the titles of several of his books on it, and handed it to her. That evening when we were closing, I found the list on the waiting room floor.

THE WOMAN WAS wearing one of those fox neckpieces with the mouth of one dead animal chewing on the tail of another.

"Tell her to go to a private doctor," Ethel muttered as she and I passed on our way to and from the alcoves.

The card Fania handed me said Mrs. Alfred Whitehurst was twenty-nine, had been married for five years, and had four children.

"Maybe this is terrible, Mrs. Sanger, but I don't want any more. I thought you'd be able to understand, only having two yourself."

I turned from the model of the reproductive organs and stared at her.

"I saw a photo of you and your two boys in the newspaper," she explained.

I let it go. Neither the photograph nor the message it sent was her fault.

We were closing the clinic that night when Fania showed me a two-dollar bill.

"Remember Mrs. Whitehurst?" she asked.

"The one in the dead foxes?" Ethel said.

Fania nodded. "It's from her. I told her registration cost ten cents and the pamphlet she bought was another twenty-five, but when I started to hand over her change, she said she wanted to make a contribution to Mrs. Sanger's clinic."

Fania lifted the lid of the metal cashbox, but I took the bill from her before she could put it in, then picked up an index card from her desk, wrote on it, and carried it and the bill to the bulletin board. Ethel, Fania, and Elizabeth stood reading over my shoulder as I pinned up the money and the card.

"Received from Mrs. Arthur Whitehurst of the New York Police Department."

ELIZABETH WASN'T AT the clinic that morning, but Ethel, Fania, and I had been at work for several hours when they arrived. I'd expected to be arrested, but I hadn't anticipated a raid by the vice squad. I was just emerging from the alcove behind a patient when I saw Mrs. Whitehurst coming through the door. She was in plainclothes, but she wasn't wearing the fur piece. The three men who pushed their way in after her weren't in uniform either, but I had been roughed up on enough picket lines to know they were police. Their faces were hard as granite, their eyes dead from all they'd seen.

One of them leaned over a woman sitting with a baby in her lap and demanded her name. Another pulled a woman out of a chair and pushed her up against the wall. The police were shouting, and women were screaming, and children and babies were crying. I tried to pry the man off the woman he was holding against the wall. He pushed me away with one hand while he went on holding her with the other.

I whirled around to face Mrs. Whitehurst. "Tell your men to behave themselves. This is a clinic, not a bordello."

"Just as bad," Mrs. Whitehurst shouted back. "You're under arrest, Mrs. Sanger."

Behind me, I saw one of the plainclothesmen yank open a

drawer of a filing cabinet and begin pulling out the folders and dumping them into a cardboard box. Fania tugged at his shoulder. He threw her off. She went sprawling. As he turned back to the files, he noticed one of the wooden models of the female reproductive organs. He picked it up in his big hands and stood turning it one way and another. Ethel tried to grab it out of his hands. He lifted it above his head to keep it out of her reach, like an adult tormenting a child.

Mrs. Whitehurst grabbed my arm and began pulling me toward the door. "Just come quietly, Mrs. Sanger."

I shook her off. "Keep your hands off me. I'll go of my own volition."

"Volition. Pretty fancy talk for a criminal."

Outside the clinic, a mob of curiosity seekers mingled with the line of waiting women. I recognized a reporter from the *Brooklyn Eagle*.

"Did you bring a photographer?" I shouted, as Mrs. Whitehurst tried to push me toward the paddy wagon.

"He's on the way," the reporter shouted back.

Another policeman was shoving Ethel into the wagon. I came up behind him and began pulling him away from her.

"We'll go," I shouted above the noise, "but on our own. We'll walk to the stationhouse," I shouted in the direction of the reporter from the *Eagle*.

"This ain't no Fourth of July parade, sister," the policeman said.

"Let her walk." Mrs. Whitehurst laughed. "She'll be cooped up soon enough."

I reached up to pull Fania down from the wagon, then linked one arm through hers and the other through Ethel's. We started down Pitkin Avenue.

The crowd began to fall into line behind us.

"Shame!" a woman shouted at the police.

"Shonda!" others took up the cry.

"Vergogna!"

Suddenly a woman came darting through the mob. Beneath the battered hat she held to her head as she ran, her hair flew wild.

"Mrs. Sanger," she cried as she panted after me. "Mrs. Sanger. Stop. Please stop. I need help."

I didn't stop. The photographer from the *Brooklyn Eagle* had arrived. A picture of Margaret Sanger, the birth control advocate, being dragged down the street by the police couldn't hold a candle to a photograph of Margaret Sanger being pursued by a distraught woman with outstretched arms, wild eyes, and a mouth open in a wail of desperation.

Nineteen

ETHEL WENT ON trial first. When she was found guilty and sentenced to thirty days on Blackwell's Island, she announced that she would go on a hunger strike.

I tried to dissuade her. So did Kitty Marion, the British actress-turned-suffragist who sold copies of my new magazine, *Birth Control Review*, in front of Macy's, in the Grand Central Station, out at Coney Island, and other places where she was heckled and roughed up. Kitty had been imprisoned in England for suffragist demonstrations, gone on hunger strikes, and been force-fed repeatedly. She said the procedure was agony and her body had never entirely recovered. But Ethel refused to listen. A hunger strike, she said, would call attention to the cause.

I agreed that it would and never added that it would also call attention to her. She had been our mother's favorite, but our mother was gone, and now it couldn't be easy for her having a famous older sister.

ETHEL BYRNE

Maybe I did want to upstage you, Marg. No one ever said sisterly love was uncomplicated. Mary was our rock, Nan our compass, but you and I were two sides of the same coin, inescapably bound, hellishly competitive. We were so close that a few years later you managed to forget which of us went on the hunger strike and was force-fed.

At first I thought your letter was a joke. I'd heard about the plan to make a movie of your life. According to Hedda Hopper—I never thought I'd be reading Hollywood gossip columns to find out what was going on in my glamorous sister's life, but we were seeing less of each other by then—it was to be called *First Lady of the Century* and star Ida Lupino. At least they'd chosen an intelligent feminist actress and director for the part.

The idea of the movie didn't surprise me, but your asking me to sign away part of my life did. I understood that for dramatic effect you should be the one to go on a hunger strike. Never mind the daily headlines in all the papers reporting my condition. Never mind your public tribute to the historic importance of my sacrifice. As you pointed out, the public's memory is short.

I was sorry the movie never came off. It would have been a nice tribute to you. And they could have hired me as what I believe is called a technical adviser, because if there's one area where I have expertise, it's the misery of a hunger strike and the pain and helpless horror of being force-fed. You have a vivid imagination, Marg, but even you aren't up to that.

The matron had it in for me from the moment I arrived.

She was always coming by my cell with taunts and temptations.

"If you hadn't been foolish, you wouldn't be here," she said.

"Why don't you have a little soup. I won't tell anyone," she whispered.

"At least take some water." She held a glass out to me. The liquid glittered like crystal in the light from the bare bulb. I turned away from the sight.

But she wouldn't give up. At night, when she went up and down the cellblock calling out offers of a last glass of water, she lingered in front of my cell.

"Just a glass, Mrs. Byrne. Just a swallow."

Through the high narrow window of my cubicle, I heard the East River rushing by and imagined the sensation of cool water running down my sandpaper throat.

But she wasn't heartless. She sneaked me a newspaper. Or perhaps she was heartless. An article on the front page said that the next day I would be force-fed. According to the piece, I had gone without food or water for one hundred and three hours. I had to take the police commissioner's word for it. I'd lost count. The rest of the article described what was in store for me. I've often wondered why those men, who prided themselves on their noses for news, wouldn't waste a paragraph on women dying in childbirth or the attempts to avoid it but couldn't get enough of one woman trying to starve herself. Maybe the idea that women could take control of their own bodies scared them.

"It's a simple painless process," the commissioner told the reporters. "We roll the inmate in a sheet to keep her from struggling, run a tube down her throat, and put in a mixture of milk, eggs, and brandy. If we can't get the tube down her throat, if she tries to bite it or resists in any way, we insert two smaller tubes into her nostrils."

Until then, I hadn't thought of biting.

The next morning I lay on my cot drifting in and out of consciousness. I'd been doing that a lot lately. Sometimes when I floated off, I dreamed of food. Gradually I noticed the murmur of the matron's voice mingling with a man's, or men's—how many did they need?—coming down the corridor toward me. A key scraped in a lock. I tried to sit up, but before I could, hands were lifting me.

"Be gentle with her, boys," the matron said, but she laughed as she said it.

They dropped me into a wheelchair, pushed me through a steel door, and started down a long corridor. Narrow openings high up in the wall on one side let in a trickle of thin winter light. The only view was of a frozen white sky. I could still hear the river. The sound made my mouth pucker.

We reached another metal door at the end of the hall. One guard opened it, and the other wheeled me into a small room. Four men in white coats stood around an examining table. A lot of manpower was being expended to feed one diminutive woman. The men were strangers to me, but I recognized the expressions on the faces of two of them. They wore the smug superiority of the doctors I was supposed to bow and scrape and curtsey to at the hospital. The other two—orderlies, I guessed—looked more nervous.

A smaller table stood beside the large examining one. Among various instruments and vials and containers, a rubber tube lay coiled. It was an ordinary piece of equipment. I had used it on patients myself. But now, in this bare chilly room, it looked lethal as a poisonous snake.

The two orderlies lifted me onto the table as easily as if they were picking up a child. They started arranging my arms at my side. I flailed. The guard who'd wheeled me in pinned me to the table while one of the orderlies held my legs and the other began wrapping a sheet around me. I tried to thrash, but I was no match for six burly arms. They went on winding the sheet. All I could think of was the shroud Mary and Nan had wrapped around Mother. When they finished, they stepped back with a look of pride at a job properly done. They had rendered me limbless, ineffectual, inhuman.

One of the doctors stepped forward and looked me over. He tugged the sheet to make sure it was tight enough. "Well done, lads," he said.

He nodded to the two orderlies, and they moved in again. One held my feet; the other leaned over me to grip my shoulders. Again I tried to struggle, but it was hopeless. Panic was rising in me like a tide.

I sensed the second doctor standing behind my head. He slid a cap over my hair, then splayed his fingers on either side of my jaw and pried it open. I tried to twist my head to bite him, but his hands were like a vise on my face.

The other doctor stepped forward, pulled the overhead light down, and began to examine my throat. I felt him prodding and palpating.

He disappeared from my view, then returned holding an atomizer over me and began to pump it. I knew from Kitty that it was a mixture of cocaine and disinfectant. It went up my nose and down my throat like a swarm of stinging bees.

He disappeared from my line of vision again. This time his hands returned holding the rubber tubing. I tried to thrash. The orderlies tightened their grip. I tried to twist my head to bite the doctor again. He slapped my face with his free hand. "It will be easier if you cooperate." His voice was strangely kind after that slap.

He began working the tubing down my throat. It felt sharp as a razor cutting its way through my body. The pain began to radiate, through my nose, out to my ears, across my chest, down my spine. It came in waves and went on and on and on. My body began to spasm. I prayed I'd lose consciousness. The light overhead grew hazy. The doctor's face looming above me was fuzzy. But I could still feel the pain.

I couldn't be sure, because the world had become a blur, but I thought the doctor's hands were above me again, a funnel in one, a pitcher in the other. The pair of hands holding my jaw clamped tighter. I sensed movement. They were inserting the funnel into the rubber tubing. The pitcher passed over my face again. A stream of ice rushed through my body. The liquid was going in. I was shivering and sweating and convulsing. The ice kept running in and the hot pain kept radiating out. It went on for what felt like eternity. I saw the blur of white that I thought was the pitcher disappear from above my face and felt the tube being pulled out. This must be what evisceration was like.

Then suddenly it was over. The doctor let go of my jaw. The two orderlies stepped back. My vision began to clear. The four men turned away from me, but before they did, I caught the looks on their faces. Again, they wore the satisfied expressions of a job well done. No, more than that. They wore a look of postcoital pride.

That, Marg, was the force-feeding I never endured and you did.

. . .

THEY FORCE-FED ETHEL twice more that first day, once in the afternoon and again in the evening. They wouldn't let me see her, but the commissioner continued to release medical bulletins. Her blood pressure, heart, and respiration were all normal, he said. Her pulse rate was only slightly accelerated. She had not regurgitated.

"Force-feeding is not so terrible," he added with a politician's public-courting grin. "We do it to drunks and dope fiends all the time."

The analogy infuriated me. The statements about her health didn't fool me. I knew he was lying even before J.J. arranged for a woman who worked in the jail and was grateful to him for taking her son under his wing to smuggle out reports.

The force-feeding continued three times a day. Ethel grew steadily worse. Her vision was blurred. Her heartbeat was irregular. She lapsed in and out of consciousness.

While she was fading, a battle was raging in newspapers and other public forums. The police commissioner, the mayor, and the men who ran the city continued to issue their lies about her condition. The Committee of One Hundred, dozens of women, J.J., and I fired off statements to the press and demands to officials.

When they wouldn't let J.J. in to see her, though she was his client, he threatened to get her out of prison on a writ of habeas corpus.

"Just try," the commissioner said.

The Committee of One Hundred sent a letter to the mayor. "We maintain that it is no more indecent to discuss sexual anatomy, physiology, and hygiene in a scientific spirit than it is to discuss the functions of the stomach, the heart, and the liver."

When that had no effect, they turned their guns on the governor and demanded he commute Ethel's sentence.

The protests came to a boil at a mass meeting at Carnegie Hall.

A throng of three thousand, most but not all of them women, crowded into the red plush interior, grandmothers fighting for their daughters and granddaughters, high school students battling for their future, poor women who paid twenty-five cents to sit in the balcony, club women who ponied up seventy-five cents for a seat in the orchestra, and elegantly dressed society matrons who subscribed to whole boxes. Ushers moved through the audience selling the *Birth Control Review* for fifteen cents a copy.

Behind me on the stage, I had placed two dozen Brownsville mothers. "These are the women we're fighting for," I told the newspaper photographers before the program started, and their flashbulbs went off like Fourth of July fireworks.

Dr. Mary Hunt, a radical who wasn't afraid of the medical profession's censure, stepped to the podium and launched into an attack on Fifth Avenue doctors who practiced birth control in their own families, and helped their rich patients to do the same, but opposed the dissemination of the information among the women who could least afford another mouth to feed.

She turned and bowed to the Brownville mothers on the stage behind her, and the crowd roared its approval. When she introduced me as the woman who was building a bridge over which womankind could pass to freedom, the cheering grew louder. I stepped forward into the applause and raised my hands for silence.

"I come to you tonight not from the stake at Salem, where women were burned for blasphemy, but from its modern-day equivalent, Blackwell's Island, where women are tortured for what men in power call obscenity. Where my sister Ethel Byrne is risking her life to protest an unjust law."

Again the crowd clapped and shouted its support.

"Theodore Roosevelt goes about the country telling people to have large families, and he is cheered."

Now there were boos.

"But my sister Ethel Byrne and I try to give women information about their own bodies, and we are arrested and molested."

There were cheers for me, and boos for the police, and the word "shame" whirled through the audience like a tornado.

"We must repeal an unjust law."

I hadn't thought the cheering could grow any louder, but it did.

"No woman can call herself free until she can choose when and how often she will become a mother."

The crowd was on its feet now, chanting my name. I held up my hands again and waited for the applause to die.

"Ethel Byrne," I said. "My sister Ethel Byrne is the one you should be cheering."

And they did.

DESPITE THE FORCE-FEEDING, Ethel's condition continued to deteriorate. I couldn't let her go on with the strike, though I knew she wouldn't thank me for stopping her, or for the way I went about it. She'd told me more than once what she thought of my new friends. She couldn't understand that the movement was becoming increasingly respectable. These days it required more will than guts, more accommodating of the people who could make things happen and less thumbing of noses at their prerogatives. I was moving on. She couldn't forgive me for that. And, I admit it, I resented her assumption of moral superiority. The mutual resentment was one more snarl in our tangled connection.

Ethel disliked most of the society women I was turning to for support, but she'd taken a particular antipathy to Juliet Rublee and Gertrude Pinchot, perhaps because they had taken a special shine to me.

Juliet was a restless Chicago heiress. Gertrude was a well-connected suffragist and philanthropist. Both women knew Governor Whitman. Nine days after Ethel went on her hunger strike, six after they began force-feeding her, Juliet, Gertrude, J.J., and I took the train to Albany. At first, I hadn't wanted J.J. to come along. I was sure the easiness between us, the pull between us, would give away our affair.

"You think you're the only one who can fool people, Peg?"

I found the statement vaguely unsettling, though I wasn't sure whether the implication was that I wasn't fooling him or that he was fooling me.

An aide ushered us into a large office hung with portraits of great men in New York State history. The governor rose from behind his big desk, flanked on one side by the state flag, on the other by that of the United States.

"How nice to see you, Mrs. Rublee," he said.

"How are you, Mrs. Pinchot?" he asked.

I was back in Mrs. Graves's class, a shamed outcast.

The governor held out his hand to me. "It's a pleasure to meet you, Mrs. Sanger."

"I appreciate your seeing us, Governor." Where had I picked up that accent? My consonants were clipped, my vowels plump as oysters.

J.J. and the governor shook hands; then Whitman gestured us to chairs in front of his desk and sat behind it.

"In view of Mrs. Byrne's health," he began, "I am prepared to pardon her. If she will agree to abide in the future by the current laws."

It was the same paltry peace offering. Agree to live by an unjust law we were trying to overturn and the men in power would pat us on the head and send us off like the good little girls we were, or should be.

"I cannot promise you that, Governor." My accent, I was relieved to hear, was returning to normal.

The governor's smooth mask of cordiality developed a hairline crack. "I thought the purpose of the meeting was to obtain a pardon for Mrs. Byrne."

"The law you want my sister to obey, Governor, is the unjust law she is starving herself to overturn. I cannot agree to your terms without her consent."

"Margaret—" Juliet began.

"Think of your sister's health," Gertrude said.

J.J. sat watching me. He had been through this before. He knew argument was futile.

"I'm thinking of her moral health," I answered.

"Surely you can understand my position, Mrs. Sanger," the governor said. "Mrs. Byrne was convicted of knowingly and willfully breaking the law. I cannot pardon a woman who intends to go on knowingly and willfully breaking the law."

"I have a suggestion." It was the first time J.J. had spoken, and we all turned to him. That was one of the things I loved about J.J. Bill had bombast. Hugh had whimsy. Havelock had depth. But J.J. had gravitas. When he spoke, people listened. "The commissioner won't permit Mrs. Byrne visitors. If you can arrange a pass for Mrs. Sanger to see her sister, perhaps she will be able to persuade Mrs. Byrne to agree to your terms."

The governor looked as if he were the one who had been pardoned.

A NURSE LED me down the hall of the workhouse infirmary. They'd moved Ethel from her cell to a room in the medical wing. The nurse came to a closed door, opened it, and stood aside for me to enter. I stepped into the room, then stopped. This wraith in a hospital gown could not be my sister. Her skin was yellow as a tallow candle, and covered with dark blotches. When she turned her face at the sound of my steps, her eyes rolled in their sockets like a blind woman's. Patches of her once lovely auburn hair lay on the pillow. Her scalp showed through the bald spots.

I crossed the room, sat on the side of the bed, and took her in my arms. It was like holding a rag doll.

"Ethel," I said.

She didn't respond.

"Ethel, can you hear me?"

Her filmy eyes rolled in their sockets again.

"It's Margaret."

A sob racked her limp body.

I asked the nurse who was still standing in the doorway to go downstairs and tell Mrs. Pinchot to telephone the governor. Ethel was in no condition to give her consent, but I was. Perhaps she'd hate me for it, but holding that limp lifeless body in my arms, I felt a rush of love, and responsibility. I couldn't risk another Peggy.

The governor didn't waste any time. In less than half an hour, two orderlies came into the cell, lifted Ethel off the bed, and began half carrying, half dragging her down the hall. Her head lolled from side to side. Her legs dragged behind her, the tops of her feet scraping the floor.

"Stop!" I shouted. "Can't you see she needs a stretcher?"

"Commissioner's orders, m'am. He says the reporters got to see the prisoner walking out on her own two feet."

I ran ahead of them and stopped in the corridor blocking their way.

"Get her a stretcher."

The orderlies stood for a moment, looking around the corridor for a higher authority.

"Do I have to call the governor again?" I took Ethel in my arms and pushed one of them away. "Get a stretcher!"

The other orderly and I stood with Ethel between us as the man went down the hall and came back with a stretcher. By now Gertrude had arrived.

The orderlies put the stretcher on the floor, the three of us arranged Ethel's inert body on in, and the men picked it up.

"Wait." I turned to Gertrude and took the lapel of her sable coat between my thumb and forefinger. "Do you mind?"

"Not at all." Gertrude slipped off the coat and held it out to me.

I took it, placed it over Ethel, and tucked it in around her. "All right," I said to the orderlies.

They carried the stretcher with my sister's wasted body out to the crush of reporters who had come across the East River to see the little woman who had almost starved herself to death for the right to contraception.

"No single act of self-sacrifice in the history of the birth control movement has done more to awaken the conscience of the public or arouse the courage of women," I told the reporters, as Gertrude and her chauffeur maneuvered my sable-swathed sister into the waiting limousine.

"Some shroud," Ethel said when I got into the auto. She managed a rictus of a smile, then passed out again.

Twenty

T HE COURTROOM WAS bedlam. Spectators fought for seats. Reporters jockeyed for position. Thirty women, whom the district attorney had subpoenaed because their names had appeared in the clinic records that the police had confiscated in the raid, crowded onto the benches with children and bags of diapers and newspaper-wrapped food. I spotted several I remembered from their visits to 46 Amboy Street. Behind them, members of the Committee of One Hundred sat in their expensive furs and handsome hats, but their lavender soap was no match for the smell of kosher pickles, salami, and garlic.

As I made my way down the aisle, carrying a bouquet of crimson American Beauty roses the committee had sent, the reporters and photographers surged toward me, snapping pictures and firing questions.

"Look this way, Mrs. Sanger."

"Do you think you can get a fair trial, Mrs. Sanger?"

"If you're convicted, will you go on a hunger strike like your sister, Mrs. Sanger?"

I kept smiling and pushing my way through the crowd, until a reporter shouted another question.

"Are you worried that the subpoenaed women will testify against you, Mrs. Sanger?"

"I'm worried *for* the women who were subpoenaed," I said. "Most of them have no place to leave their children, as you can see. They can scarcely afford the carfare to get here. Yet the district attorney threatened them with fines of two hundred and fifty dollars each if they failed to show up to testify to what I readily admit. I disseminated contraceptive information. In my opinion, any law that makes it wrong to help the poor is unconstitutional. And the burden the district attorney has placed on these women is unconscionable."

A wave of applause ran through the courtroom. Flashbulbs exploded. A dozen pairs of nicotine-stained fingers scribbled on notepads. Then the cry of "All rise" rang through the courtroom, and the three judges entered.

They took their places on the high massive bench without a glance at me or any of the other women in the room. Perhaps no women were real to them except their wives and daughters, and possibly not even them. Their faces were closed and impassive. They might have been thinking about the case before them, or court politics, or what they were going to have for lunch.

The presiding justice, John Freschi, was a Catholic, as was Judge George O'Keefe. J.J. said our only hope was the third judge, Moses Herrman, an elderly Jew. As I sat watching them settle in, I knew J.J. had picked the wrong horse. Judge Herrman's hair and face were gray, his expression stern, his eyes small and sharp. In his black robe, he looked like a cartoon image of the Grim Reaper. All he needed was a scythe.

The district attorney called Mrs. Arthur Whitehurst to the stand. She was wearing the fox neckpiece again. As she told the court about her visit to the clinic, she stroked the skins.

If the court wanted a definition of obscene, she was giving it to them.

The district attorney asked Mrs. Whitehurst to tell the court what she had found on her first visit to the Brownsville Clinic. She described the line of women that went halfway down the block, the crowded waiting room, the children in tow, Fania behind the desk.

"She was registering the women. During the forty-five minutes I was there, she registered twenty women and charged each of them ten cents."

"So this clinic was a moneymaking enterprise?"

J.J. was on his feet. "Objection!"

"Sustained," Judge Freschi said.

"How were these women registered?"

"Name, address, age, number of children."

"Were the women asked if they were married or unmarried?"

"They were." Mrs. Whitehurst hesitated, the better to deliver her punch line. "But they were all registered whether they said married or single."

Out of the corner of my eye, I saw the reporters scribbling rapidly. This was the juicy part.

"Mrs. Whitehurst, did you have any financial transactions while you were in the clinic?"

"I paid a registration fee and bought a booklet."

"You paid for the booklet?"

"Twenty-five cents."

"Was this booklet written by the defendant, Mrs. Margaret Sanger?"

"It had her name on it."

"What was in this booklet?"

"Contraceptive information."

"You mean information to prevent the birth of children."

"Yes."

"Mrs. Whitehurst, from your experience on the police force, how would you characterize the Brownsville neighborhood?"

"The people there are very poor."

"Do they belong to a certain race?"

I could not imagine what the district attorney was driving at. I looked at J.J., but his attention was riveted on the DA.

"Most of them are Jewish. There are some Italians and other foreigners."

"But most of them are Jewish?"

"Yes."

"Would you agree then that by selling this contraceptive information to Jews, Mrs. Sanger's intention was to do away with the Jewish race?"

J.J. was on his feet even faster this time. "Objection!"

"Sustained," said Judge Freschi.

The district attorney did not try to pursue the point, and I thought that was the end of it. It embarrasses me now to think how naïve I was.

The district attorney called Mrs. Pincus Berger to the stand. A plump woman in a shawl handed her baby to her neighbor, edged her way out of the row of mothers, and made her way to the witness stand. Her back was straight as a Prussian soldier's, her chin high.

The clerk swore her in. She settled herself in the chair and arranged her shawl around her shoulders.

"Can you tell me, Mrs. Berger, why you went to 46 Amboy Street?"

She looked at him as if he were a slow child.

"To have her stop the babies."

"Who?"

She pointed at me. "Mrs. Sanger."

"And did she give you the information you wanted?"

She nodded and smiled at me. "Yes. Good information."

The district attorney nodded and returned to his seat.

J.J. stood and made his way to the witness box.

"How many children do you have, Mrs. Berger?"

"Eight."

"How old is the eldest?"

"Twelve."

"Did you lose any in birth or miscarriages?"

"Two died, three miscarriages."

"Is your husband employed?"

"A presser in a sweatshop."

"How much does he make a week?"

"Sixteen dollars a week."

"Do any of your children work?"

"Sure they work. Good children I got. They do piecework. Just like me."

It went on that way for some time. One after another, the women handed over their babies, made their way to the witness stand, and told the district attorney that they had gone to the clinic at 46 Amboy Street to get information to stop the babies, and that I gave it to them. More than one of them glanced over at me with a smile of gratitude.

When the district attorney finished with each woman, J.J. took up the questioning. One after another, they cataloged the misery of their lives. Miscarriages, stillbirths, and infant deaths; tuberculosis, undiagnosed illnesses, and female complaints. Husbands who earned fifteen dollars a week, husbands who could not find work, and husbands who never looked for work.

The district attorney called Mrs. Guido Giuseppe to the stand. She handed over two babies and made her way out to the aisle. She was so thin her bones seemed to protrude through her shirtwaist. Her skin had the grayish cast of a threadbare sheet that's been washed too often, without bleach. When she reached the witness stand, she held on to the railing for a moment to steady herself.

The district attorney asked his questions. She answered in a voice so soft it was barely audible. Then J.J. stepped up to the stand.

"How many children do you have, Mrs. Giuseppe?"

"Twelve."

"Could you speak up please, Mrs. Giuseppe?" Judge Freschi asked in a voice that was almost deferential.

"Twelve," she repeated.

"And how many did you lose?" J.J. asked.

"Three from miscarriage. All the time, I was so sick the doctor say I die. One baby die."

"At birth?"

"Two years."

"Does your husband work?"

"When he can find it."

"What is the most he makes when he does find work?"

"Ten dollars a week."

Most of the spectators were concentrating on the witness, but I was watching Judge Freschi. He had his elbow on the bench, and his forehead was resting on his hand. His fingers shielded his eyes from view, but I could see his mouth. He was grinding his teeth. Suddenly he dropped his hand from his face and looked up.

"Enough!" he shouted. "You've made your point, Counselor. Court is adjourned until tomorrow morning at nine."

If there's one thing I love to see, it's a man's awakening.

·ᴈ · ᴋ·

I CONGRATULATED J.J. and thanked him, but I never mentioned a thought that had passed through my mind as I'd watched him questioning the women in court that morning. For the first time since he'd begun talking about marriage, I could envision it. Not the domestic aspect. That was the point. J.J. wouldn't want to lock me up in a dream house. He'd want me out in the world fighting injustice, just as he was. I'd battle for the cause in clinics and meetings, on the podium and the printed page, and he'd fight for me in court.

The romantic in me fell for the fairy tale. The rebel scented the sham.

That night I dreamed I was back at Wantley, in bed with Hugh. I spread my legs and arched my back and shuddered with pleasure, and when I opened my eyes, I was shocked to discover that I was making love to J.J.

THE JUDGES FOUND me guilty. Four days later, I was back in Special Sessions court for sentencing. This time Judge Freschi looked at me as I approached the bench. I wouldn't swear to the other two judges, but I knew he'd heard the stories the women had told.

"Mrs. Sanger," he began, "if you promise to obey the law faithfully in the future, this court will exercise extreme clemency."

I told him I would obey the law pending the decision of the appeal. Of course, we were going to appeal.

The judge frowned.

J.J. pointed out that if I disobeyed the law after the appeal, I would be subject to another arrest.

"Mr. Goldstein, what is the use of beating about the bush? We are not looking for blood, only a promise by Mrs. Sanger that she will obey the law." He turned to me. "Mrs. Sanger, if you will state publicly and openly without any qualifications whatsoever that you will be a law-abiding citizen, this court is prepared to exercise the highest degree of leniency."

"This is a test case, Your Honor. I can promise to refrain from my activities only pending an appeal."

The judge closed his eyes for a moment, as if he were praying for patience. "We will take your word if you will give it, Mrs. Sanger."

"I cannot respect the law as it exists today."

Behind me, murmurs of approval were beginning to build.

The judge rapped his gavel. "The court must have an answer, Mrs. Sanger. Yes or no?"

"Yes."

Behind my back, a collective gasp went through the spectators.

"Pending the appeal."

Applause rippled through the courtroom, and a few shouts of approval rang out. The judge gaveled them into silence.

"The judgment of the court is that you pay a fine of five thousand dollars or be confined to the workhouse for thirty days."

This time only a single voice was raised. "Shame!" It had become the cry of my supporters.

I CHOSE THE thirty days.

"Mrs. Byrne's experience has persuaded me," I told the reporters, "that I can do more good by serving a sentence than by paying a fine. Conditions on Blackwell's Island are unconscionable. I propose to expose them."

"What about a hunger strike?" a reporter shouted.

"Are you going on a hunger strike like your sister?" another yelled.

I was not going on a hunger strike. The doctor had warned that one would exacerbate my tuberculosis and most likely kill me. But my health was not the only argument against it. A little more than two years earlier, I'd fled the country because I'd known that as long as men were fighting and dying in trenches abroad, no one would care about one woman's battle for justice at home. Now the struggle was drawing closer. The Kaiser had declared unrestricted submarine warfare, and America had severed diplomatic relations with Germany. It was only a matter of time before we got into the fight, and once we did, editors wouldn't need hunger strikes to sell newspapers. But I did not tell the reporters that. It sounded too self-serving and calculated. It also sounded, after Ethel's heroism, cowardly. I told them I hadn't yet made up my mind.

THE WORKHOUSE ON Blackwell's Island refused to take me. Ethel had given the prison a black eye as well as a great deal of trouble. The warden wanted no more obstreperous Higgins sisters. I was sent to the Queens Women's Penitentiary. It wasn't a walk in the park, but it was better than the workhouse. I had a private cell. Sometimes I read aloud to the other inmates, most of whom, either prostitutes or drug addicts or both, were illiterate. I also taught them about sex and birth control. The matron was livid.

"They don't need no teaching about that. They already know more than is good for them."

The only real hardship was celibacy. The visits from J.J., who was working on the appeal, made it even harder. We sat across from each other in the dim light of a bored guard's observation. Sometimes, when the guard glanced away, I ran my foot up and down J.J.'s calf beneath the scarred wooden table. He pulled his leg away. Sometimes, I moved my hand on top of the table until it was resting against his. He withdrew his hand. "Be serious, Peg," he whispered. But when I held his glance with mine, he couldn't help himself.

The only brutality I was subjected to came as I was about to be released. Actually, it was more indignity than brutality, and I gave as good as I got.

Perhaps because I had come by way of Blackwell's Island, the Queens officials had neglected to fingerprint me when I arrived. Now that I was being released, the warden wanted to take my prints. I refused.

"Regulations," he explained.

"Regulations for common criminals. I'm a political prisoner."

"We can't release you until we got your prints on file."

"Then you'll have to hold me."

He called in two guards, told them to take my fingerprints, and left the room. I should have suspected what was coming, but I was too busy enjoying the warden's flight. One of the guards had moved behind me. He threw a hammerlock around my shoulders and chest and frog-walked me to a table where an ink pad and paper sat ready. The other guard grabbed my right hand. I tried to pull away, but between them they must have had more than two hundred pounds on me. The guard holding my arm managed to get my thumb onto the ink pad.

"Now that's a good girl," he said, as he pressed my thumb

against the paper. I stopped struggling. He relaxed his grip. I smudged my thumb back and forth across the paper.

We went through the tussle again, and twice more after that. I had ink smudges all over me, but so did they. Finally the warden came back and said my attorney had protested the delay. He would release me without taking my fingerprints. He didn't look at me as he said it.

J.J. was waiting in the outer office. "Welcome back to freedom, Mrs. Sanger."

A month had passed since I'd been outside. The frigid air came as a shock. I blinked against the glare, though the day was overcast. A crowd of women standing in front of the jail came into focus. There must have been a couple of hundred of them, friends of the movement, women we'd treated at the clinic, society matrons from the Committee of One Hundred, and Ethel.

"They've been standing out here in the cold since early this morning," J.J. said.

He added something else, but I didn't hear him, because the women had started to sing.

Allons enfants de la patrie,
Le jour de gloire est arrivé

As I stood listening to them, fighting back the tears, I heard other voices behind me joining in. I turned my head and looked up. In the second-floor windows, the women who moments ago had been my fellow prisoners were gathered shoulder to shoulder, looking down at me, and humming along. They didn't know the words, they probably didn't even know they were French, but every one of them understood the sentiment.

Who could call this sacrifice?

Twenty-One

J.J. FILED THE appeal. The court upheld the verdict, as we'd expected. Section 1142 of the state's obscenity law prohibited laymen and -women from disseminating birth control information. But the judge's ruling went further. He wrote that physicians were permitted to prescribe contraception on medical grounds, and here was what J.J. called the kicker, the twin kickers. The judge defined medical grounds in broader terms than venereal disease. And he included women as well as men. Birth control clinics were legal as long as they were staffed by doctors.

That night in the small apartment on West Fourteenth Street, I sat alone in the living room as I had the night after I'd given birth to Sadie Sachs. Unlike Bill, J.J. didn't come into the parlor to try to persuade me to return to bed. He knew me better.

I sat wrapped in a blanket, my bare feet tucked under me, remembering that earlier night and thinking about how far I'd come and how far I had yet to go. And as I did, I felt Peggy's presence beside me.

. . .

THE APPEAL RULING was a victory, but I still had powerful enemies outside the movement and, almost as frustrating, misguided colleagues within it. Mary Ware Dennett was the most annoying. I won't dignify her by using a stronger word. She thought she could change unjust laws by lobbying legislators to rewrite them. She didn't understand that no politician would stand up for a cause that carried the faintest whiff of sex, especially sex for women. I knew the only way to change the law was to break it and have the court rule, as it had in my appeal. Mary also had a bias against physicians. I recognized their limitations and arrogance, but I would have joined forces with the devil if the devil could have got contraceptives into the hands of the women who needed them. I forgave Mary her naïveté, even her stubbornness, but I could not abide her pettiness.

The incident occurred at a dinner party at Juliet Rublee's. Juliet had a husband who was busy serving in President Wilson's cabinet in Washington, D.C., and did not have children. A botched surgery in her youth had taken care of her contraceptive problems. She also had boundless energy, a good deal of unspent passion, and a fortune. I had a movement that needed all three. It was a marriage made in heaven. It was, come to think of it, my most successful marriage.

Still, I hadn't wanted to go out that evening. My body ached, my head throbbed with fever, and outside my window a drenching rain turned the street to patent leather. But I couldn't let Juliet down. Every few weeks, she invited ten or a dozen of her well-heeled friends to dinner. When they were all gathered around the long dining table, silver glowing in the candlelight, wine shimmering in crystal goblets, men growing rosy with good food and drink, women turning well-coiffed heads from one dinner partner to the other as the courses changed, she steered the conversation to birth control and asked my opinion on some aspect of it. That was my cue to go into my song and dance. So I put on the silk evening dress that brought out the green in my eyes, bundled into my raincoat, and went out into the wet night.

Mary Dennett was there that night too. Mary came from a Boston Brahmin family and never let you forget it. Excuse me. I swore I was not going to sink to her level.

By the time the women stood to leave the men to their cigars and brandy—even a rebel like Juliet still separated the sexes for digestive purposes after dinner—Juliet could tell from the flush on my cheeks that I was burning up and suggested that while the women returned to the drawing room, I go into her dressing room and lie down on the chaise for a few minutes.

"We'll let Mary carry the flag," she said, and we smiled, because fund-raising was not Mary's strong suit. A woman who is brought up to believe talking about money is bad form is rarely any good begging for it.

At first I didn't know where the voices were coming from. Then I realized Juliet's dressing room communicated with another bathroom as well as her private one, and the door to the second had been left open a crack.

"Oh, Mary, you are wicked," a voice I didn't recognize said.

"I'm sorry, but it's true," Mary, whose voice I did know, replied. "I admit she's a charming vision in that green satin gown, and a genuine spellbinder, but oh, her English, and her facts that aren't facts, and her logic that isn't logic, and her amazing faculty for being the whole moomunt! The woman can't even pronounce something she claims to be the head of."

My cheeks were flaming, and not only from my fever. As I stood, slipped into my shoes, and smoothed my hair, I decided that the next day I'd sign up for elocution lessons. It was time to get the bottom of the hill out of my mouth for good. After all, I made my living as a public speaker.

MARY WARE DENNETT

I'm sorry if you didn't like the imitation, Margaret, but your accent really was dreadful, and you did have a habit of bending the facts to your own ends. That didn't stop me from suggesting that for the good of the movement we cooperate. We were fighting for the same cause. We'd even suffered similar heartbreak. I was divorced from my architect husband. I had lost a daughter in infancy. But you didn't want colleagues or friends; you needed followers and admirers. No, more than that, you needed lackeys and sycophants. And you had them in droves, though I will never understand the spell you cast. Men fell in love with you. Women, not only the poor women in the tenements whom you helped but those in the movement, were willing to lay down their lives for you, despite the fact that you were impossible to work with—demanding, unforgiving, credit-stealing. The last was the worst. To hear you tell it, Margaret Sanger created the birth control movement as single-handedly as the Lord created the universe. She just took a little longer.

. . .

LATER, WHEN I was recognized as the mother of the birth control movement, the fearless advocate who had saved the lives of millions of women and children around the globe, my leadership would come to seem preordained, almost an act of God, or at least fate. It was more complicated than that. It always is.

Twenty-Two

AS THE UNDISPUTED leader of the movement, I had to be
more careful than ever, not only about the sexual side of
my life but about another aspect as well. I could not afford to
have doctors and scientists, philanthropists and policy makers,
dismiss me as a crank any more than I could have them censure
me as a loose woman. That was why I told few people about my
study of Rosicrucianism. I was even more secretive about the
séances I attended.

Yes, I attended séances. Is that so awful? Are we so sure the
spirit world doesn't exist merely because our limited powers of
reasoning can't prove it? I refuse to believe that the bonds of love
formed between souls cease to be once the bodies that housed
those souls are no longer with us. I refuse to let the limitations
of the human mind define the possibilities of the human spirit.
There is more to life than birth and death and the daily drudg-
ery between. I was determined to find out what. So the evening
in question, the evening that would finally usher me into that
other sphere, I went to hear the Parsi Indian speak. Juliet Rublee
went with me. She was searching too.

The speaker was spellbinding. Life, he explained, is a temporary state, but so is death. When time ends and the final renovation arrives, the souls of the dead will return to life in their undead form. Perhaps I'm not describing this well, but he made it all clear.

Afterward, Juliet and I were standing on the sidewalk in front of the hall, waiting for her touring car, when a small woman approached. She seemed to know who I was. I assumed that she'd heard me speak or seen my photo in a newspaper. She explained that she was a psychic. I was immediately on my guard. I believe in the spirit world, but I'm skeptical of people who accost strangers on the street, proclaiming their powers. I kept walking to Juliet's car, which had pulled up at the curb. The woman put a hand on my arm. I started to shake it off. Then she spoke again.

"I have been in communication with Peggy."

I stopped. This couldn't be a scam. The world couldn't be that cruel.

"Moonbeams danced on her blond hair, and she was running like the wind. Without a brace," she added.

How could she know about the brace? I stood on the sidewalk unable to move. Juliet, who was stepping into the car, turned, saw me, and came back.

"Are you all right, Margaret? You look shaken."

"She's seen Peggy."

Juliet looked from me to the woman. "Is this true?"

"Didn't you hear the talk tonight? I do not deal in falsehoods."

I wanted to believe her, but still, she could have seen a photo of Peggy. Perhaps there was even one with a brace that Bill had taken and never shown me.

"Tell me more about her," I begged.

"She is with Doma."

Any doubts I still harbored evaporated in the breath of that one word. Doma had been Peggy's name for Bill's mother. No one outside the family knew it.

"With Doma," I repeated and clutched the woman's arm. "Please tell me more. Anything."

But she slipped out of my grasp and disappeared into the crowd.

I swore Juliet to secrecy and told no one else about the incident. I'd battled with Bill over Peggy's body; I refused to fight over her soul. The boys were too young to understand. J.J. would say that the woman was a con artist out to exploit my grief. When he caught me sitting alone in a room, holding a hair ribbon or toy or old sweater, he didn't try to comfort me, and that was the only comfort I could hope for. But he wouldn't be able to let this pass. Be reasonable, Peg, he'd say in that maddeningly reasonable tone. So I kept the secret of Peggy and her reentry into my life to myself.

Twenty-Three

I WENT ON ANOTHER speaking tour. The schedule was even more demanding and the crowds larger. By the time I returned home, I was exhausted, weak, and ailing. The doctor prescribed a holiday. I couldn't manage a holiday, but I could take Grant to California for several months. I would write a book, and we would get to know each other. Peggy had given me the idea.

The encounter after the Parsi lecture had left me suddenly hopeful. Peggy's spirit was here among us. It was only a matter of time until she contacted me. But as the days and weeks passed and she gave no sign, I felt the intensity of the loss all over again. It was as if she had abandoned me a second time. Still, I refused to give up. I went to séances. Other souls appeared, but Peggy remained elusive. I consulted mediums. Patience, they counseled. You cannot rush the spirits. So I pretended to myself, as if the pretense would fool Peggy, that I was not waiting. And then, when I really had given up hope, she began to appear in my dreams. I know what the skeptics will say. We all dream of those we're longing for. But not with this vibrancy. Her presence was so real, so vivid, that it lingered long after I awoke. It was as if she were in the room with me. Soon I heard the echo of her voice. Again the skeptics will jeer. We all carry the voices of loved ones around with us, they'll say. But they're wrong. The memory of a voice fades faster than the recollection of words or appearance or habits. Ask the women whose husbands went overseas in the war. They cherished photographs. They read and reread letters. But no matter how hard they tried, they couldn't conjure voices. That's how I knew Peggy's voice whispering in my ear was real.

And because I believed, because I trusted, she began to leave signs. Photographs turned up in drawers where I was sure I hadn't left them. Grant's letter telling me how much he missed me was lying on my desk when I returned home from the doctor who'd told me I needed a holiday. The connection was as clear as if Peggy had written the prescription.

I had another more practical motive for going to California. J.J. was still talking about marriage.

"Can't you see it, Peg? A real home. I'm not talking about a house in the suburbs. I know you'd hate that. But a decent apartment with a room for the boys. No more boarding schools."

"They love their boarding schools."

"That's what they tell you."

"Are you saying the boys lie to me?"

"The boys don't want to worry you. Don't you know that much about them yet? But you see what they're like when they have to go back to school. Worse still, when they can't come home for a holiday, because you're off lecturing somewhere."

"Now you sound like Bill."

"That's not what I mean, and you know it. All I'm saying is that even if you were off lecturing, the boys could be here with me. We'd keep the home fires burning until you got back. Admit it, Peg, it's a rosy picture."

His rosy picture looked too much like Bill's rose window. It had been a mistake to say yes to the window, but I couldn't seem to say no to J.J. I was counting on three months in California to give me courage, or at least perspective.

Grant and I settled into a cottage in Coronado. It was surrounded by palm trees that whispered and clapped in the wind, thick vegetation exploding in flamboyant flowers, and raucous birdsong. I promised Grant we'd learn the names of all the local flora and fauna. Peggy had been right when she'd told me to take him out of boarding school to spend a few months with me. He misses you, Mama, she'd whispered to me in my dreams.

He started public school and made friends with the neighborhood boys. They spent hours cruising the well-kept streets on their bicycles, exploring the tidal pools, and doing whatever eleven-year-old boys do after school. He was flourishing.

One afternoon I felt him hovering in the doorway of my study but didn't look up. I was in the middle of a thought and afraid of losing it.

"Mother," he began.

I held up my hand, palm toward him. He knew what that meant and stood waiting. My fingers flew over the typewriter keys. I finished the paragraph and looked up. The sun had bleached his hair and darkened his skin.

"What is it, handsome?" I asked.

"May I ask you a favor, please?"

He was such a polite boy. More than polite. He was so protective. He'd been that way with Peggy. He was that way with me.

"Of course."

"Please don't tell people here that you were in jail."

Peggy was right. He needed time with me. I'd open his eyes to worlds beyond bourgeois convention.

But despite the fact that Grant was thriving and my book was going well, my spirits were low. I blamed it on the weather. The constant eye-searing light, the ever-changing blue sea, the crimson sun sliding into it in a balmy farewell each evening— these were narcotics intended to dull the pain and suffering of the real world. But I refused to run from reality. My old friends Jack Reed and Louise Bryant were on trial in Washington for making Bolshevik statements. Emma Goldman had been deported. Free speech was dead, and now that the war was over, all the country cared about was having a good time. Hemlines were rising, sexual inhibitions were falling, and women were breaking free. I celebrated all that, but I bemoaned the lack of seriousness. People needed contraception more than ever, but everyone seemed to be too drunk on jazz music and bootleg liquor to fight for it.

My fevers returned. The doctors recommended X-ray treatments. They didn't help. Other doctors prescribed iron injections. They were just as ineffective. I was eating like a stevedore, and my clothes hung on me as if on a hanger.

At the end of April, Grant and I boarded the train for the trip home. He would finish the school year in the East. I had a manuscript in my suitcase, a new closeness to my son, and several months of rest, and I still felt terrible. The most recent letter from J.J. didn't improve my mood. It was about marriage, and strangely enough, he used the same words Bill had the day he'd hired the horse and buggy and lined up a minister. It's now or never, Peg.

The ultimatum came on the heels of several letters in which he'd mentioned a woman called Harriet Lowenstein. I'd met

Miss Lowenstein when he'd brought her to one of my talks. She'd worn her conventionality like a sandwich board.

I'D WIRED J.J. to tell him which train we were taking, and he was waiting on the platform. I saw him from the window before the train stopped. He spotted me coming down the steps from the Pullman car with Grant and a porter in tow. We shouldered our way through the crowd toward each other. Suddenly, after months, we were inches apart. We stood that way for a moment; then I held out my hand. He took it. In those days respectable people did not kiss on station platforms, and we would not have even if others did. Newspaper photographers often met the more glamorous limited trains, and while I wasn't a movie star and he wasn't a baseball player or senator, if none of those was arriving, a photographer might settle for a picture of the birth control champion and the lawyer who fought her court battles.

He turned to Grant. Grant imitated me and held out his hand. J.J. ignored it and swallowed him in a bear hug. I waited for Grant to recoil. He would think he was too old for such flamboyant displays of affection. But J.J. had pegged him better than I had. Grant closed his eyes and hung on for dear life. When they released each other, J.J. ruffled Grant's hair, Grant gave J.J.'s arm a playful punch, and then they slipped back into their masculine dignity. How could I not marry this man?

GRANT SANGER

That's what I was thinking the day he met us at the station, Mother. I wanted it so badly. Stuart and I both did. If you married J.J., we'd be a normal family. You do know that's what children long for, don't you? But I think even then I knew that was the last thing you wanted, because by then I had got to know you. I grew up on that trip, Mother. I suppose realizing that a parent is only human, the old feet-of-clay story, is part of growing up. I just did it sooner and more precipitously than most.

You were determined to open my mind, and you did. You made me challenge the accepted pieties they passed out at school. You forced me to question the injustices of the world that our neighbors in that elegantly aloof paradise ignored. You introduced me to unusual people with extravagant ideas. And you trucked a stream of besotted men through the house. I hated you for that. I felt as if you were betraying not only J.J. but Stuart and me too.

I remember one night some neighbors had a luau and hired Hawaiian dancers for the occasion. I can still see your face as you watched the firelight gleaming off the oiled bodies of the half-naked men. I was on the edge of puberty and had to look away, because I sensed something that I didn't understand, and didn't want to understand.

Don't get me wrong, Mother. I didn't lose faith in you during those months. In some ways, I came to admire you more than ever. I had never known, I still don't know, anyone who is as open to new experiences and ideas. You seemed to be always in a state of wonder. But for the first time I saw you whole, your deviousness and dishonesty and selfishness as well as your strength and compassion and sense of justice. At first the realization was frightening, but somehow I learned to hold all of you, the black and the white, the Jekyll and the Hyde, the arrogance and the insecurity, the hell-bent ambition and the capacity for love, in my mind at once. Stuart never got the chance to. Maybe that's why he's still angry.

WE TOOK A taxi to the Pennsylvania Station and put Grant on a train back to school.

"I'll miss you." I stood on the platform mouthing the words up to the window.

Grant looked down at us. He was trying to smile, but the effort to fight back the tears turned the expression into a grimace. "I'll miss you too," he mouthed back at me.

The train started moving, slowly at first, then gathering speed. It carried him away like an outgoing tide. I fought the urge to run after him. I'd felt it before when I'd said good-bye to the children, but never as powerfully. We'd grown so close in California. I stood, my hands clenched, my eyes closed, wishing that I were like other women. I hung on for another beat. The moment passed. I was myself again.

In the taxi going downtown, J.J. and I sat at opposite ends of the backseat. On the way up the stairs to the apartment, I felt his eyes on me, but he kept his hands to himself. When we reached the landing, he opened the door and stepped aside for me to go in before him. He closed the door behind us. We put down the luggage. And there against the wall, still in our hats and coats and shoes, he went down on his knees, and I pulled up my skirt and pushed down my bloomers, and afterward I was no closer to an answer to him than when I'd left.

We moved to the bedroom and made love in slow motion as the sky outside the window turned from blue to mauve to black, and the streetlamps went on, and a full moon swung up over the roof of the building across the street. Later, we lay side by side in the sex-rumpled sheets, our bodies pale in the stream of streetlamp light flooding through the window. His breathing still had a jagged edge. I didn't want him to speak, but I knew he would.

He rolled over on his side, rested his head on his hand, and looked down at me. "Can I take this as an affirmative?" His voice was tentative. He knew that for me sex was not an affirmation of anything but sex. Still, he was hoping.

I shimmied out from under his gaze and sat up with my back against the iron headboard. "Why do you want to marry me, J.J.?" I wasn't being coy. He knew I didn't believe in marriage. He also knew I was no good at it. Why was he asking for trouble?

He sat up beside me and shook his head. "Because I love you. And you say you love me. When people are in love, they usually get married."

"We're not people. We're rebels," I said, though I knew he wasn't.

"Even rebels get married. If they didn't, there'd be no little rebels who grow up to be revolutionaries."

"That's another thing. I don't want any more children. You do."

"I've got all the kids I can handle. Stuart and Grant. The entire membership of the Grand Street Boys. What I want is you."

The conversation went on that way for some time. We stopped to go out to dinner and came back and made love again, but the sentences spun out and circled back on themselves. We begged each other to see reason. He raised his voice. I did too. He got out of bed and paced the apartment. I laughed.

He whirled on me. "What's so funny?"

"This apartment is too small for pacing."

He looked at me with the expression of a man who's itching to get his hands around a woman's throat, and not in affection. A moment passed. Then he burst out laughing and came back to bed. Somewhere around dawn I told him I'd marry him.

I AWAKENED WITH a vague feeling that something was wrong. It took me a moment to figure out what it was.

I turned over and saw J.J. was gone. A frisson of relief, cold and quick as ice going down my back, ran through me. A moment later I recognized his step on the stairs. The door opened and he was standing there with a loaf of bread in one hand and a bunch of roses in the other. I could have taken one or the other, but the two together undid me. I didn't want the crumbs of daily living littering the rose-strewn bed of passion. As I watched him come toward me, smiling a promissory note good for the rest of my life, I knew it was hopeless. I could never be faithful to one man. It was against my nature. It was against my creed. It would be giving in to the forces of convention and small-mindedness and bourgeois prejudice. It would be a betrayal of my essence. It would be taking the easy way out.

"I can't do it," I said.

JONAH J. GOLDSTEIN

Sometimes I try to remember how I felt that morning when I walked in the door and saw your face. Before you said a word, I knew you couldn't go through with it. I was miserable. I was furious. But I must have been just a little relieved. As crazy in love with you as I was, I must have known

I was getting off easy. You broke my heart that morning, Peg. But if you hadn't, you would have wrecked my life. You had my number about that. I wasn't worldly like those English intellectuals and American Romeos you played around with. I thought free love was a lot of hooey. Someone always pays in the end. In our case it would have been me. From what I heard, your second husband did through the nose, although gossip said he never caught on. If he didn't, he must have been deaf, dumb, and blind. But I wouldn't have been. Still, standing there like some domesticated stage-door Johnny with a bouquet of flowers in one hand and a loaf of rye bread in the other, I hurt like hell.

DAISY, THE WOMAN J.J. had hired to come down from Harlem to take care of the apartment and the boys when they were home, had finished cleaning and was about to leave when the telegram arrived. I didn't tear it open immediately. I had a sixth sense of what it said.

I took my time walking to my desk, finding a paper knife, slitting open the envelope.

HARRIET AND I MARRIED IN LONDON THIS MORNING
STOP JJ

I stood in the circle of yellow light from the lamp staring at the piece of paper. Daisy asked if anything was wrong.

I looked up and pasted a grin on my face. "No, nothing wrong. Good news, in fact. Mr. Goldstein got married."

She went on staring at me for a moment, then put on her hat, buttoned her coat, and shook her head. "For a smart lady, you sure do some dumb things."

"I'm sure he'll be very happy."

"I was talking about you, not him. Who'd he marry, that nice Miss Lowenstein he brought round after you came back from California?"

"Yes, that nice Miss Lowenstein."

"She'll make him a good wife."

I started to say that was exactly what Harriet would be. A good little wife, loyal, tame, a one-man woman. Why not get a golden retriever? Then I caught myself. I refused to be that petty. Harriet would be all those things, but she would be more than that. She'd make J.J. happy. And she'd be happy herself. As a woman who'd dedicated herself to improving other women's lives, I had to rejoice. And I did. Really I did.

Twenty-Four

I DIDN'T REGRET MY decision. I don't believe in regret any more than I do in guilt. They're merely two sides of self-indulgence. Worse than that, they're two sides of self-pity. And I was too busy for either. I was writing another book. I was on the road constantly, not just in America but around the world, giving talks, organizing conferences, meeting with people who had the power and position to advance my agenda.

Albert Einstein wrote me a letter of support.

Gandhi invited me to his ashram. What a disappointment that was. I'm not suggesting he wasn't a great man. He was one of history's true saints, canonized not by an absurd and political church ritual but by his natural goodness. Like so many saints, however, he was pigheaded. He lived in a criminally overpopulated country, festering with illness and suffering and death, and saw the solution not in the science of contraception but in the so-called virtue of chastity. He would not have been out of place in the parish church in Corning. Instead of a black robe and turned-around collar, he wore a white loincloth; instead of threatening damnation, he beamed beatifically. But the message was the same. The celebrated thinker I went halfway around the world to meet was as naïve and wrongheaded about sex as he was about irrigating the land with old-fashioned water wheels. More so. His agricultural schemes merely denied scientific and technological progress. His family-planning methods flew in the face of human nature.

But the point is, I was too busy to miss J.J. And any number of men were eager to console me, not that I needed consoling. Havelock still welcomed me every time I went to London. Wantley was still a heavenly escape from town. And H. G. Wells entered my life. The spark between us was immediate. Later he admitted he'd expected it to flame briefly, then go out. It always did for him.

"But you're not like other women," he said. "You don't cling."

"You're not like other men," I countered. "You don't smother."

He was an intense lover, but a playful one. I still have the notes he sent commemorating our meetings, often with sketches. In my favorite, squiggles suggesting the electricity that we gave off decorate the margins of the page.

One afternoon in his hotel room, he got out of bed and walked to the desk. I lay back on the pillow, watching the play of light and shadow on his skin as he moved through the shaft of sun flowing through the window into the shadows and came back again carrying a manuscript. I looked at the top page. SECRET PLACES OF THE HEART was typed across it.

"I want to read you something," he said, as he got back into bed.

And lying there beside him, I heard about V. V. Grammont, a young American who was the embodiment of the New Woman, a fearless pagan who took sex where and when she liked, without sin or shame, entanglements or regrets. She—and I loved this—was better read in the recent literature of socialism than the male protagonist, and had a most unfeminine grasp of economic ideas.

Later, critics in the know would say that one of the greatest writers of our time had immortalized me. I prefer to think that I had inspired one of the greatest writers of our time.

So you see, my life was too full of love as well as work to give a thought to J.J., though once, on a train going from Los Angeles to San Francisco, I looked away from the blinding Pacific seascape to see a man across the aisle who reminded me of him. As I went on watching him, it occurred to me, the similarity wasn't of looks but of manner. He was with a little girl of about five or six. Perhaps she was the one who'd caught my eye, though she was dark and looked nothing like Peggy. Something in the way the man was speaking to her, not talking down in the singsong voice most adults use with children, but carrying on a normal conversation that gave her her due, reminded me of the way J.J. had been with Stuart and Grant, and for a moment the ache of loss, of all the losses, blindsided me.

I began gathering up my belongings. A porter was at my side in a moment. He asked if anything was wrong. I told him the car was too smoke-filled and I had to change my seat.

Then, years later, on a rainy afternoon during the war, I ran into the real J.J. on Constitution Avenue in Washington. I was walking with my head down and my umbrella tipped forward against the wind, so I didn't see the other umbrella coming at me until we collided.

Running into former lovers is always a dicey business. It's too easy to slip into paranoia on one hand or self-aggrandizement on the other. Does the shocked expression on his face mean I've aged that much, or is it a sign that even after all these years my presence still unhinges him? I was glad, irrationally since

I was wearing a raincoat, that Juliet and I had gone on that all-citrus diet that had knocked off four pounds. But I couldn't tell whether J.J. was love- or horror-struck. His face gave away nothing. He might have been parsing legal niceties instead of standing inches away from a woman he'd lived with and loved and pleaded to marry.

We huddled under our umbrellas as wet pedestrians hurried past our vapid duet of how-are-yous, and I'm-fines, and I-saw-the-piece-on-you-in-this-or-that-newspaper. He was a judge now, and there were rumors of a mayoral candidacy. We asked each other what we were doing in Washington.

I explained that I'd come down in hope of persuading the Women's Army Corps to distribute contraceptives to WACs. Unfortunately, the people I had to convince were men, and from the expressions on their faces as we'd sat around that conference table that was polished to as high a gloss as the brass on their uniforms, you'd have thought none of them had ever heard of sex without benefit of clergy. You'd certainly never have guessed that the army was spending millions of dollars passing out condoms to GIs, and plastering walls with warnings about Mata Haris who spread venereal disease, and showing ghoulish training films intended to instill a terror greater than the fear of war. But I knew better than to frame the argument in terms of sexual equality. I'd spoken only of the war effort. Did they want to beat Hitler and Hirohito, or did they want half the WACs in uniform mustering out because they were lonely and scared and found a little solace with some GI who was just as lonely and twice as terrified? The officers around the table hadn't bought it. They'd frowned and cleared their throats and explained that if they made birth control available to military women, the women would behave as badly as military men, and the officers around that table knew how bad that was.

"Any success?" J.J. asked.

"What do you think?"

He shook his head and explained that he was on his way to a press conference to announce that he was resigning from the American Bar Association, an organization so backward and benighted that it refused to admit a Phi Beta Kappa Yale graduate because he was a Negro.

Standing there in the shelter of our umbrellas and our moral rectitude as the rain puddled around us, I had a sudden flash of what our life together might have been. Then it passed.

I'M NOT SUGGESTING I wasn't happy. For one thing, I had married again.

Noah Slee was a God-fearing, churchgoing, conservative businessman. He was also rich. We met at another of Juliet's dinner parties. You might say he was my mark that night. Juliet had told me he gave generously to good causes. All I had to do was persuade him that birth control was a good cause.

I went after Noah for his money, but I was also intrigued by him. Most of the men I knew wanted to fix the world. He was satisfied with it the way it was. Of course, it had been awfully good to him.

He wasn't handsome, but with the exception of my two Hughs—de Selincourt and Brodie—I have rarely fallen for superficial traits. He had a head of silver hair, a kind face that tended to flush when he was excited, and a stocky body, but he carried himself with a sense of his success that made people pay attention. And there was the sex. There must always be the sex. Even before he told me about his wife, I knew I was preparing a feast for a starving man. I saw it in the way he looked at me that

234 / Ellen Feldman

first night. Nothing obvious or vulgar, simply a gaze so intense it was almost a physical touch.

NOAH SLEE

I hate to think of how close I came to not going that evening, Margy. In those days, I was living off and on at the Union League. There wasn't much point in going home to Dutchess County. Mary didn't want to see me any more than I wanted to see her. All I did want that night was dinner at the club, a brandy, a cigar, and the newspapers. The last thing I was in the mood for was one of Mrs. Rublee's dinner parties with all those swells who painted or danced or hatched formulas for saving the world. Not one of them could have come up with a real formula, like the one I developed for my Three-in-One Oil, if their lives depended on it. I wasn't in the mood for Mrs. Rublee either. I never could understand how her husband put up with all her harebrained enthusiasms.

Then you walked in and there was no other place I wanted to be. I suppose the way I cut through all the other guests to get to you was unseemly, but I wouldn't have got where I am today if I worried about seemliness. I'm a plain businessman, not a parlor snake.

You were sweet as honey to me that night. These days you tell people that you almost fainted when I talked about my work at St. George's Sunday school down in Stuyvesant Square, but you sure hid your surprise then. You asked about the school, and wanted to know the size of the families in the congregation, and talked about how those women had access to contraception while poor women didn't. That was my turn to almost faint.

I couldn't believe this little lady looking up at me with those big green eyes would talk about birth control as if she was discussing the weather. I'd never seen anything like it. I'd never seen anything like you. Mary never mentioned sex. Wouldn't talk about it. Wouldn't commit it. Every time I managed to, she called her mama the next morning crying. But I've already told you about those calls. Mother, she'd wail, he did it again.

You made me feel so big that night. Was it an act? Were you laughing up your sleeve in the backseat of my town car as my chauffeur drove us down to your apartment? I must have sounded like a rube to you, a rich rube, but a rube all the same. Even then I knew my money was part of the attraction, but that was all right. My money was part of me. I'd made it myself. When I told you about driving around the countryside as I was just starting the company and seeing barns that were in need of a paint job, then offering to paint the barn for the farmer if he'd let me put a sign for Three-in-One Oil on the side facing the road—I figured if he hadn't been able to paint it then, he wouldn't be able to in the future, and the advertisement would stay for a while—you said what a clever idea and I must be a very forward-thinking man to have hatched it. By the time I got out of the car to see you to the door, I was ten feet tall. When you agreed to have dinner with me, I was over the moon, as your English friends would say. I'd give a lot to have those days back.

NOAH AND I got along better than we should have, at least in the beginning. If he minded about the other men, he didn't say so. I can't believe he didn't know. Let's just say he was wise enough to pretend ignorance.

I'd known his money would be a boon to the cause, but I hadn't suspected he'd be useful as well. My proper business-man husband became a bootlegger for the movement, smuggling German and Dutch diaphragms into the country packed in his Three-in-One Oil containers. He also managed to get his hands on the German formula for a spermicidal jelly to be used with the smuggled diaphragms—he wouldn't say how, but he couldn't stop grinning when he told me about it—and began producing it in one of his factories in New Jersey.

He put my finances in order too. Suddenly the organization wasn't on the verge of bankruptcy, and I wasn't living hand to mouth. Noah was generous, at least in the beginning. He built me my own Wantley, complete with a man-made lake on a hundred and ten acres in Fishkill in Dutchess County. It was a handsome Tudor mansion—I know the word is vulgar, but there's no other way to describe the house—a short drive from New York. Willowlake was my home on the hill, and now I was one of those enviable matrons who floated over green-as-legal-tender lawns through soft summer nights. I even took up tennis and golf.

I enjoyed living well, but now that I had money, I thought about it even less. Manufacturers of contraceptives offered me fees to endorse their products. I refused. A firm in the Midwest tried to capitalize on my reputation by calling itself the Margaret Sanger Company. I sued. When the Crash came, Noah lost his seat on the stock exchange, and we cut back, but all I had to do was look around me at families suffering in Hoover-ville tents in Central Park, men selling apples on street corners, and women writing to me desperate for ways to prevent having another mouth to feed to know that we were still living uncon-scionably well.

Each year seemed to bring a new triumph for the movement. In 1936, the Supreme Court ruled that contraceptives could be sent through the mails to doctors. In 1937, the American Medical Association endorsed birth control. Contraception was becoming so respectable that the Sears, Roebuck catalog advertised what it called "preventives." CBS invited me on national radio to deliver a talk on family planning. For years the airwaves had banned me. The FCC gave a license to Aimee Semple McPherson, that snake-oil saleswoman whom I'd seen in London the night I'd stumbled into a religious meeting, with her healing-through-the-air-waves scam, but they'd refused to let me near a broadcast studio. Now suddenly they decided I was worth listening to.

As the years passed, the honors and accolades poured in. Tokyo gave me the key to the city. Smith College awarded me an honorary degree. I heard that President Johnson wanted to present me with the Presidential Medal of Freedom, but feared antagonizing the Catholic Church. I was feted as Woman of the Century at a dinner attended by more than a thousand people, including the Duke and Duchess of Windsor.

ETHEL BYRNES

The Duke and Duchess of Windsor, well la di da. My sister, the former socialist, the former *Irish* socialist, was beside herself because she was going to meet the king of England, who'd abdicated, and the climber who thought she could sleep her way to being queen. Poor Marg. You never could make up your mind whether you hated the people at the top of the hill or loved them. Perhaps that's one more reason you're not as happy as you want the world to believe.

If you ask me, all this talk about your achievements and your honors sounds a lot like whistling in the dark. If life was so sunny, if you were so fulfilled, why did you take to your bed every November 6? You refused to see anyone. You wouldn't even talk to me on the phone. I'm not faulting you for that. I'm merely suggesting that maybe if you'd stop insisting you don't believe in guilt, if you'd permit yourself some ordinary—I know how you hate that word—emotions, you'd have an easier time of it.

Or maybe not. Owning up to the guilt doesn't necessarily dull the pain. Especially when it comes to your children. I'm proof of that.

Twenty-Five

I HAD WON THE fight to make contraception legal and available to large numbers of women, but I hadn't found a way to make it simple or easy or even feasible for the millions of women who lived in urban tenements without adequate plumbing or privacy, or rural hovels with outhouses, or anywhere without access to doctors who could fit a diaphragm and explain how to use it. I wanted a form of birth control that could be effective in all those circumstances. I dreamed of an injection or a pill or a miracle drug of some kind. Dream on, skeptics told me. But if science could develop vaccines against diphtheria, tetanus, and whooping cough, surely it could find a substance that would prevent conception. I had no intention of giving up until it did.

KATHARINE MCCORMICK TO
MARGARET SANGER

Boston, Massachusetts
November 18, 1950

Dear Mrs. Sanger,

My late husband's estate has been settled, and I find myself with some funds in hand. Do you have any suggestions about how to put the money to the best use? What is the status of contraceptive research, and where would contributions do the most good?

With sincere regards,
Katharine Dexter McCormick

Tucson, Arizona
December 1, 1950

Dear Mrs. McCormick:

Contraceptive research needs tremendous financial support. At present, Dr. Gregory Pincus of the Worcester Foundation in Massachusetts has proved that repeated injections of progesterone stops ovulation in animals. Do not be put off by the fact that he is working in a small underfunded laboratory, which he started with a colleague, rather than at a large university. He was formerly at Harvard, but was denied tenure. Some say he was bypassed because of his controversial in vitro fertilization of rabbits, which raised a moral brouhaha. Others ascribe his situation to academic politics, anti-Semitism, and plain old jealousy. Whichever it is, he has achieved excellent results, and I believe funding his work will yield success for our cause.

With sincere regards,
Margaret Sanger

Boston, Massachusetts
June 14, 1954

Dear Mrs. Sanger:

Dr. Pincus was here yesterday for two hours, and I feel so encouraged by his progress. As you know, the price of progesterone was $200 a gram, economically feasible for thoroughbred horses, but not for the average woman in need of contraception. However, Dr. Pincus reports that progesterone is now being made with synthetics.

The problem going forward will be the clinical tests. I pointed out to Dr. Pincus that we are unlikely to find a cage of ovulating females. He is thinking of Japan, Hawaii, or Puerto Rico.

With sincere regards,
Katharine Dexter McCormick

NEW YORK TIMES, May 10, 1960

U.S. APPROVES PILL FOR BIRTH CONTROL

My legacy was secure.

GRANT SANGER

Your legacy was secure, Mother? I'm only glad you don't see half of what's written about you these days. I can't understand how it happened. You had no prejudice, except perhaps against the Catholic Church. You went to jail for trying to help those poor Jewish and Italian women in Brownsville. You set up clinics in Harlem and the South. You spoke at a Mother's Day service at the Abyssinian Baptist Church. You gave interviews to Negro newspapers saying the white man had to be educated to overcome his bigotry. You disturbed the peace by inviting those two Negro doctors to your talk at a white club in Oklahoma City, then pretended you'd had no idea they wouldn't be welcome. Later, when Hitler began rounding up Jews, you fought the bigots at the State Department and managed to bring over doctors and researchers who were being hounded out of their own countries. For a while there, *Willowlake*, as they called it, looked like a refugee center. You were so much on the side of the angels that the Nazis burned your books. So what I want to know is how in hell did you end up being compared to Hitler and accused of genocide by every crank with a typewriter and an ax to grind?

ISN'T HINDSIGHT WONDERFUL? Doesn't it make us wise? But if you want to understand what really happened, you have to forget what came later—Hitler, concentration camps, gas chambers, ghoulish experiments on human beings—and return to the way the world was in the earlier decades of the twentieth century. I can remember that more vividly than I can recall what I had for lunch yesterday.

Eugenics was in the air. Everyone was intoxicated by it. We were going to wipe out illness and eliminate defects by engineering reproduction. We were going to cure society's ills by breeding, not a master race, but simply new and improved human beings. Perfection was just around the corner.

I was as idealistic as the next reformer, but I had a more practical motive as well. Eugenics was a reputable science. Serious thinkers and respected officials espoused it. Colleges and universities offered courses in it. But despite the successes I'd had, in certain circles birth control was still regarded as shady. Politicians were afraid to touch it. I was hoping the science of eugenics would paste a fig leaf of decency over the naked effrontery of contraception.

But eugenics turned out to be sham rather than science. And I became fair game for every crank enemy of contraception. The Catholic Church compared me to Hitler. Critics said, as the district attorney had so many years earlier, that I was trying to wipe out the Jewish population. But here's what I want to know. Why didn't those cranks and critics take out after Justices Oliver Wendell Holmes and Louis Brandeis, who ruled that enforced sterilization was legal? Why didn't they blame W. E. B. Du Bois and Roger Baldwin of the ACLU for subverting civil rights? I'll tell you why. Because they were men with impressive credentials and seemingly serious causes. I was a woman talking about sex and tampering with their cherished male prerogatives. I had to be discredited. More than that, I had to be disgraced.

They did a good job. I've seen the books calling me a Nazi and accusing me of trying to engineer a master race. I've read the way they've trimmed and twisted my words by taking them out of context. I know the way they've demonized me and discredited my cause. But their slurs can't undo what I achieved. I changed the world for the better. Nothing can take that away from me.

Twenty-Six

T HE FIRST THING I saw when I opened my eyes was the pink blush creeping over the distant peaks. My house spreads out on the desert floor like a fan, and every room commands a view of the mountains.

When I bought the land next to Stuart and his family, I asked my friend Frank Wright to design a fitting home for my soul's development. I was still studying Rosicrucianism and was determined to nourish my life-force as well as my aesthetic sense. But he said the piece of land was no more than a handkerchief and anything built on it would look like a pig's sty. Frank doesn't mince words, but he ate those once he saw the house another architect friend built for me. Every room pulsed with light. The lines were spare and clean without a hint of hand-me-down Spanish fraud. How could a woman not be happy here? And I was most of the time, no matter what Ethel said. But November 6 was always a day out of my life.

I turned on my other side and closed my eyes. I knew I wouldn't fall back to sleep, but I had no reason to get up. I made no appointments on November 6. I did not see people. I did not even work. I devoted the day to my children. Stuart and Grant would call. They always did. Peggy would come to me, if I was patient.

I lay there thinking about my little girl. I had changed with the years. My hair had turned from ginger to rusty to gray, and grown thinner. Lines that had been no more than suggestions of life to come had deepened into ravines giving away my past. My wide almost-green eyes had gone into hiding beneath heavy lids. The alterations—no, the insults—had piled up year after year. But Peggy remained the same, a yellow-haired daisy of a girl with the smile of an imp and the eyes of an innocent. Even after all these years, those eyes staring through my memory made my heart ache.

My own eyes flew open. The day had been stalking me for weeks, it always did, but I hadn't given a thought to the year. November 6, 1965. Fifty years of November sixths. Half a century of taking to my bed to mourn, and to wait for her. How could that be? How could I have lived so long? So much longer?

I turned on my other side again and stared at the photograph on my night table. It had been taken in front of the building across from the Luxembourg Gardens. In it, Stuart's corduroy Norfolk jacket and knickers are disheveled from play. Grant stands with roller skates strapped to his feet and dirt smudges on his face. And Peggy stares into the camera from beneath blond bangs that fall like a silk curtain from the brim of her hat, daring the world, or me, to make her smile. The children do not look happy, but it is better than the other photograph, the professional one that J.J. persuaded me to have taken. I never should have done it. I almost hadn't. On the way to the photographer's studio, I'd lost my nerve.

"I can't do it," I said, standing on the sidewalk, somber in the gray dress with the scalloped white collar. I had started to put on a black skirt, white shirtwaist, and tie that morning, but J.J. had said the uniform of the suffragist was too provocative.

"Can't do what?" He stood facing me with a hand on each boy's shoulder. "Have a picture taken?"

"Exploit the situation. Exploit her."

"You're not exploiting her, Peg. You're giving her meaning. Didn't you always say the cause was for her?"

I closed my eyes again and lay in the faint early-morning light, waiting for her.

The ringing of the phone shattered the silence. It was too early for Stuart to call, but Grant lived on the East Coast. I started to reach for the phone, then shrank back. Suddenly I remembered not the half century of calls from him on November 6, seeking and offering solace, commiserating in our shared grief, but the first November 6. He'd laid on his stomach and kicked his small brown oxfords against the floor. They took my sister to the hospital and they brought back a dead body, he'd cried over and over.

The outcry was directed against the world. He was too young and too terrified to turn on his mother.

Twenty-Seven

I F THERE WERE any truth in advertising, they'd call this place not House by the Side of the Road but House at the End of the Road. That's what I've come to. The end of my road. I've run out of tricks to keep the memory at bay. The truth lies exposed in the heartless sun that beats into my room in this spirit-crushing prison they call a nursing home. It's as intrusive as the attendants coming and going on their soft-soled cheerfulness. The memory is all that's left. I am face-to-face with it, finally.

OCTOBER 1915

I had a premonition that night in Boston, but when I reached Ford Hall and found the police stationed around the auditorium, I was arrogant enough to think my foreboding had to do with nothing more than another attempt to silence me. At the last minute, the Boston city fathers, egged on by the Church, had decided they could not permit a birth controller to speak in a public forum.

An officer met me at the door and handed me a piece of paper. It said, in a garble of legalese, that Mrs. Margaret Sanger was prohibited from speaking at Ford Hall or anywhere else in the city. I wished J.J. were there, though I doubted he could have done much. Even if the order wasn't legal, and I had a feeling it wasn't, the police were determined to gag me.

The minute the word *gag* took shape in my mind, I knew what I had to do. I sent a young woman volunteer out to get a roll of surgical tape. It was lucky I was a nurse. (Oh, how the irony of that thought struck me later.)

"Are you hurt?" she asked.

"Just get the tape and meet me in the ladies' room."

I went to the ladies' room and, while I waited for her, took a notebook from my handbag, tore out a page, wrote a brief paragraph, and put it back in my handbag.

She returned with the tape. I took the roll from her and sent her back to the auditorium to find Professor Arthur Schlesinger. His wife, who was active in feminist circles, had written that she would be coming over from Harvard with her husband for the speech.

I had to use my teeth, but I managed to tear off a piece of tape about five inches in length. If it were any longer, it would get in my hair and removing it would be painful and, even worse, ruin my hairdo. The memory of my vanity on that night goes through me like a knife. I faced the mirror and fastened the tape over my mouth from ear to ear. When I was sure it was secure, I took my handbag and headed back to the stage. Professor Schlesinger was there, waiting for me.

I mounted the steps to the stage, Professor Schlesinger and I shook hands, and I gave him the paragraph I'd written. He studied it for a moment.

"Can you read it?" The words came out muffled from behind the surgical tape.

"Perfectly," he said.

We turned to face the audience. I stood with my head up, daring the police and the world, while he read.

As a pioneer fighting for a cause, I believe in free speech. As a propagandist, I see immense advantages in being gagged. It silences me, but it makes millions of others talk and think about the cause in which I live.

When he finished, the applause shook the room.

Someone was helping me remove the surgical tape, and I was trying to keep it out of my hair, and people were crowding up to the stage. A guard cut through the throng and handed me a telegram. I tore it open. It was from Bill. These days he wrote and wired only to harass me. I started to stuff the sheet of yellow paper in my pocket. I would not let his badgering spoil my triumph. Then one word jumped out at me. Peggy.

I HAVE NO idea how I got to the station or who bought my ticket. All I remember is sitting in the unforgiving light of the Pullman car, reading and rereading Bill's wire. It was anemic with lack of information.

I crumpled the telegram and sat staring out the window. There was no view, only an occasional light carving a desolate hole in the darkness, and my own reflection.

I smoothed out the piece of paper in my lap and read it again.

PEGGY RUSHED FROM STELTON TO MT SINAI WITH

PNEUMONIA STOP COME AS SOON AS POSSIBLE STOP
LOVE BILL

I lifted my eyes to the night-blackened window again. My mother's face stared back at me. Now you know, she said.

Outside the Grand Central Terminal, the city was still in darkness, but overhead a beam of thin autumn light had snagged on a water tank on one of the roofs. A queue of taxis stood waiting in front of the station. I stepped into the first one. "Mount Sinai Hospital," I said.

The smells of the hospital, the forced cheerfulness of the early-morning activity, the sagging faces of the nurses going off duty and the sleep-softened ones of those coming on—these were all familiar, but everything about my being there was strange and alien and wrong. This was a mistake. It had to be.

The woman behind the desk gave me the room number. Peggy was here. There was no mistake.

The elevator inched up. I stepped off it and started down the hall. Even before I reached the room, I heard the noise. That tortured rasp could not be the breathing of a five-year-old. It must be coming from another patient, a dying old man, a stranger.

I reached the room. The sight of that small body struggling for air stopped me in the doorway.

FOR THE NEXT three days, or five, or ten—I didn't know then; I can't remember now—I could not leave her side. I didn't dare. I was her mother. It was up to me to save her. Another nurse, even Ethel, would not get the compress cold enough, or warm the chill metal bedpan sufficiently, or sponge-bathe her as lovingly. They would manhandle the weakened fragile body. They would fail to get all the mucus from her lungs. That was the worst part. That was why I could not trust anyone else to do it.

I leaned over her, forcing myself to pound her skinny chest with the cruel hammers of my hands, again and again and again. Tears streamed down my face and fell onto hers. The skin that used to be smooth and translucent was crepey as an old woman's. Once, when I finished the procedure, I complained to Ethel about the noise down the hall.

"That was you, Margaret. You were the one who was screaming."

The lung procedure was agony. Inactivity was worse. What kind of nurse was I, what kind of mother, to sit by the side of the bed helpless while life leaked out of my baby? I demanded to see the doctors. I would not let other nurses in the room. I hated having Bill there. He was always getting between Peggy and me. He was always putting a sympathetic hand on my shoulder. I shrugged it off. I couldn't stand his touch.

I was with her when it happened. Her body convulsed, then went limp. I threw myself across the bed and clutched her to me. I would hold her in this world by physical force. But I could not hold her here. She was gone.

-⊁ · ⊰-

I CANNOT PUT the days that followed in any kind of order.

Tears stream down Bill's face.

Stuart clings to me as he has not in years. Stuart hides under a bed and will not come out.

Grant pummels the floor with his hands and feet and bays at the world.

A churning sea of faces. Ethel. J.J. Sisters and friends and women in the movement. Sorry, they say, so sorry.

Sorry. What a puny lisping word. I could not stand to hear it. I could not stand to see all those people who were still alive. I could not stand myself. I went back to my room at the Rutledge, locked the door behind me, and put the box with Peggy's ashes on the table. It was so small it barely took up any space at all.

Twenty-Eight

EVERYTHING IS SO white. No, not white, blinding. Blinding and silent and floating. Is this what death is like? Or am I dreaming again? Why do I dream of dying so often? My journal is full of death dreams.

Oh, now I understand. I'm in Mabel Dodge's white apartment with everyone arguing and drinking, making trouble and making love. John Rompapas prowls the perimeter of the room, sending a shiver down my back, and Big Bill Haywood sleep-moans his socialist dream, and poor Emma Goldman twists in the cruel attentions of a roving-eyed Romeo.

The sound of a knob turning clicks through the silence. Rubber soles make sucking sounds across the linoleum. I turn my head on the pillow to see who it is, but all I can make out is a blur. The blur is getting closer. More white. Light glinting off glasses. But the face is a smudge.

A hand circles my wrist. It's gone. Fingers open my gown. Cold metal presses against my chest. The touch is gentle but impersonal.

The hands disappear. Shoes move across the floor again. The door clicks. Does this mean I'm alone? I close my lids against the eye-stinging whiteness.

I open my eyes. How long has it been? Is it morning, afternoon, almost nighttime? The room is still dazzlingly bright. Did I miss the darkness or hasn't it fallen yet?

The doorknob turns again. These shoes click smartly. High heels tap toward me. Almost dancing. Bill crashes through the circle of doctors surrounding me and reaches out, and I take his hand and step into his arms. I'm Bill Sanger, he says, and you're going to marry me.

"Grandmother?"

The word stops the music of our dance. Bill disappears.

"Grandmother, it's me. Margaret."

I turn my head on the pillow. A figure comes into focus. The face takes shape. My daughter-in-law Barbara? No, not Barbara. Her daughter. Margaret.

"Margaret," I whisper through cracked lips.

"I brought the baby to see you."

She is holding something out to me. A package? The mattress shifts as she puts the bundle down next to me. I narrow my eyes to make it take shape. A little girl in a pink dress with a smocked top sits staring at me with the bright ruthless eyes of an infant.

"It's Peggy, Grandmother. Hasn't she gotten big?"

"Peggy?" My voice rasps.

"Margaret. The fourth generation of Margarets. But we call her Peggy."

Now I remember. Peggy. I lift my head from the pillow to see better. Peggy. It's Peggy. I maneuver my hand out from under the cover. I must touch her. I must make sure this is not another trick shaken loose from my memory. Her curls are silky. Her skin is softer than down.

"Peggy. My own little Peggy. I knew you'd come back to me." Tears run down my face. A sob racks my body. I hear the keening of grief, and this time I know it's coming from me.

The baby is gone. I did not see her go. I did not hear the click of high heels on the floor. A woman looms into my vision. Or is it two? There are too many hands for it to be only one. A voice is telling me everything is all right.

"I killed her," I shout.

Shh comes the sound.

I try to struggle up from the bed.

"I killed her."

Hands press me down to the mattress.

"They were right. Stuart and Grant and Bill. I killed her. It's just as they said. I'm a monster. A sacred monster, they called me."

The hands are still holding me down. Something sharp pricks my arm. The white world shimmers, then fades away.

PEGGY SANGER

Can I ask you something, Mama?

Of course, darling, ask me anything.

If you could do it again, would you do it the same?

. . .

I'm waiting for an answer, Mama.

. . .

That's what I thought.

THE ROOM IS back again. But Peggy is not here. I try to sit up to get a better view. I fall back against the pillows and close my eyes. Peggy. I am crying again. Peggy.

The door opens. I hear shoes moving across the floor, one pair, two, four, dozens, rubber soles and high heels and heavy boots and rustling bare feet. Voices begin to whisper. I can't make out the words, but I hear the timbre. Women's voices, soprano, alto, contralto. Whispering, shouting, singing, laughing. A chorus of women speaking in a babble of tongues.

I open my eyes. The room is packed. The women who sat in court, rocking children on their laps, holding bags of food and diapers, shouting "shame" at the judge as he pronounced the verdict, rally around the bed. Clients from the clinic push in, their eyes wide with wonder, their smiles lighting up a world dark with ignorance. They jostle one another, pressing closer, reaching out for me, clamoring. Thank you, Mrs. Sanger. A saint, Mrs. Sanger. My life you saved, Mrs. Sanger.

I feel them swirling around me, high-kicking, unafraid, free. They toss their untamed hair in rowdy celebration and open their mouths wide to let out the laughter and the words.

We're your daughters too, they cry. And you saved us.

Sources and Acknowledgments

FOR THEIR GENEROSITY with materials and guidance, I am grateful to Esther Katz and Cathy Moran Hajo, director and editor of the Margaret Sanger Papers Project; Amy Hague, curator of manuscripts at the Sophia Smith Collection of Smith College; and Patrick Kerwin, manuscript reference librarian of the Manuscript Division of the Library of Congress. Ellen Chesler's *Woman of Valor: Margaret Sanger and the Birth Control Movement in America* proved invaluable in researching Sanger's life and the complexities and crosscurrents of the movement she helped found. The Margaret Sanger Papers Project online is a treasure trove of information about Sanger and her struggle to make birth control legal and accessible.

I am indebted to Alex Sanger, who was kind enough to share memories of his grandmother with me; and to Jay Barksdale, former director of the Allen Room of the New York Public Library, and Carolyn Waters and the entire extraordinary staff of the New York Society Library for help in research and for creating safe harbors for writers.

Many friends and colleagues were generous with information, inspiration, and support during the research and writing of this book. I am grateful to Andre Bernard, Jakki Fink, Edward Gallagher, JoAnn Kay, Meredith Kay, Judy Link, Sara Nelson, Mark Schwartz, Michael Schwartz, Ann Weisgarber, and Brenda Wineapple, and especially to Liza Bennett and Richard Snow for their time and generosity in listening to endless talk about Margaret Sanger and reading the manuscript so carefully and perceptively.

And finally, I am beholden to my superb agent and dear friend, Emma Sweeney, and to Jennifer Barth, whose vision, perseverance, and kindness make her the kind of editor every writer dreams of.

About the Author

ELLEN FELDMAN, a 2009 Guggenheim Fellow, is the author of five previous novels, including *Scottsboro*, which was shortlisted for the Orange Prize for Fiction, and *Next to Love*. She lives in New York City.

Insights,
Interviews
& More . . .

An Interview with Ellen Feldman

This interview was conducted by Rosanna Boscawen at Picador. *First published on Picador.com URL: http://www.picador .com/blog/january-2015/an-interview -with-ellen-feldman.*

Which writing do you find yourself returning to and why?

Every decade or so I read *The Great Gatsby, Madame Bovary,* and *Middlemarch.* I don't say that I reread them, because at each stage of my life I find that I'm reading a different book. A friend, who is another *Middlemarch* devotee, puts it ingeniously. Why would you bother with a self-help book when you can read *Middlemarch*?

Which other author would you most like to have for dinner and why?

That's always a dicey question, because the writers I admire most would not necessarily make the best dinner companions. I'd love to meet F. Scott Fitzgerald, but he was a nasty drunk, and would probably get blotto before dinner started, hurl crockery and cutlery during it, and insult me mightily.

What's your favourite film?

I have two favorite films, both of which I discovered decades after they ran in theaters. *Dodsworth*, based on the novel by Sinclair Lewis and better than the book, was known as the first grown-up American movie. *The Best Years of Our Lives* is a beautiful story about homecoming after World War II. I loved it so much that years ago when I first saw it I tried to track down the book on which it was based. I naturally assumed it was a novel, and when I couldn't find it in the fiction section of my library, I was sure that the whole world had discovered the movie too and beaten me to the book. It turned out that the movie was based on a long narrative poem. I'm still amazed that some earnest moviemaker persuaded a Hollywood mogul to risk filming a long narrative poem.

What's the last thing you do at night?

The last thing I do at night is scratch Charlie, our mixed terrier foundling, behind the ears, tell him he's a good boy, and read fiction.

Tell us the first thing you do in the morning.

The first thing I do in the morning is scratch Charlie behind the ears, tell him he's a good boy, and read the paper.

What continues to inspire you?

I'm not sure if I'd say inspire, but I am endlessly intrigued by the variety and complexity of human nature, not only how some people can be so honorable and altruistic and others so venal, but how the same individual can be so high-minded one moment and vicious the next.

What advice would you give your fifteen- or twenty-year-old self?

Take more chances. ⌒

The Difficulty of Writing a Difficult Woman

This essay "The Difficulty of Writing a Difficult Woman" was originally published on the Amazon Book Review and is reprinted courtesy of Amazon.com, Inc.

Books are writers' children. Asked which is our favorite, we scrupulously reply, I love them all. Asked which gave us the most difficulty, we say each had its challenges and rewards. But I'm going to break with custom here. Of the several novels I've published, *Terrible Virtue*, based on the life of Margaret Sanger, was the hardest to write. It also had the longest gestation period, ten years from first inspiration and early research to publication.

I gave up in despair and abandoned the book once, a twice, a third time. I could not bring Margaret Sanger to life on the page, but Margaret Sanger would not let me go.

The day I tossed it out for the first time, or at least put it in the dormant file, I ran into a friend. When he asked how I was, I confessed that I had just given up on more than two years of work. He was so appalled that he told the story at a dinner party that evening, and for several weeks I got calls and e-mails of condolence. They were kind, but they

4

didn't make me feel any less a failure or a traitor. I was deserting a friend I had lived with, intensely and intimately, for two years. After writing another novel in the interim, I tried again. A year later, I put the novel aside a second time. Would I never learn, I chastised myself, and once again turned my hand to another book. The third time I returned to the idea and again failed, I was furious at myself for throwing good months and years after bad. Why couldn't I relinquish this obsession, which clearly was ill-conceived?

The answer to why I couldn't give up the book is the same as the answer to why I was having so much trouble writing it—Margaret Sanger, her singular genius, her towering achievements, and her maddening contradictions. How do you bring to life a woman who was at once selfish and altruistic; loyal and ruthless; arrogant and insecure; devoted to improving the lot of all women and fiercely competitive with other women; determined to expose society's hypocrisies and a maker of her own myths; a breaker of sexual taboos who somehow managed to maintain a spotless public persona; a woman who married twice, but didn't believe in marriage, and had countless affairs to prove it; a mother who loved her children but was hopeless at caring for them, and endured the worst heartbreak a parent can know?

It would have been demanding enough to capture this charismatic larger-than-life character in a biography; it was daunting to try to penetrate her mind and heart, which any successful novel must do. But the near impossibility of the endeavor is what attracted me in the first place. As a young woman, I had admired Margaret Sanger and her triumphs, but the more I read about her, the more her incongruities confounded me, and the more determined I became to try to figure out what made this towering figure tick. For that only fiction will do. And in fiction, perhaps more than in any other literary form, what we leave out is as important as—perhaps more important than—what we put in.

Therein lay the key to writing Margaret Sanger. I had been adhering too closely, not to the facts—I was determined to stick to those, and I have—but to the minutia of Sanger's life. I was sacrificing the essence of the woman to the details of ▶

5

The Difficulty of Writing a Difficult Woman (*continued*)

her existence. I was losing the magic of the individual to the particulars of her struggles, strategies, marriages, affairs, and encounters with her children. I had become a bore on the subject of Margaret Sanger rather than a novelist bringing to life her indomitable spirit. When I realized that, when I took a step back to see Margaret Sanger whole, she began to come alive in my imagination and on the page.

I have lived with Margaret Sanger for a decade. Even when I was writing about other characters and times and places, she occupied a corner of my mind. I can't say she is always sympathetic, but I can say she is superb company—exhilarating, inspiring, passionate, brilliant, capable of great love and petty hate, canny about her cause but often blind about her personal life, and always deeply human. She is, in the end, the woman who not only wrought a major social revolution but, more than any other single person, fashioned the sexual landscape we inhabit today.

And here's a footnote to the story behind the book. While I was doing the research for *Terrible Virtue*, I had a recurrent surreal sensation. The contemporary headlines I was reading with my morning coffee were uncannily similar to those of a century ago that I was unearthing in libraries and archives. The experience made me realize that from her opening of the first, then illegal, birth control clinic in America in 1916 through her founding of Planned Parenthood to her role in helping develop the Pill in the 1960s, Sanger's story is alive with yesterday's struggles and as timely as today's headlines. ❧

Contraception as a Plot Device in Fiction

Out-of-wedlock pregnancy, followed by misery, mayhem, or disgrace, has long been a plot device in fiction. In *The Scarlet Letter* by Nathaniel Hawthorne, both Hester Prynne and the Reverend Dimmesdale pay mightily for their indiscretion. In Theodore Dreiser's *An American Tragedy*, Clyde Griffiths either murders his pregnant girlfriend, Roberta Alden, or lets her drown. Though the child may not be unwanted in Ernest Hemingway's *A Farewell to Arms*, Catherine Barkley dies in childbirth. While all of these plots, and scores of others, hinge on pregnancy, none of them mentions ways to avoid it.

The appearance of contraception in fiction would seem to be a function the modern era, but in a sixteenth century collection of tales, *Ecatomiti* by Cinthio, one character tells his beloved of "marvelous secrets, which I have tested a thousand times with others, and have found so effective that they have never failed me once." Unfortunately, they do fail, the young woman gets pregnant, and misfortune follows.

Contemporary post-Margaret-Sanger references to contraception tend to be more effective at preventing pregnancy, but often lead to other plot complications. Here is a brief selective list of novels and short stories in ▶

which contraception or its absence or failure plays an important role.

The Group by Mary McCarthy (1963). In one of the most humiliating scenes ever written about birth control, Dottie Renfrew, at the suggestion of the man with whom she has lost her virginity, goes for a pessary or diaphragm to a doctor modeled on Hannah Stone, the physician who ran Margaret Sanger's clinic. The medical visit is a success, but afterward, Dottie spends the day waiting for her lover in New York's Washington Square Park. Finally, as night falls and he still hasn't turned up, she leaves the package containing the new device, along with her romantic illusions, under a bench.

Goodbye Columbus by Philip Roth (1959). Brenda Patimkin also gets a diaphragm at the urging of her lover, Neil Klugman. Brenda's experience is, at first, more lighthearted. When she comes out of the doctor's office to the square across from Bergdorf Goodman where Neil is waiting and he asks where it is, she tells him she's wearing it. But when Brenda goes back to Radcliffe in the fall, she leaves the diaphragm in a drawer for her mother to find, thus sabotaging the affair.

A Stroke of Good Fortune by Flannery O'Connor (1949). In this short story, the form of birth control is never actually mentioned, but the narrator Ruby clearly relies on it, though her husband, Bill Hill, is the one responsible for it. Ruby, who watched her mother wither and die from too many children, will not admit the possibility of, or even mention the word, pregnancy, despite evidence of it. "Not me!" she insists, "Oh, no, not me! Bill Hill takes care of that . . . Bill Hill's been taking care of that for five years!" The implication is that Bill Hill has taken care of it, but not in the way Ruby wants.

Lives of Girls and Women by Alice Munro (1971). In this novel of a young girl's coming of age in rural Ontario in the 1940s, Del Jordan's iconoclastic mother warns that if she lets herself get distracted by a man, her life will never be her own. "You will get the burden, a woman always does." Del replies glibly, "there is birth control nowadays," rejects her mother's message that "being female made you damageable," and resolves to live like men who are "supposed to be able to go out and take on all kinds of experiences and shuck off what they didn't want and come back proud."

Girls in Their Married Bliss by Edna O'Brien (1964). Unlike Del Jordan, who finds freedom in contraception, Kate and Baba, the eponymous protagonists of *The Country Girls* trilogy, are trapped by the lack of it in fiercely Catholic Ireland. Sex permeates the trilogy, which was banned in her native country, but not until this final novel is contraception mentioned, and then it's remarked on only obliquely and for its absence. Baba reports that the man she will end up marrying is, "Bad in bed. But . . . It made him a hell of a sight nicer than most of the sharks I'd been out with who . . . wanted some new, experimental kind of sex and no worries from you about might have a baby, because they liked it natural, without gear." Later, a distinctly kinky lover pleads with her to promise him she won't get pregnant. "He was an imbecile. On second thoughts I was the imbecile. I suppose he thought with the tights and the elaborate bathrooms I knew all there was to know."

Mothering Sunday by Graham Swift (2016). In 1920's England, contraception presented no problem for the wellborn. On a genial outing—"afterwards they'd gone to a cinema"—Paul Sheringham, an aristocratic young man who's about to make an appropriate marriage, takes Jane Fairchild, the servant he's sleeping with, to a "doctor chappie" he knows to get a "Dutch cap." Since she wears a little white cap as a maid, she sometimes thinks of herself as wearing two caps, but easy as it is, she can't help wondering how it would have changed her life if she had got pregnant.

Peyton Place by Grace Metalious (1956). In this risqué-for-its-time novel, which shocked the nation, exasperated critics, and ▶

sat on the best-seller list for more than a year, there's a great deal of sex, which results in illegitimate birth, abortion, and other socially unacceptable consequences, but little concern with contraception, except for one crucial occurrence. After a steamy interlude on the beach, mill worker Betty Anderson turns on Rodney Harrington, the mill owner's son, because he was less experienced than he'd pretended and hadn't even known enough to "wear a safe." Five weeks later, Betty is pregnant.

Keep the Aspidistra Flying by George Orwell (1936). When I first read the novel, I was shocked by the protagonist's—and by association, the author's—screed against birth control. On the verge of having sex, Rosemary stops because her lover Gordon refuses to use a condom. "This birth control business!" he lectures her, "it's just another way they [capitalists] have found out of bullying us." He goes on to speak about the "estranging shield", a phrase Orwell takes from his poem "St. Andrew's Day, 1935," which some suggest is the first reference to a condom in English poetry.

Rabbit, Run by John Updike (1960). Rabbit Angstrom has a similar aversion to contraception, but he objects to it on physical and aesthetic rather than political grounds. When Ruth Leonard, the "hooer," whom he's giving fifteen dollars "toward [her] rent," is about to slip into the bathroom to insert what he calls a "flying saucer," he stops her with the argument that he's "very sensitive." "Do you have the answer then?" she asks. "No, I hate them even worse . . . If you're going to put a lot of gadgets in this," Rabbit, who has abandoned his pregnant wife and child, goes on, "give me the fifteen back."

Couples by John Updike (1968). Eight years later, in his novel about rampant infidelity among a group of young married couples in Tarbox, a small town in Massachusetts based on his own Ipswitch, Updike not only embraces birth control, but identifies it by brand name. The first time Piet and Georgene, married to other people, have sex, he worries about "making a little baby," and she's surprised to find that he doesn't know about Enovid. "Welcome to the post-pill paradise," she tells him, and the "light-hearted blasphemy . . . immensely relieved him." Birth control as a literary device has come into its own. Without reliable contraception that makes no demand on the "sensitive" male, *Couples* could not have been written.